CURTAIN CALL

ROSEVILLE ROMANCES

Book One: Picture Imperfect
Book Two: Finding Harmony
Book Three: Curtain Call

CURTAIN CALL

by

Alyssa Roat and Hope Bolinger

MBI

Curtain Call
Published by Mountain Brook Ink
White Salmon, WA U.S.A.

The website addresses shown in this book are not intended in any way to be or imply an endorsement on the part of Mountain Brook Ink, nor do we vouch for their content.

This story is a work of fiction. All characters and events are the product of the author's imagination. Any resemblance to any person, living or dead, is coincidental.

The Team: Miralee Ferrell, Nikki Wright, Kristen Johnson, Cindy Jackson
Cover Design: Indie Cover Design, Lynnette Bonner Designer

Mountain Brook Ink is an inspirational publisher offering fiction you can believe in.
Printed in the United States of America

HOPE'S ACKNOWLEDGMENTS

A calling starts with a Caller. Thank you to God who called me into publishing. I know I often want to quit, so I'm grateful that you always provide a way just before I'm tempted to.

To Alyssa who often prevents me from quitting. You don't ever let me quit even though you beg me to let you. It's a never-ending cycle of us not allowing the other one to stop writing. I don't know what I would do without a co-author.

To the numerous friends and relatives who also won't let me quit (sensing a pattern, readers?). To James, Sonya, Carlee, Jess, Tyler, my family, Nikki, whatever the Cyle group is called now, the Pizza Squad, and to my really fat cat Twix who sits on me and impedes writing progress (he unfortunately passed after I wrote these initial acknowledgments...I miss him sitting on me all the time now).

To the people who took chances on me and made me believe in myself such as Tessa and Miralee. I can't believe Alyssa and I wrote an entire series in less than the span of a year. In one year, I wrote five books, and man does it take it out of you. But I am so grateful for the numerous opportunities presented to us. This really confirms our calling and tells us we've veered onto the right path.

To all the people integral to my theatrical past: Mom, Mrs. King, Tracy and the Taylor University Theater program, Weathervane Playhouse, all the community theaters I was a part of, and the wonderful casts of sixty shows in which I have been in.

To my fourteen-year-old self who wrote plays and thought she would write nothing else. Joke's on you.

To the wonderful Mountain Brook Ink team who worked on this book. As well as the cover revealers, endorsers, reviewers, launchers, promoters, and anyone who got the word out. We couldn't put on "a show" without you, and are so, so, so beyond grateful for you.

And, of course, to the readers. A director's biggest worry is that no one will show up for the performance. But you did. I am so grateful that you have ventured with us on this journey.

ALYSSA'S ACKNOWLEDGMENTS

This book hit so many personal topics for me. I've never been in a play (well, other than church Christmas productions), but the topic of calling is one Hope and I wrestle with. I have so many people to thank who have supported me in pursuing my calling.

First off, to our Lord and Caller, who has made it very clear I was called to write and hasn't let me quit. Thank you for the joy You bring me through the written word and for giving me a loving shove every once in a while.

To Hope, who is often the vessel of the Lord's gentle encouragement and loving shoves, and continues to amaze me as a co-author and as a person.

To my family, who, unlike many of the family members in this book, have always been my biggest fans and encouragers, making it possible for me to be where I am now. I was blessed with supportive parents, grandparents, aunts, uncles, cousins, and sister.

To everyone in the home school community who were fabulous, to co-op teachers and most of all my amazing mother who provided the best educational experience a book-loving nerd voracious for knowledge could ask for. (What I lack in theatrical background I make up for in knowledge of the home school experience. Hope and I learned a lot from each other in this book.)

To all of the friendos who unceasingly support us—the Cyle folks, the Prowrites, Juli, Nikki, the Pizza Squad.

To Miralee and the MBI family. I praise God all the time I stumbled into this amazing publisher. Definitely the work of the Lord.

To you, readers. Thank you for joining us on this journey, supporting us in our calling. I hope you enjoy reading this book as much as we enjoyed writing it.

HOPE'S DEDICATION

To James, a wonderful thespian, director, and ridiculous friend who won't let me quit writing. This is for you since the previous book dedicated to you probably will never get published.

ALYSSA'S DEDICATION

*To Nana and Papa, who have unswervingly, generously,
and lovingly supported me in every peak and valley in
pursuing my calling. Hearts and flowers, hearts and flowers.*

Chapter One

Hadassah Wright shivered in a late-November gust as she ushered five of her younger siblings through the doors of the Roseville Public Library.

"Hold on, let's hang our coats first," she called before the gaggle could storm the stacks. Once the coats were shed and properly hung on the library's community rack, Hadassah corralled the kids through the reference books into the children's section of the library.

"Come on, Obadiah." She took the hand of the youngest boy and led him away from the shelf he was trying to climb. "We're going to pick out some picture books. Maybe with dinosaurs?"

"Dinosaur, roar!" He bounced up and down.

Hadassah winced at the shout, but she gave him a wide smile. "Right. Let's go find those."

Why did the designers of this library think it was a good idea to put the children's section in the back corner? Clearly they didn't anticipate broods of home schooled children tromping through for their weekly book haul.

They emerged from the stacks into an open, colorful room with whimsical paintings on the walls of animals reading books. As the five kids dispersed, Hadassah imagined herself letting chickens out of a coop into a yard of freshly-scattered corn.

She plopped into a squishy chair and shed another one of her outer layers, folding the sweater over her arm. The chill outside didn't carry into the building, which she suspected was heated to the preference of the elderly head librarian.

She made a headcount. *One, two, three, four, five.* Good, all five accounted for.

She'd left her next oldest sister, Elizabeth, home with the two tween boys to finish their math homework. The fifteen-year-old's pleading eyes when Hadassah announced the upcoming library visit had made her take pity.

"Liz, why don't you stay home with Matthew and Luke?" Hadassah had said while searching her siblings' messy desks in the schoolroom for library books to return and stuffing them in her tote bag. "They need help with math."

"That's a good idea." Mom had poked her head in, fresh from the kitchen with flour on her apron and cheeks flushed from preparing for Thanksgiving tomorrow. "We don't want to be doing any school this weekend."

Elizabeth's shoulders relaxed. "Sure, sounds good." Then, as Mom left, she turned to Hadassah and mouthed, "Thank you."

Hadassah leaned back in the library chair. Poor Liz. Being an introvert in a house of eleven meant a day without the littles might be the highlight of her sister's week.

Obadiah ran toward her, a book held over his head. "Dinosaurs!" He thumped the hardback into Hadassah's lap.

She turned it over to look at the cover. "Those are frogs, Obie. Frogs are cool, too."

"Oh. Okay." He ran off again.

Thank goodness the children's section was fairly empty the day before Thanksgiving. Hadassah had watched too many near-collisions from her brother's lack of spatial awareness. She set the frog book beside her, the first of the impending stack. Each child could pick up to three books a week, and they almost always checked out the maximum.

Her eyes roved to a nearby bulletin board displaying posters of library and community events. Read-aloud with Santa, a food drive, an ornament-making class...and auditions for the community theater's Christmas play.

She stood and drifted toward the board. She hadn't been able to do anything theater-related since running the skits at Vacation Bible School this past summer. Once the school year began, teaching co-op classes and younger siblings had consumed most of her time.

She scanned the poster advertising a popular Christmas play. The production would probably draw a large audience. She'd seen it performed before, and she could think of several roles she'd love to play.

A thud drew her attention. She whipped her head toward the sound, clutching her cardigan. She relaxed once she saw one of her sisters picking up two books she had dropped. Those hardcover picture books could make enough noise to wake the spirits of Christmas Past, Present, and Future.

And they could make excellent bludgeoning weapons for young boys. She'd confiscated more than a few.

Her attention returned to the poster. What day were auditions?

Bzzt. Bzzt.

She dug in her skirt pocket for her phone, taking a moment to both appreciate the depth of the pockets she had sewn and lament how difficult that made finding things. Locating the device, she pulled it out and read the text on the screen.

Mom: Guess who's back in town?

Hadassah smirked to herself as she responded.

Hadassah: Santa Claus?

Mom: You are so silly. No, Byron Young.

Hadassah's smile faltered. Byron?

The Wrights and the Youngs had been best friends as long as she could remember. Dad and Mr. Young had gone to college together, and Mom and Mrs. Young basically ran the Roseville chapter of their home school group. The Youngs had had all girls—except for Byron.

Hadassah: I'm glad the girls will get to see their brother again.

That was neutral enough, right? *I just hope I don't have to see him.* After what happened the last time the two of them had interacted... She shook away that thought and watched her siblings poke through the shelves until her phone buzzed again.

Mom: You know Byron has been running his dad's branch in Seattle? Apparently it has been doing very well. They're so proud of him.

Ah, yes. Everyone was proud of Byron. The star student, the college graduate, the junior partner in his father's financial firm doing...whatever they did. Hadassah didn't really understand finances.

But the part she envied the most about Byron, that she wouldn't tell a soul, was how much she wished she could have studied theater like he did in college. She didn't envy his degrees in finance, but to work with some of the country's best thespians...

Hadassah: Yes, I've heard a lot about what he's up to from his mom. What a nice Thanksgiving for the Youngs.

She slid her phone back into her pocket and focused on the poster for the play, holding in a sigh. No, she couldn't do a Christmas play. Not with the busyness of the holiday season.

Turning toward the wider library, away from the children's section, she noticed a familiar broad-shouldered form with a bounce in his step heading in her direction. Her stomach did a leap. Griffith, the director and playwright at the community theater.

She'd gone to the local coffee shop where he worked, She Brews, at least once a week for a while. She had told herself she just liked his eclectic drinks, but she would stay to hear him talk about what was happening at the theater.

Until Mom had an intervention with her about her "caffeine addiction" and spending money on overpriced beverages when they had plenty of tea and lemonade mix at home. Hadassah hadn't been back to She Brews in a few months.

Griffith's eyes met hers across the row of books. Her cheeks flamed. Oh, no. Had she been staring? She wasn't sure. Curse her tendency to space out.

He raised a hand in greeting. "Hadassah," he said, once in range. His whisper carried, part of his natural projection that he couldn't quite seem to leave behind on stage. "I haven't seen you in a while."

She fiddled with her skirt, then forced herself to stop. "Yeah." She gave a small laugh. "Things got busy."

He glanced toward her siblings swarming over the children's section. He grinned. "Kids can definitely do that." He clutched a folder stuffed with papers to his chest. "How many siblings do you have, again? I'm sorry for not remembering."

"No problem." She played with the bottom of her long braid. *How many* are *there?* was everyone's question. "There are ten of us. I'm the second-oldest." She searched for a change of subject. "What brings you to the library?"

He tapped his folder. "Critique group. A few of us are looking over each other's plays that we're working on and giving feedback."

"Oh, nice." She wished she could listen in on their meeting. She'd never tried to write a play—and she doubted she could write a very good one—but she would love to learn what went into a production from a writer's perspective.

"Yeah." He shifted on his feet. Was that nervous energy? "It's certainly helpful. Sometimes a little intimidating."

"What is your play ab—"

A crash interrupted her sentence. She spun toward her siblings and cringed. A row of books displayed on one of the low shelves had toppled, and two of her brothers held their hands up, looking far too innocent.

She glanced back at Griffith. "Sorry, I should go take care of that."

"Do you need help?" His brow furrowed at the chaos.

"Oh, no, this is normal. Boys, right?" She huffed a laugh.

"Okay, if you're sure." He gave a little wave. "I should probably get going too if I don't want to be late. I'll talk to you later. Good luck."

"You too." She waved her fingers, then dropped her arm. *What sort of wave was that?* Why did she always act so awkward around Griffith?

Now wasn't the time to ponder. She turned and strode toward her brothers, adopting her stern older-sister look.

"I'm sorry, Griffith." Byron clicked a red pen in his fingertips. "But there's just not a whole lot of positive things I can say about your writing sample."

Griffith Williams's foot tapped against the carpet. He paused the movement, wondering how long he'd been doing that.

He swallowed, but his throat had gone dry. "What do you mean?"

The timbre of his voice caused him to wince. The critique group had met today in an upstairs conference room that liked to echo. Never mind that he'd never quite gotten the concept of "inside voice." Not after his parents had put him in charge of skits in the Dominican Republic all those years ago.

His brows drew toward the bridge of his nose.

No, he didn't want to think about them now. Images of the latest photo they'd posted on Facebook, of his parents beaming proudly at his brother Hudson, flashed across his retinas.

Too late.

"Well—" Byron said.

Byron cleared his throat and drew Griffith's attention back to him. Byron raked fingers through his autumnal-hued hair. Something about the brazen red color told Griffith that it looked dyed.

Beside Byron, a woman—in a Thanksgiving sweater featuring a turkey that said, "Gobble, Gobble, I'll improve your FOWL mood"—dabbed at the corners of her eyes with a tissue. She hadn't quite recovered from Byron's critique of her minutes before. Where he'd said, "Frankly, Ellen, I think you need to take out the first ten pages of your opener." Even though the play had been, from what Griffith could tell in the critique group emails, thirty pages in total.

"—for starters, Griffith, this seems like a rip-off of a Christmas play I did back in"—his nostrils flared, like he'd caught a whiff of some bad Thanksgiving stuffing—"community theater."

Byron pinched his eyebrows together, thumbed his chin. Then his fingers snapped.

"Ah, yes, I remember. *The Best Christmas Pageant Ever.* Honestly, Griffith, it's a good thing you don't have a title for this thing yet. Luckily you're not too far in and you can start from scratch."

Too bad his untitled play had already been completed, ninety pages in all. The critique group hadn't met in a while because of conflicts with the high school football season. Three of the group members had students who attended that high school and played on the team.

Griffith's foot started tapping again. His large hands forced themselves on his quads to get his legs to stop. "How so? I was once in *The Best Christmas Pageant Ever.* It's not that similar, right?"

He tried to ignore the sniffles from Ellen and forced a grimace. *What's wrong with me? I've gotten plenty critiqued in my college program when I did a playwriting elective.*

But his critique group then had favored spending most of their time over a refreshments table filled with tea and chocolate-covered cookies. The worst criticism he'd receive during those meetings was, "Maybe you should add in more action beats."

However, now faced with *the* Byron—a man who claimed to have worked with professional regional theaters in his master's program—he'd hoped for...well, better news.

Should've seen it coming with the emails he sent.

Right before he'd bumped into Hadassah downstairs, he'd scrolled through one such message from Byron.

Greetings, fellow playwrights.

Thank you all for sending me ten pages of your plays and screenplays for this week's critique group. As it was explained to me by your chapter leader Ellen Jenkins, all six of you bring ten pages apiece per meeting, and we peruse them ahead of time.

I know most of you read them on your computer, but I've taken the liberty of printing them out at home and marking them up.

Don't be alarmed by how much scarlet ink you'll find on your pages. As my professor and former Broadway actress Yvonna Remmington says, "If your paper bleeds, it means that I care."

Having worked with the best in the business, I am so thrilled to be able to convene with some fellow script writers. Looking forward to making these the best they can be.

Best,
Byron Young

Crimson spattered Ellen's pages so much that Griffith could hardly make out any white space.

"—also, Griffith, you have a woman who is trying to get a bunch of ragtag kids to put on a Christmas play."

Whoa, how long had he been zoning out? Griffith caught himself staring at the refreshments table. Mulled apple cider scent churned his stomach. If only he'd grabbed something to eat after working a double shift at She Brews today.

He could use all the money he could get. Especially after purchasing Christmas gifts for his theater friends.

Griffith cracked his knuckles, a bad habit he'd never seemed to rid himself of. "Well, besides the fact that I have a play about a woman helping troubled children in her community put on a theater show...Byron, are there any other similarities?"

Byron shrugged. "Can't tell. You only turned in ten pages, you know. Of which, I'd suggest cutting the first four." He passed a stack of papers to his left, which wound its way around the wooden table toward Griffith. Byron appeared to read Griffith's expression and added, "Not to worry, pal. It takes a lot of work to hone those skills. You'll get there."

Fire ignited in Griffith's forehead. He had to take a deep breath to cool the flames.

Relax. He has lots of experience. This is making you better, right?

He had to force himself not to text the director of the Roseville local theater to tell her to boot him out of the show due to his apparent lack of competence, according to Byron. The director, Lilian Kron, had appointed Griffith as stage manager for the winter play—their biggest seller every year.

She often let Griffith direct one of his own plays he wrote during the summers. But even now, he didn't think he could make cue calls backstage without messing up. Maybe she should hire someone else to take his spot, like Byron. After all, Griffith had put years into his position at the theater. What did he have to show for it? No pay, nothing.

Maybe that was Lilian's nice way of telling him that she only kept him on out of pity.

Papers landed on his lap. Everything in him wanted to slide further into the wooden chair until he disappeared under the table.

"Too much dialogue."

"Cut this character."

"Why is this stage direction even here?"

The red pen remarks, scrawled in the most perfect handwriting he'd ever witnessed, burned into his brain.

How he wished he could call back that warm glow in his chest when he saw Hadassah. *She has such a friendly face.* Right now, he felt like lead filled his veins.

Someone else cleared their throat, a woman in a pencil skirt with thin eyebrows. His shoulders relaxed at the sight of Zinnia, crossing her arms. She'd helped serve as a stage manager in his last show he'd directed.

"Why don't we take a break and go through the rest of the scripts later?"

Everyone, except Byron, murmured in agreement and bolted to their feet. Griffith shoved his chair back against the wall and nodded at Zinnia—too afraid that the "thank you" he wanted to mouth would echo in the cinderblock room.

He ambled to the refreshments table and ladled cider into two Styrofoam cups for them. Zinnia nodded at the door and they stepped onto the landing of the staircase. Cool air brushed his cheeks. Downstairs, a family bundled in scarves entered the library.

"Thanks." Sure enough, his word reverberated. He wondered if it made it all the way to the children's section.

Good thing I waited until we left the room.

He glanced over his shoulder and watched Byron take a bite into a frosted turkey-shaped cookie. Ellen, beside him, tried to argue with him about some of his markings on her manuscript.

"Eh, I'm a theater kid." Zinnia set her cup beside her feet and placed her arms on the banister. "Back in college directing classes, they would be ruthless about how we performed our monologues. I don't think I left my dorm for two days after one particular incident." She frowned back at the room. "Although, I don't think anyone has *ever* reamed me as much about dialogue as"—she placed her index finger on her nose, to make it resemble a pig's snout—"Byron."

Griffith sniggered.

He recalled how much Zinnia's cheeks resembled cherry pie filling when Byron slashed through her screenplay. When Byron told her that she'd clearly fashioned the main character after herself, she'd gripped her pen like a dagger.

If Griffith hadn't suggested they move on to the next script at that moment, they may have had a murder case on their hands.

Zinnia tapped him on the shoulder. "Don't let him get to you. You've been called to theater for a reason."

A buzzing filled his pocket before he could utter another too-loud "thanks." He dug his phone out and mouthed an apology. Zinnia threw him a wave of dismissal. "No problem. But don't be too long. Or Byron may not make it out of the library alive."

A glint filled her pupils before she disappeared into the conference room.

Griffith caught the name "Lilian" on the screen before he swiped the green answer button.

"Hello?"

"No time for greetings. Did you get the email I sent?" Lilian always talked like an auctioneer, fast and sometimes too hard to understand.

He recovered from the initial shock of her thunderous voice. "No?"

Considering Griffith perused his inbox about half an hour before, Lilian must've sent him something not too long ago.

"A theater in too close a radius is putting on the winter show we were planning on doing."

A long pause—well, long for Lilian—filled the air.

"What do you mean by that, Lilian?"

"The play publisher got back to me. It's a rule that you can't have too many theaters within a certain radius putting on the same play. They told us that we can't put it on."

Griffith's large palm slapped his forehead. How could he have forgotten that piece of information from his scriptwriting class in college? Then again, his days at the university ended three years ago. A lot had happened since then.

"Oh, gosh." He didn't know what else to say.

"You have a play, right? With lots of kids? Lots of parts? Do you think we could put that on?"

Shakiness filled his arms. He gripped the railing to the stairs. Any more shocks would send him flying down the staircase.

"I mean—" He winced back at the room. Byron stood by the door, taking his red pen once again to Ellen's manuscript. Ellen stood by and screwed up her face. No doubt, the waterworks would make a second appearance. "Sort of. I don't know if it's ready yet."

"Great. Send me a finalized copy by Black Friday."

He grimaced. "You need me to send my play in two days?"

"I'll send you another email detailing exactly how many parts we need, so we can match the original play we were going to put on as much as possible. We've already posted the audition listing, so I want to make sure we can have the same actors who were planning on coming. Also, since I haven't had time to look over the script and do preliminary work, and since you know this piece better than anyone, I'm going to have you direct it."

Gravity overtook him. He steadied himself, avoiding a near-tumble.

"Direct it? Me?" he yelped. Cleared his throat. Oh goodness, the whole library had to hear that. He hissed, "Direct the winter play? You mean the one we sell out every year?"

A sigh sounded from the receiver. Perhaps Lilian had, for the first time in her life, run out of breath.

"I know. Big responsibility. But honestly, Griffith, if you can pull this off—and do an outstanding job—it'll prove to me that you're ready for next steps here."

"You mean—"

She had mentioned wanting to retire soon and appointing a successor to take over. That would signify a full-time job at the theater, and no more shifts at She Brews. He'd been tempted to suggest himself as an applicant over the past few months. But he didn't feel like he had enough directing credits yet.

Critique group certainly hadn't helped today...

"Yes, yes. Now get me that script with some additional things I'd like you to add. I'm sending those to you now. I'm counting on you. Don't make me regret it."

The line went dead. Numbness filled him as he took in all the information. Someone slurped behind him, jolting him from his stupor.

Byron blew on the contents of his Styrofoam cup and nodded inside the classroom. Had he heard the whole conversation?

"Come on, Griffith, these scripts aren't going to critique themselves."

Chapter Two

Hadassah gripped the electric mixer, plunging the beaters through steaming potatoes in a gigantic mixing bowl. "Okay, Tabitha, now add in the cream very slowly."

Her eight-year-old sister bit her lip, concentrating on tipping the measuring cup of cream into the bowl as Hadassah rotated the potatoes. Hadassah smiled. Tabitha looked so cute when she scrunched her nose while focusing. Hadassah was glad to pass on the tradition of making Mom's famous Thanksgiving mashed potatoes.

"Yocheved is here!" Obadiah screeched, tearing through the kitchen.

Tabitha jumped, dumping the rest of the cream into the potatoes. A bit splattered onto Hadassah. "Oops, sorry."

"That's okay, cooking is messy. Can you grab the butter?"

While Tabitha wove around Mom, Elizabeth, and Priscilla—all the other Wright females—Hadassah craned her neck toward the front door.

With the open floor plan, she could see Matthew and Luke vie for the coveted task of opening the door while Obadiah bounced around them. Dad beat them both and threw open the door, revealing a lovely petite brunette holding a stack of pies and a man with a neat beard and an easy-going smile. "Hey there, strangers."

"Hi, everyone." Yocheved beamed at her younger siblings. She handed the pies to Matthew and Luke, half for each of them. "Can you take these to the kitchen for me?"

The boys bounded toward the cooking chaos while Yocheved and her husband, Aaron, came inside and began hugging the family.

"Here's the butter." Tabitha tossed two sticks into the mashed potatoes.

"Oh." Hadassah winced as hot potato splashed across her shirt and into her face. She gripped the bowl, arm aching as she struggled to control the whirling mixer. "Thank you, Tabi. Next time, we're going to cut them into a couple of pieces first before putting them in, okay?"

"Okay." Then she was gone, running toward the front door to greet their older sister.

Mom intercepted the pies and set them on the counter before wiping her hands on her apron and bustling toward the commotion at the front door. "Come in, come in. Oh, I'm so glad to have you here."

Hadassah focused on finishing up the potatoes threatening to run away, taking a few seconds to stir in the rest of the butter before grabbing a dish towel to wipe off her face and shirt while the other ten members of the household crowded the entryway and living room. No one could resist Yocheved's infectious charm.

It had always been that way. Growing up only thirteen months apart in age, Yocheved and Hadassah could have been twins—Yocheved, the outgoing one, Hadassah, her willing, quiet accomplice. They'd sworn to be best friends forever.

Until Yocheved met Aaron four years ago, married him a year later at the age of barely nineteen, and moved an hour and a half away.

Hadassah joined the fray of hugging and chattering in the living room. Dad, Aaron, and the older boys were already planning a game of backyard football while Obadiah clutched Yocheved's skirt and the girls clustered around.

"How *is* the church doing?" Mom fussed with the silky waves framing Yocheved's face. "Dad said Aaron might be invited to guest preach at our church. Wouldn't that be nice?"

Yocheved turned glowing eyes toward her husband. "We've had a lot of growth lately. Especially with the children's ministry."

Ah, yes. Yocheved had married a man in seminary. Which

meant, three years later, she was the wife of a young pastor of a new church plant, and with her duties as a pastor's wife, she often didn't have time to come visit.

Not that Hadassah could complain about any of that. It was wonderful for her sister. No one deserved happiness more.

She tried to shove down the hollow feeling in her chest.

"Speaking of growth, and children." Mom gave Yocheved a sly look, pushing a graying lock behind her own ear. "Might I expect grandbabies anytime soon?"

"Mom..." Hadassah grimaced.

Yocheved gave an awkward laugh. "Not yet, unfortunately."

"I had both you and Hadassah by your age, you know." Mom placed a hand on Tabitha's head before the girl could wriggle away. "Children are such a blessing."

"They certainly are." Yocheved blinked quickly. Most people wouldn't be able to tell, but Hadassah could see that her sister's warm smile looked forced.

"Mom, is that your casserole I smell?" Hadassah sniffed the air. "Is it burning?"

"Oh!" She hurried toward the kitchen.

Yocheved turned a genuine smile toward Hadassah. She spread her arms, and the two sisters fell into a hug. "Thank you," Yocheved whispered.

"Of course." Hadassah squeezed her sister one last time and then took her hands. "Want to help me decorate the cornucopia?"

The co-conspirator grin blossomed on Yocheved's face. "Always. I have our decorations in the car."

Between family chaos, preparing and laying out the feast, and the usual prayers and going around the table sharing what each person was thankful for, Hadassah hardly had a chance to talk to anyone until the family had cleared their plates and started on seconds.

Hadassah and Yocheved smirked at each other across the table when their younger siblings giggled about this year's centerpiece—a mini traffic cone filled with pinecones. Ever since the two oldest sisters had accidentally crushed the wicker family cornucopia in kindergarten and tried to replace it with a party hat painted brown in hopes no one would notice, the tradition held that each year, they had to decorate the table with a new homemade cornucopia. From a funnel to a trumpet to a vacuum cleaner attachment, they had always delivered.

"You two outdid yourselves this year." Mom gestured at the neon orange traffic cone with her fork.

Dad chuckled, cutting into his second piece of turkey and dunking the chunk in his third helping of mashed potatoes. How he maintained the physique of a beanpole, Hadassah would never know. "Hadassah's idea, I'd guess." He raised his voice over the chatter and winked at her. "She's always had a knack for the theatrical."

Hadassah glanced at her sister and giggled. "Yocheved procured the supplies. Churches apparently often have traffic cones lying around."

"Speaking of theatrical." Mom looked up and down the table, as if waiting for an audience to settle.

Instead, the boys continued arguing about football while Obadiah picked his nose. Hadassah nudged him with her foot and gave him a look.

That must have been enough for Mom, because she plunged onward. "We're having the Youngs over on Sunday for dinner after church. Byron will be here, too." She waggled her eyebrows at Hadassah.

Not at the dinner table. Not in front of everyone. Why did Mom have to do this? Hadassah felt her cheeks warm. "That will be nice. We haven't had a chance to hang out with the Youngs much lately."

Yocheved's expression darkened as she glanced between Hadassah and Mom. "What's Byron doing back in town?"

From Mom's clasped hands and delighted smile, it seemed that was exactly what she'd been hoping someone would ask. "He finished his master's program this spring—while helping direct his father's branch there. He's taking some time to be with family and invest in the local community this winter. It's so nice to see a young man prioritizing family."

Hadassah shot a quick "help me" look at Yocheved. If anyone understood Hadassah's feelings toward Byron, her sister did.

"His masters is in theater or something, right?" Yocheved spooned more cranberry sauce onto her plate. "That seems a little odd, considering the family business."

"I'm sure he'll be ready to take over for his father once Dave decides to retire. Men sometimes need to get their impractical interests out of the way while they're young." Mom raised an eyebrow at Dad. "Right, John?"

Dad paused with a loaded fork halfway to his mouth. "Uh. Yes." He turned his attention back to his food.

Hadassah doubted he knew what he'd even agreed to.

Mom beamed at her. "You two were always together as children. Wouldn't it be nice if—well, I shouldn't say anything yet."

Yocheved nodded. "Probably best not to think too hard about a gathering with family friends." She cast a worried glance at Hadassah. "Especially since we don't know what anyone's intentions are."

Unfortunately, Hadassah had a sinking feeling she knew exactly what Byron might be planning.

Hands down, this was the most stressful Thanksgiving Griffith had ever endured.

Yes, he often had "Friends-giving" at his friend Ryan's apartment. Ryan's two-bedroom resided one floor up from Griffith's studio. Because Griffith's parents often spent their Novembers in the

D.R.—Dominican Republic—and Ryan had a lot of friction with his parents, the two of them often brought four dishes together and watched a movie.

But today, both of them had work. Ryan cloistered himself in the second bedroom—his "photo and video editing suite." Griffith snuggled onto Ryan's red-carpet colored couch.

In front of him sat a huge projector and sheet where Ryan liked to host movie nights. Griffith didn't have the heart to tell his friend he probably couldn't make most of the ones leading up to Christmas, now with a ton of rehearsals in the pipeline.

An apple cinnamon candle on a table flickered and wafted sweet scents throughout the room. He blinked the glaze out of his eyes and forced himself to stare at his computer. On the couch, Ryan's huge husky Balto inched ever closer to his lap.

"Silly boy." Griffith scritched Balto's ears. "You won't even come close to fitting on my legs."

Griffith could relate. Built like a wrestler, his whole life strangers would plague him with questions about whether he played football or if he could help them carry moving boxes.

Seemingly satisfied with his pets, Balto placed his chin back on the couch cushion. Griffith returned his focus to the screen and pulled open a Word document. Over the span of twenty-four hours, Lilian had bombarded his Messenger on Facebook with "additions" she wanted to see in the script. Now, with less than a day left to make edits, he perused the most recent ones she'd sent in the past hour.

He'd put them in bullet points on the document.

- Oh, can you make sure to have lots of kids' parts? The original play we were going to put on had thirty speaking parts: eighteen children and twelve adults. Can you get your script to have close to that number?

- Make sure to have lots of ensemble parts too. Tons of nonspeaking ones for our actors who need a little help, well, acting. I'll make sure to give the 'no small parts only small actors' speech at auditions.

- Can you send me the title of your play? I want to update the audition listing before the end of the day so the actors have more than twenty-four hours to prepare.

- While we're at it, send me the cast descriptions. Make sure to have age, gender, ethnicity, etc. Maybe a little bit about the character. A sentence or two per part is fine.

- Oh, and can you find a replacement stage manager, since you'll be directing this? Thanks.

Dizziness swam in his skull. Just when he thought he'd finished with edits, another notification dinged on his computer from Lilian.

He dug out his phone from his pocket and shot off a text to Zinnia.

Griffith: Any chance you could stage manage for the show? I know it's last minute. Sorry.

He'd already had to send tons of apology messages this morning. To She Brews for the fact that he couldn't work many shifts from now until after Christmas, to his family that he couldn't make as many video calls because many rehearsals went well past midnight...

His shoulders drooped and he opened the newest version of his untitled play.

Time to chop up these parts into smaller parts.

He had plenty of adult roles in the script, but only ten kids. Buzzing vibrated the couch, which caused Balto to lift his head. A message from Zinnia burned on the screen.

Zinnia: Was just about to text you asking if you needed a replacement. I'm all for stage managing another show. Just send me the script as soon as you can so I can be as prepared as possible.

Relief washed over him. At least he could tick another item off the list.

Let's hope Lilian doesn't send any more today.

"Heya, pal—"

A voice from the hallway caused him to jolt in his seat. Ryan emerged from the editing suite and shoved a pair of blocky glasses up his nose. He reminded Griffith of a Clark Kent, if Clark Kent suffered from asthma during pick-up basketball games.

Oh...those basketball games they liked to play in the winter...he'd have to break the news to those guys that he didn't have time for those this year. At least, not until January.

"—what say we take a break and heat up some of the Thanksgiving delicacies we brought?"

The minute Griffith had arrived at the apartment, they shoved their dishes into the fridge. Ryan's black and gray Maine Coon cat, Buttercup, patrolled the kitchen. She marched back and forth between her food bowl and the refrigerator, perhaps hoping for some food to materialize.

Griffith frowned at the screen, wincing in anticipation for yet another message from Lilian to pop up. Then, despite himself, he shut the lid to the laptop. "Sounds good."

Ryan had pried open the door to the fridge and held Buttercup back with his leg. Quite unsuccessfully, it seemed, because the cat leapt over Ryan's foot and launched toward the top shelf of the fridge. Ryan pulled her out with an eye roll, tossed her in the direction of the family room, and slid out a glass dish filled with corn casserole.

"Lilian been keeping you busy?" Ryan nodded at Griffith's laptop and plucked a serving spoon out of a cup stationed near the microwave.

"It's been nonstop today. Now I have to come up with a title. No pressure, right? You?"

"Don't get me wrong, editing wedding photos is fun." Ryan dug a glob of browned corn onto his plate. Griffith's oven, which prepared the concoction, always heated up too fast and burned most items placed into it. "It's definitely not what I want to do for the rest of my life. Kind of drains me, you know?"

Griffith grunted in assent and moved to the kitchen to grab dishes to set on the small, high-top table near the family room. He opened the cabinet doors and pulled out two cups and a plate for himself, since Ryan already had one.

"So if you don't want to do wedding photos, what do you want to do?"

Ryan grabbed a rotisserie chicken—the store had run out of turkeys—out of the fridge and banged open the silverware drawer. He hoisted a knife and began to saw off a leg. "I'd love to do more indie film...but the wedding photos pay a whole lot more." He sighed. "It's hard when your calling has to be a part-time thing."

"Agreed." Griffith placed the plates and glasses on the table and avoided tripping on Buttercup, who now circled his legs.

She often did this when someone had a dish in hand. Perhaps in hopes that they would lose their balance and send all the contents onto the wood floor.

"Speaking of the title for your play. Why not *In the Wings*?" Ryan twisted off the tag on the Hawaiian rolls bag. "You had me read an earlier version. Doesn't your main character talk about being 'in the wings' a lot? That's a theater term for being off to the side of the stage, waiting for your cue, right?" He placed two rolls on his plate. "Like, being backstage and wishing they could be on stage more?"

True. He had created the lead role "Emily Willard" as a reflection on how he felt about working at She Brews. Much as he enjoyed creating concoctions out of foamed milk and syrups, like Ryan said, the job "drained" him.

Just earlier today he had written the character description for Emily, because Lilian needed those for the adjusted audition listing.

Emily Willard (late 20s, early 30s, any ethnicity): Emily has always dreamed of starring on the stage. In high school and college, her directors made her do stage managing instead. Now the town has tasked her with putting on a Christmas show with some troubled kids from a foster home. She's struggling to balance her new calling of directing, while wishing for her old one—being able to take center stage as a main role.

"Hmm." Griffith frowned. Something about the title *In the Wings* didn't feel right. Back in college, when he wrote ten-minute plays for class, the right title would ring like a beautiful note.

This one didn't.

He looked over his shoulder back at his laptop. Balto nestled his chin on the humming computer.

Griffith didn't have much time to mull over titles or little details. One of his professors, back in college, had said something along the same lines.

"Most of you will end up doing theater as a part-time gig. You may wish you could spend more time on character depth or on scenes...but when something you're passionate about is on the back burner, you have to learn when to trim the fat."

He cracked a knuckle and blew out a breath.

Guess I'll have to sacrifice a great title for a pretty good one.

"*In the Wings* sounds all right." He scooped up his plate and ambled to the kitchen, while Ryan popped his plate into the microwave. Right as Griffith did so, he heard a buzzing from his phone. He set everything down and reached for his device.

Maybe Lilian had other things she needed from him.

Instead, a notification from his mother blinked on the screen.

Mom: Know you don't have much time for FaceTime. Just letting you know that Hudson, your dad, and I will be in town for Christmas. Will stay with relatives. Plan for some time to spend with us.

Oh, Mom. I love you. When am I going to have time?

During his parents' last visit, they lectured him about how he spent way too many hours in the theater. What would they do now when he had to allocate double the amount for this show?

Knowing them, they'd want to do all the usual Christmas festivities when they visited, from caroling with neighbors to watching the handbell choir perform in the town square to sipping peppermint hot chocolate near a crackling fire.

Warm creamed corn and chicken scents spilled from the kitchen. Glints from the microwave lighting showed on Ryan's glasses.

"More theater stuff?" Ryan asked.

Griffith's temples pounded. "More stress, that's for sure." He pinched the bridge of his nose. When would he get a day off?

Chapter Three

Hadassah halted in the hallway of the children's wing of the church, one arm full of craft projects, coloring sheets, and snacks while she held Obadiah with the other. Four really was too old to be carried, but with the milling children around her, she didn't want to lose him.

Plus, he'd lost a shoe, which she'd tasked her sister Elizabeth with finding.

Children ran into her legs and flowed around her like salmon in a stream while she scanned the flyer posted on the bulletin board. Hadn't the local theater planned to do a production of *The Best Christmas Pageant Ever*? Yet overnight, it seemed that all the posters had been replaced with this new one, advertising a show called *In the Wings*.

Obadiah squirmed. "I want to show Enoch my picture."

"Just a minute, Obie." Hadassah squinted at the fine print. She'd never heard of this show before.

There, in tiny lettering. "Written by Griffith Williams."

They're putting on his play for the big Christmas season? That had to be huge. He hadn't mentioned that at the library on Wednesday.

According to the paper, auditions opened on Monday, and adults needed to perform a monologue from memory. If someone saw this for the first time today, it would be difficult for those unaccustomed to theater to memorize and polish something that quickly. They must be in a rush.

Anyway. Not important right now.

Hadassah turned to retrieve Enoch from his kindergarten

classroom, just as Elizabeth appeared, shoe in hand, with Priscilla, Tabitha, and Isaiah trailing behind. Teachers had joked that the Wright family made up half the Sunday School classes.

"Thanks, Liz." Hadassah held out Obadiah, and Elizabeth wrestled the sneaker back onto his foot. Then Hadassah set him on the ground and took his hand. "We just need droids Four, Five, and Nine."

Elizabeth saluted. "Roger roger, D-Two."

Once they'd hit about seven kids and started joking they were practically the Clones from the *Star Wars* prequels, they'd given themselves birth order numbers and began calling each other droids, much to Mom's dismay.

Especially when she would scold the boys for bad behavior and they began responding in their best Obi Wan impression with, "These are not the droids you're looking for."

Dad's old *Star Wars* DVDs mysteriously disappeared after that.

By the time they'd rounded up the final droids—or the droids plus a Jedi Master, since D-Five liked to complain, "I should be Luke Skywalker, because we have the same name"—and made it out to the parking lot, Mom and Dad had pulled the white fifteen-passenger van around to the front.

"Hop in, everyone," Mom trilled, her hand fluttering like a caffeinated bird. "We don't want to be late."

Hadassah bit her lip. She wished she could be late enough to miss their lunch with the Youngs entirely.

Instead, she'd been up early, helping Mom prepare food before church so the meal would be ready once they got home and would only need to be heated.

She barely heard the commotion in the van all the way home. Hardly registered her actions as she heated casseroles—some of them Thanksgiving leftovers in disguise—and instructed the girls to set the table while Mom flurried through the house, tidying up last minute messes and yelling at the boys to put their shoes away properly.

Then the doorbell rang.

From the kitchen, Hadassah watched Mom open the door in slow motion. Watched Mom and Mrs. Young embrace, and Dad and Mr. Young shake hands while the four Young girls, aged eighteen to eight, greeted the Wright children.

A young man in his mid-twenties entered last, dressed in a style that seemed to be attempting to be scholarly, professional, and trendy all at once—a goal which, in Hadassah's opinion, he did not achieve. The noise level rose as greetings flew.

All Hadassah could notice was his *hair*. It had always been a mousy brown, but now the locks shone a dramatic auburn. She snorted.

Eyes turned toward her right as the knife in her hand slipped. She gasped in pain as blood spurted from her finger onto the pecan pie she'd been prepping.

"Oh, Hadassah!" Mom's hands flew to her chest.

"I'm fine." On instinct, she stuck her bleeding finger in her mouth and whirled for the sink, face burning. Her ears flamed as the metallic taste of blood spread across her tongue. Why did she put her finger in her *mouth*? She shoved the wounded digit beneath the spigot and turned on the water in the sink, watching red rivulets run down the drain.

That's more blood than I expected. A wave of nausea ran through her, spots appearing in front of her vision.

Suddenly, the counter rose toward her, and black overtook her vision.

The next thing she knew, girls were shrieking, boys were yelling, and someone held her slumped in their arms.

"Does anyone have a first aid kit?" The voice resonated from the person supporting her, clear and projecting. "We also need to apply pressure to the wound."

Thoughts coalesced, connecting the voice to the person. Byron. *Byron* had caught her fall.

She stiffened and stumbled forward.

"Whoa, whoa." Byron kept his hands on her arms, holding her steady. "It's okay. I caught you." His eyes met hers, and he smiled. "Hello, Hadassah."

"Byron," she croaked.

Mom shoved a handful of paper towels toward them. "Use this."

"Thanks, Mom." Hadassah took the wad and broke away from Byron, pressing the paper towels to her finger.

Mrs. Young bustled forward, skirts swishing. "Oh, you poor dear. Byron, I can't believe you moved so quickly. Hadassah, you could have hit your head."

"It seems I've been unknowingly preparing for this moment for years," Byron said with a chuckle. "I've caught plenty of women swooning on stage before, but I must say, never in real life." He winked. *Winked.*

"I don't know what happened," Hadassah said, holding out her hand as Elizabeth gave a subtle eye roll, plunked down the first aid kit, and began cleaning and bandaging the finger. Both Hadassah and Liz had plenty of practice with first aid with five rowdy younger brothers. "It must have surprised me."

"She doesn't usually have such a delicate constitution," Mom confided to Mrs. Young.

Constitution? Was this eighteen-twenty? *Lord, help me.*

"I brushed some glue on there to keep it closed, and you should be fine," Elizabeth said, wrapping a Band-Aid around the finger. "It does cross a joint, though, so try not to bend it."

"Thanks, Liz." Hadassah headed back to the pecan pie. "Okay, I'm going to check on how much of the food I ruined."

Mrs. Young gave a wide-eyed look. Hadassah doubted the woman's four demure daughters—or Byron, for that matter—got into many scrapes. A sliced finger didn't hold a candle to the braces and splints and giant bandages the Wright children had all sported at various points. Doctor's visits were reserved for only the worst cases.

With the drama over, the two families quickly turned to other topics. The Wright girls set the table, and the Young sisters helped carry food to the dining room, where a smaller table had been set up for the youngest kids.

To Hadassah's dismay, she ended up sitting across from Byron—no doubt due to Mom's machinations.

After prayer, Byron leaned forward, too-white teeth flashing. "Hadassah, it's been so long."

She stabbed a carrot with her fork, eyes focused on her plate. "Yes, it has."

From two seats down, Mom shot her a raised eyebrow.

Byron scooped up a mouthful of green bean casserole with a spoon, like a psychopath. "What have you been up to? The last we saw one another, I believe you were looking at colleges."

A rock settled in her stomach. "I changed my mind. The co-ops let me teach anyway since I have that dual enrollment certificate I got from the community college."

"Ah, yes. I did dual enrollment in high school as well."

We know. As the oldest of both the Young and Wright clans, Byron had set the standard for their home school experiences. Yocheved, Hadassah, and Byron's oldest sister had followed in his footsteps, earning a two-year degree from the local community college during high school.

Unlike Byron, Yocheved and Hadassah never went further in education.

Yocheved never minded. After all, she had fallen head over heels for Aaron, and she'd always wanted to be a pastor's wife. Hadassah hadn't expected her sister to get married so quickly.

She hadn't expected to suddenly be Mom's second-in-command over eight children. Between her and Yocheved, someone had to stay to help.

"We should get coffee sometime this week to catch up more." Byron's voice brought her back to the present.

"Oh, I wish I could, but I'm teaching co-ops and helping with the kids all week."

In the home school community, co-op classes operated so that individual parents didn't have to teach all the subjects to their kids by themselves. A teacher, often a mom, would lead a particular subject for a group of students, and the other families would contribute either by paying for classes, or by trading to instruct a different subject.

Thanks to Hadassah teaching a handful of middle-school English, math, and science classes, the Wrights never had to pay a cent for the Wright children to enroll—and she even made the occasional pocket money.

"I love how dedicated you are to your family." Byron took a sip of his drink. "What about the evening? We could get dinner."

No, no, no. She cast about for a solution. What could she say? Mom would tell her to go in a heartbeat if she tried to make some excuse about Mom or the kids needing her in the evenings, too. She couldn't act pleasant for an entire dinner with only Byron for company.

Act. That was it.

"Actually, I'm trying out for the new play at the community theater tomorrow. If I get a callback...well, I don't know what my schedule will look like this week."

"You're doing theater?" Mom blurted. "I didn't know that."

I guess I am now. "Yes, I'm very excited for this Christmas play. It seems like a great way to get involved with the community and work with the local kids."

Mom softened. "That's sweet. Just don't overwork yourself."

Success. Hadassah glanced back at Byron.

For some reason, he smiled. "I'm glad to hear it. Maybe we'll see each other sooner than you think."

With that, his attention diverted to Dad asking a question, leaving Hadassah wondering what his words could mean.

And what on earth she would recite for the audition tomorrow.

Griffith nearly spilled his drink onto his pants when he stumbled into the theater. He spotted Byron sitting in the back row of the auditorium with his arm draped over a cushioned seat.

Strange, auditions don't start for half an hour.

Did Lilian know Byron was in the theater early? Had he come to audition?

Speaking of Lilian, she stood in the center aisle, deep in conversation with the theater's newest hire, a dramaturg who wore too many neon and yellows—perhaps revelling in his theater days from the '70s.

Lilian on the other hand had bedecked herself in her usual shawl. Gray, matching the streaks of silver in her black hair.

She craned her neck over her shoulder and waved Griffith toward her. He noticed a sticky sensation overtook his hand. A dollop of whipped cream had spilled from the cup onto his fingers when he'd spotted Byron.

He licked the sweet cream off his thumb and strode briskly to Lilian.

"I have another addition for you." Lilian pressed the tip of a pen to her lips. She always carried one, taking constant notes during rehearsals to give to the actors.

Griffith forced a smile and hoped he didn't give the wince away by how much he crinkled his eyelids. "Yeah?"

"You have a dog, yes?"

How could he forget his Westie named Chekhov? Monikered after Griffith's favorite comedic playwright, Chekhov too had a flair for the dramatic. It usually materialized with Chekhov licking Griffith's face to death at five in the morning to take him out on a walk.

"Sure, Lilian. He's a little booger."

"Great. I need your booger for this show." She pointed her pen at the stage. Remnants of the previous production, *The Importance of Being Earnest*, hadn't yet been torn down. Mainly, the blue paint they used to cover the floor of the stage.

His stomach plummeted.

He thought he'd reached the end of the tunnel in terms of edits. Now Lilian wanted to throw a canine into the show.

"I, uh"—he palmed his neck—"I don't know where a dog is going to fit in the script. There's already a lot of moving parts."

He knew, from experience, that anything and everything could go wrong in a show. *Especially* if someone introduced an animal into the mix. One college production of *The Wizard of Oz* gone wrong had assured him of that.

Lilian picked a piece of fuzz off her shawl and let it drop to the carpet. "Nothing huge, just need the dog in all of Emily's house scenes. Dogs sell tickets, you know. We can use all the help we can get. Ticket sales will already drop as soon as people hear we're putting on an unknown show."

Griffith's shoulders drooped.

How could he argue against that? She'd already given him such a huge opportunity to put on his play during their highest volume season. He could make some allowances, right?

"No problem, Lilian."

"Great. Make sure to bring Chekhov to callbacks tomorrow. We'll see how the actors do with him." Her eyes widened, something that happened often when she got an idea for an addition to a scene. "Oh, I already took care of one of your items on your to-do list for you."

With a grand sweeping gesture, her arm motioned to the figure in the back row. Byron didn't appear to notice, immersed in some playbook he was reading.

"Griffith, meet your new stage manager."

"Stage manager—?"

He paused and an icy cold sensation gripped him. Not unlike how the chilly weather froze his veins outside moments before he entered the well-heated lobby of the theater. He'd forgotten to inform Lilian about Zinnia.

For the last few days, he'd spent agonizing hours over sending her the play and cast descriptions. Once Lilian received those, Griffith started to work his way through the script to figure out just how he'd direct the scenes.

In most cases, directors had months to do preliminary planning for how they'd bring their vision to life.

Lilian gave him two and a half days.

Telling her about Zinnia must've fallen off his to-do list. He'd written some reminder on the wall of sticky notes near his bed, hadn't he?

"Yes, and thank our lucky stars he has a lot of experience. Worked at major regional theaters for his masters' program. He'll make a fine addition."

Byron looked up over his book and flashed a grin. "Anything to give back to this community. I'm glad I could join at the last minute."

Right as he spoke the last word, the double doors to the auditorium flew open again.

Zinnia rushed in with a salad bowl container in hand. She poked at the contents with a fork. "Sorry I'm a little late to being early. The line was out the door and"—she paused, a piece of lettuce dropping to her slush-coated boots. She narrowed her eyes at Byron. "Never mind. I'm here now."

Griffith bit his lip. Oh boy, how could he convey to his friend, who had volunteered her time to help him, that Lilian replaced *his* replacement?

"Hey, Zin." He ambled to her as she propped her back against a column near the doors. His shoes squeaked from the wetness of the snow outside. Not all of it had melted yet from his soles. "Umm, so I guess Lilian appointed another stage manager."

Her face fell as she crunched into a cucumber slice. She swallowed and grimaced.

"Not a problem. Glad she was able to find someone." She wrinkled her nose in the direction of Byron.

"We could always use an ASM—assistant stage manager. I need someone to call lighting cues during the show and be here for rehearsals when Byron can't make it."

"Oh, I've been an ASM before. That sounds fine." She skewered a radish sliver with her fork. Then she leaned forward and hissed, "I would prefer to be in the lighting and sound booth anyway. As far away from *him* as possible."

Griffith's lips twitched. "You and me both, sister."

Whoops, his whisper came out a lot louder than he'd hoped. Byron didn't move. Perhaps he hadn't heard.

Lilian waved them over ten minutes later. "We should probably go over a few last-minute things before the auditionees start showing up. Griffith, anything in particular you want us to know about the cast list and your vision for the show?"

"The most important parts are Emily and the foster kid Oliver."

Oliver, in the show, gave Emily a hard time. Until she helped him discover his love for acting and that he didn't need to lash out. He could get his energy out through telling a beautiful story on stage.

The character reminded him of one kid in particular he'd worked with in a DR village.

"I want the actors for those parts to be spot-on. I'm okay if everyone else is rough around the edges. This is community theater, after all."

Byron's nostrils wrinkled at the last sentence. They each took their places in the center seats of the auditorium and brought forth the evaluation sheets Griffith had printed in the theater office ahead of time. Items on the criteria sheet included projection, expression, characterization, energy, etc.

The audition listing told the adults they had to memorize a monologue. For the kids, they could print one off and read from it. They also had to bring in an acting resume—with a list of past shows they'd performed in—and all their conflicts from November 30 through December 23, the performance.

If they had to skip more than two rehearsals, then they wouldn't make the show.

Actors filtered into the auditorium one at a time, depending on when they'd signed up for their audition slot. Most of the kids' voices didn't reach past the third row. Too bad that Griffith and the other judges were stationed six rows back.

Griffith never thought he'd have to say the words, "Please turn around so we can see your faces. The audience doesn't want to see your backside" more than five times in one day, but here he was, when the sixth kid auditionee flounced out of the room.

Once she exited, a kid in a disheveled flannel and well-worn jeans dragged his feet as he ambled onto the stage. A woman accompanied him and parked in the first row. Parents often came to the audition for their children, but the two of them looked nothing alike.

Lilian squinted at his resume and leaned over to whisper to Griffith. "From the Roseville Foster Care. His case manager said he really wanted to audition. Was surprised we had someone show up from there for a regular show."

Huh. They'd had kids from the foster home make an appearance for drama camp in the summer, but often the folks there used it as free babysitting. Most of the kids had no interest in acting.

"Leroy," the boy stated his name, gave a sigh, and stared at the paper in his hands. He read, in the most drained-of-all-life voice possible, the monologue before him.

Byron, flanking Griffith's side, groaned. He clapped his pen down on his evaluation sheet and leaned back into his chair. Great, Byron had already given up on this kid.

Fire ignited in Griffith's neck, and so he listened harder. Caught the cracks in Leroy's voice as he read. Watched how the paper shook in his fingertips. Had Leroy also counted himself out of the running?

Pity tore at Griffith's stomach.

Leroy lifted his brows at the correct moments, placed emphasis on the right parts of the words. He *got* acting. Far better than most of Griffith's peers in his theater college program.

Griffith clicked his pen and wrote one sentence on Leroy's evaluation sheet. "Ask him to come to callbacks."

This boy deserved a second chance.

Leroy finished his monologue and marched off to the backstage area as soon as he got out the last word. A woman in a denim skirt swished past him and took center stage. She cleared her throat, and Byron bolted forward in his seat, enraptured with the figure.

Griffith squinted and spotted a familiar face, Hadassah. Warmth filled his insides.

"My name is Hadassah Wright and I will be reciting Emily's monologue from *Our Town*, Act III."

How did she—how did she know? That he'd named his Emily after the main character from his favorite play?

She began her recitation, and he soaked in every word. Clung to her pleas for just a little more time in this world. During a dramatic pause, Griffith noticed that Byron had inched so far forward in his seat that he might as well have tumbled into the next row.

"Do any human beings ever realize life while they live it— every, every minute?" Hadassah closed her eyes, inhaled, then reopened her eyes. She did a small bow. "Thank you."

"Wow," Griffith and Byron said at the same time as Hadassah exited stage left.

It could've been Griffith's imagination, or the dim lighting of the auditorium, but in his periphery, he swore he caught a glare from Byron.

Chapter Four

Hadassah's heart rate had barely returned to normal by the time she pulled into the drive and turned off the engine.

She sat in the driver's seat of the old minivan—the family's smaller vehicle for excursions where the fifteen-passenger van wasn't necessary—and took a moment to compose herself.

With the Youngs over for much of Sunday, she hadn't had a chance to pick an audition monologue until Sunday evening. With little time to spend, she'd scrolled online to find a part that fit her age and what she thought might be the homey feel of the play. The monologue from *Our Town* seemed to fit the bill, so she'd read over the part several times that night, whispered the words to herself under her breath all day Monday while teaching classes and instructing siblings, and gave three dramatic deliveries alone in the car in the parking lot of the theater.

Then she'd gone inside and auditioned.

As she undid her seatbelt, her fingers continued to tremble from post-audition jitters. When she'd walked onto that stage, the last person she had expected to be sitting in the audience was Byron.

Her heart had pounded as she managed to introduce herself. "My name is Hadassah Wright and I will be reciting Emily's monologue from *Our Town*, Act III."

Byron leaned forward. She couldn't see his face very well, but she could swear he was smirking, proud of his surprise presence.

She looked toward Griffith instead, where she found a warm smile. Tension released from her jaw.

Neither of them are here. You are Emily, and you are witnessing life for the last time.

Her throat tightened with grief. The specters of her—Emily's—

family rose before her.

She launched into her monologue.

Once it was over, once the final word rang out, she closed her eyes, reorienting herself before she opened them, looking to the judges.

Griffith's mouth hung slack. Byron gripped the seat in front of him, staring.

Oh, no. Did she do terribly?

She bowed. "Thank you." Then she hurried off stage.

In the present, she sighed and slammed the door of the minivan shut, heading toward the front door of the house.

Well, if she did do awful, maybe that would convince Byron to leave her alone.

The callback email arrived so late that night, she didn't see it until morning.

"Enoch, give Obadiah his shark back," Hadassah called, eyes focused on the computer screen at one of the desks in the schoolroom.

Enoch smacked his brother over the head with the stuffed shark and then threw the sea creature at him before stalking away. Obadiah began to wail.

Hadassah pinched the bridge of her nose. *Can I not finish reading one email?* Mom had taken half the kids to their morning co-op classes, leaving Hadassah with the other half. She scanned the words as quickly as possible.

I got a callback.

She squealed under her breath and kept reading. Callbacks were tonight. She'd need to let Mom know.

Obadiah's wails intensified.

She turned toward the two boys with a bright smile that she knew didn't fit the situation. "Enoch, this is not an appropriate response. Let's make sure Obie is okay, and then we need to think about our actions."

Three sibling arguments, two co-op classes, and four hours of homework help later, Hadassah finally made her way into the theater and pushed through the doors leading from the lobby into the auditorium.

A white puffball with legs came charging down the aisle barking.

She snorted and bent down, offering her hand. "Hey there, silly dog."

The westie nosed her hand and ran a circle around her, arfing turned to excited yips. She scratched its head and then ruffled its pointy ears while the pup spun in circles, tail flying.

Griffith came running up the aisle after the dog, leash with an empty collar attached in hand. "Oh good." He held up the leash and collar. "He always slips his collar, but I couldn't find his harness, and we were running late."

Hadassah scooped up the dog, which licked her chin as she carried him to Griffith. She giggled. "He's just too friendly, isn't he?"

"Sometimes." Griffith accepted the dog. "He decides pretty fast whether he's going to spend the rest of his life barking at someone or licking them to death." He chuckled. "It looks like you made the second category."

"I'm honored." She glanced toward the front of the theater, where kids and adults milled. "Did he get a callback, too?"

"Nah, he already has the part. I'm just trying to get him used to being in the theater before he has to be on stage." Griffith cinched the collar back around the dog's neck, then fell into what Hadassah had always called a "puppy-voice," addressing the dog. "We decided that we were going to do some suspicious sniffing in the aisle, so we have to go outside to make sure we don't have any accidents. Huh, booger?"

She laughed. "Want me to take him out? I know you must be crazy busy with the callbacks." She glanced at her watch. "They're starting in less than a minute, right?"

"Actually, that would be amazing." He handed over the leash. "There's an open area to the left of the entry." He waggled a finger at the dog. "You behave for Hadassah, Chekhov."

Griffith named his dog after Anton Chekhov? Adorable. "It's an honor to escort such an esteemed playwright."

His expression registered surprise, then he grinned. "A bit of a theater nerd name, I know." He turned as someone shouted from the front of the auditorium. "I gotta go. Thank you again!"

By the time Hadassah had returned after letting Chekhov sniff every inch of the ground before finally deciding on the perfect spot, callbacks for the kids' roles were well underway.

Griffith motioned to a boy with floppy hair wearing a well-worn flannel. "Okay, Leroy. Can you read Oliver's part for me on the paper Zinnia gave you?" He gestured to another boy wearing a polo and khaki pants, as if he had come straight from one of the private schools in the area. "Tyler, you read the part of Oliver's friend."

Hadassah settled in a seat toward the back so as not to disturb them. Chekhov jumped into her lap.

Leroy, or "Oliver," cleared his throat, keeping his head down. "I don't think I'm cut out for acting," he read. "I think I should quit."

Tyler, as "Oliver's friend," responded by slinging an arm around Leroy's shoulders. "This play wouldn't be the same without you." His words echoed, each dramatically enunciated. He screwed his face into a melodramatic sneer. "It would be a lot better. I agree—you *should* quit!"

Hadassah raised an eyebrow. This kid seemed to have learned his acting skills from telenovelas.

Once kids had been rotated through various scenes and characters, Byron called out, "Will the following people please come to the front and prepare to read. Hadassah Wright, Susan Karl, May Allen..."

Hadassah set down Chekhov, her heart rate picking up. This

was it. She made her way to the front while Byron continued calling the names of women, then Griffith called the names of the—far fewer—men.

Hadassah handed Chekhov's leash back to Griffith. "Here's the star of the show."

"He definitely thinks he is." Griffith scratched the dog's head, tucking the leash under his elbow. "Thanks so much for taking him out."

Hadassah joined the others near the stage. They took turns going up on stage and reading off parts of scenes, until eventually Hadassah ended up paired across from the potential male leads, reading for the female lead of Emily.

A man with gray hair stepped up opposite of Hadassah, a swagger in his step.

"Okay, Richard, you're reading the part of 'James,' Emily's love interest," Griffith said. "And, go."

"Emily. I didn't expect to see you here." Richard/James spread his arms and planted his fists on his hips, posing like a superhero.

Oh, no. Hadassah forced herself to remain in character and gave a sweet smile that faded into a look of distress. "James, thank goodness. Do you know where I can find a reindeer?"

After Richard's posing and winking and cheesy smiles ceased with the end of the scene, Hadassah released a sigh of relief. She certainly hoped James wasn't meant to be played like that.

The next man recited all of his lines as if they were jokes, looking out to the audience after each one. Hadassah could almost hear "ba-dum-tsh" going off in his brain.

"Thank you, next." Lilian, the theater director, cut him off. "Do we have someone else?"

In the seats, Griffith shuffled his papers. "One more."

A young man who couldn't be older than eighteen sprang forward, all gangly limbs. "That's me."

They only had three options for the part of James? The only one who looked remotely the right age was Mr. Ba-Dum-Tsh.

Lilian raised an eyebrow and glanced at Griffith. "Personally, I'd like to hear more from Hadassah. Griffith, would you read opposite from her?"

His eyes widened. "Oh. Uh. I suppose I could." He wrapped Chekhov's leash around the arm of his chair and grabbed a copy of the script.

Why did Lilian want to hear more from just her? Was that a good sign? Bad sign?

Her heart thumped, and she struggled to keep her hands from shaking the pages.

Griffith flipped through the script. "Okay. Let's do Act II, Scene Three."

Hadassah found the spot, and Griffith began.

"Emily, you're an excellent director, but I know your passion lies elsewhere."

The intensity in his eyes surprised her. He had immediately jumped into character, into scene.

She sighed. "I wish I could be on the stage, becoming someone else—anyone else—but I have to be practical about this."

"Or maybe you don't." Griffith stepped forward. "Maybe this feeling, this desire in your heart, is there for a reason."

Hadassah waved him off. "You don't need me, James."

"I do need you." He paused, just long enough. "Not just for this play."

In that moment, she really did feel like Emily, gazing into the eyes of the man she'd grown to love. Griffith was no longer Griffith, but James, a man who didn't know how else to tell her that he felt the same.

"And, scene."

Byron's voice broke through the illusion. He pointed. "Griffith, your dog just ran away with your pencil."

A blur of white darted through the seats, head high in triumph.

"Chekhov!" Griffith took off after the dog.

That was fantastic. I hope I get this part. Byron had cut them off so quickly, though. Was it because she'd done poorly?

As Byron glared after Griffith's retreating form, she suspected it might be for another reason entirely.

Coffee sizzled in the greenroom—a room bedecked in, well, green paint.

A place of refuge for actors and directors alike during rehearsals and performances. Zinnia had put a new filter in the coffee machine and tossed in grounds from Colombia the moment callbacks had finished. They'd held the actors way too late, almost eleven PM, and now the group would have to determine who would make the cast of the show.

They had about one hour to do so before they'd have to email everyone the list and call them into rehearsal on Thursday.

Griffith inhaled the nutty scent of the brew and sighed. The smell had transported him back to his part-time job at She Brews.

"All right, everyone." Lilian's shawl swept into the room. Beside her, the dramaturg. The dramaturg, as Griffith discovered in college, was a person who looked into the history of a play. He or she would tell the cast in-depth analyses of plays, so the cast could better know how to portray the characters authentically.

The dramaturg at this theater, who Griffith learned went by the name of Arthur, collapsed into a chair in the most dramatic fashion an elderly man could muster at that late hour.

Posters from former shows full of autographs from the cast decorated the cinderblock bricks. Griffith had spent many an hour in here sizzling grilled cheese during rehearsals.

"Let's begin casting these roles, shall we?" Lilian nodded at Zinnia who placed a coffee mug in front of her. "Thanks, dear. Now, Griffith." She swirled a stir stick in her cup. "You ultimately have the final say when it comes to deciding who gets what part, but I do want you to take into consideration our immense expertise."

She lifted the drink to her lips and sipped.

Then she set the cup onto a round table. "Aside from Zinnia, you have the least amount of experience here." She shot a pointed look at Byron, then back at him. "You ought to mull over our feedback."

His hands twitched, and he fought the urge to roll them into fists. Instead, he grabbed a cup from Zinnia, one with a *Hamilton* logo on the front.

"Of course, Lilian. I value your opinion."

He made sure to place emphasis on the *your*. Arthur and Zinnia probably had some good thoughts as well, but Byron? He sucked in a breath and blew it out. *The man does have tons of experience. Even if he comes off as arrogant.*

"Wonderful." Lilian reached for a small cream packet from a basket and tore open the lid. She dumped the white contents into her cup. "Let's begin with the main roles, shall we? For Emily?"

"Hadassah." Byron didn't miss a beat.

Griffith parked in a soft, blue chair and flicked through his audition evaluation sheets. Sure enough, for his remark on Hadassah, he'd written one line, "If she doesn't get the part of Emily, I'll riot."

Wow, had he and Byron actually come to an agreement on something? Throughout callbacks, Byron would lean over and whisper remarks like, "Ugh, this person can't act to save their lives," even though Griffith thought they had plenty of potential. Many actors needed a little help with projection and not adding awkward pauses in the middle of scenes.

Griffith nodded. "I agree, completely. No one else came close to matching the vision I had for the part."

The dramaturg rested his chin against his fist and grunted. Perhaps in approval or perhaps to say, "I really don't care. Please let me go to sleep."

Lilian stared at Zinnia, who was busy blowing away steam from the rim of her thermos. "Whatever Griffith decides," Lilian said, "I approve. He may not have a ton of experience, but he has a knack for this thing." She lifted a brow in the direction of Byron, whose face had harshened a shade deeper.

"No arguments here." Lilian licked her thumb and flickered through her papers. "Emily goes to Hadassah. Now for the male lead and love interest. I wasn't really blown away by anyone but—" She pulled down her glasses to the tip of her nose and peered at Griffith.

His chin bent toward his hands. Warmth spread throughout his cheeks.

Reading with Hadassah had made him feel joy again. The same way that Ryan described how he felt whenever he shot movies. They did seem to share a connection—stage chemistry that was. Nothing else, right?

Why did his heartbeat double in speed right now?

Speaking of Ryan, thank the Lord he offered to come and pick up Chekhov. He even promised to take the dog for a long walk before returning him to Griffith's studio.

"I-I don't know." Byron cleared his throat and dipped his tea bag into his mug. He'd been the only one to refuse Zinnia's offer of coffee. "Wasn't there that one guy? With the hair? Didn't he do a good job?"

"Richard?" Lilian squinted at one of her papers. "I thought he played it off too cocky. Besides, the man was about fifty. We're looking at a character who is early thirties at the latest."

"Stage makeup," Byron suggested.

"My vote is Griffith, anyone else?" Lilian asked.

"Griffith." Zinnia answered before Byron could answer the question. "I'm assuming the droopy nod from Arthur means he agrees."

So Griffith would play the part. Lilian had starred in some shows she directed, but she often required the help of the stage manager to aid in the directing aspect. Rocks hit his intestines. That meant that Byron would have a lot more say in rehearsals than he'd hoped.

They made their way through the rest of the cast list, until they discussed the part of Oliver, the orphan child lead.

"That kid Tyler is perfect for the role." Byron slapped his tea bag onto a pile of napkins. "He was loud, expressive, and wouldn't require a whole lot of coaching. Most of the kids are too quiet."

Griffith frowned at his evaluation for Tyler. He'd written,

"Definitely can act, and by that, I mean <u>over</u>act. I can tell this kid has had a ton of main parts—as he noted on his resume—and he's gotten cocky about it. I'd rather work with someone who has a learning spirit and who can feel the gravity of getting a lead role."

Griffith set his sheet on the table. "Ty does have a lot of experience. However, I want actors who can grow. Who listen to direction. Who have potential. I saw that a lot in Leroy tonight."

Lilian pursed her lips. A clock hoisted in the corner of the room filled the silence with ticks.

"He would need a lot of work." Lilian grabbed another cream container. "Time that we don't have on our side. Remember my advice from earlier, Griffith. Take in the experience of those in the room."

"I know, and I value Byron's feedback. However, I just don't *see* Ty as Oliver. Leroy? He feels like he was born to play this."

Lilian thumbed her chin. "Well, as I said, it's ultimately your call."

They finalized the list about twenty minutes later and stumbled into their cars. Griffith had to defrost his vehicle for another fifteen before he could drive home. When he returned to the apartment, he scritched Chekhov's ears, handed him a doggie treat for all his "hard work," and flipped open his laptop lid.

He pulled up his email and began a message to the cast.

Thank you all for coming to auditions, and for those who were at callbacks tonight, I appreciate everyone who showed up and were willing to do cold reads from the script. I know this is a new play for everyone—except myself—so I admire you all being flexible.

I've attached the rehearsal schedule, and you'll find the cast list below. Remember that the cast is required to be at tech week, dress rehearsals, and the final show. Cast members are only allowed to miss up to two rehearsals total. Please don't miss tech week or dress rehearsals.

Please let me know by 5 PM today if you cannot perform in your part. We will find a replacement and inform them about the change.

I've also included a file of the play so you can begin memorization. You will receive a hard copy in our table reading rehearsal on Thursday. Actors will need to be off-book by Wednesday, December 15.

Without further ado, here's our cast list.

CAST LIST FOR "IN THE WINGS"
Emily: Hadassah Wright
James: Griffith Williams
Oliver:

Griffith stilled his fingertips. Lilian did want him to get this show as close to perfect as possible. Images from past winter performances flickered across his vision. Complicated dance numbers with impressive choreography, monologues that made the audience cry—he needed to compete against all of those to prove he deserved a full-time spot in that theater.

With Ty, he could get there, no problem.

However, with Leroy—Leroy was risky. If he didn't grow enough, in less than a month, by the performance, the audience wouldn't enjoy the show.

Then again...Lilian took a risk on him for *In the Wings*. Why couldn't he return the favor?

He typed in Leroy's name next to the part of Oliver.

Then he finished the list and clicked send. He rubbed his dry eyes. Man did he need sleep. Sadly, right before he could shut the laptop, he spotted an email from his mother at the top of his inbox with the subject line, "More Reasons Why You Should Join Us in the D.R."

Despite the churning in his stomach, he clicked on the message.

Hi, Sweetheart.

Another Christian site did a feature on the work we're doing, and they interviewed Hudson for it. Click on the link below to read all about our work in the Haitian villages.

We really could use a man with your muscle. Just think about it, okay? God built you to build things. Much as I love Hudson, those at the compound have given him the name, "Bean Pole." He never could quite develop that brute strength that you have.

God has given you a gift, and I just don't want to see it go to waste.

We'll talk about it more when I see you at Christmas. Love you!

Guilt soured his insides.

Had he wasted his time at the theater when he could've helped the Haitian people who were displaced in the Dominican Republic? If God wanted him to do theater, why did he craft him like a bodybuilder?

He stared at the email for another fifteen minutes, and then sleep overtook him.

Chapter Five

"REMEMBER TO TURN IN YOUR OUTLINES on Friday." Hadassah capped the dry-erase marker in her hand and turned to her class. "I can't wait to see all of your ideas."

The group of middle-school-aged students filed out of the Sunday School classroom that was used for home school classes during the week. Luke and Matthew remained sitting in the back, lounging in their chairs and looking bored.

Hadassah raised an eyebrow at them. "Do you two even know what your essay topics are going to be?"

"Do I *have* to write the essay?" Matthew slumped, arms dangling. "Mom has me in the freshman composition class too."

"Sorry, Charlie. You're still my student. You have to do this one as well."

He heaved a sigh.

Luke raised his hand, even though all the other students had left. "The dog ate my homework."

Hadassah snorted and ruffled his hair. "Nice try. Let's go get Liz and head home."

On the way back to the house, while Matthew and Luke talked about Legos in the back and Elizabeth shuffled through her homework in the passenger seat, Hadassah ran over her plans for the day in her head. Once they got home, she would hand everything off to Mom and shut herself away to read the script until she had to take the boys to soccer practice.

The script. She couldn't stop a smile from spreading. She'd almost shrieked and woken up her siblings last night when she saw the email. Not only had she made it into the play—she'd gotten the lead. The last time she'd actually been able to act had been in a church Christmas pageant, which hadn't exactly scratched the itch for theater.

The truth was, she'd never been in a real play. She loved church skits and VBS dramas, but without any sort of training, she had never felt confident enough to audition for the community theater productions.

Until it had offered an excuse to turn down a date with Byron.

"Mom, do I have to write an essay for Hadassah?" Matthew shouted as soon as he'd made it through the door.

Elizabeth gave him a gentle cuff. "No yelling across the house."

Before Hadassah could even set down her bag or take off her shoes, the three younger boys came tearing into the living room. "Hadassah, Mom said you're supposed to watch us while she teaches history because we're being pests," Enoch said all in one breath.

"Matthew and Luke need to catch up on their history because they're being *slackers*," Isaiah added with a giggle.

Luke scowled. "Mom didn't say that."

"Everyone settle down." Mom emerged from the schoolroom, a pencil tucked behind one ear and three books under her arm. "Matthew, you have to write the essay. You and Luke come in here and start your history. Elizabeth, your online class starts in ten minutes, so you better log on." She turned to Hadassah. "I'm in the middle of history with Priscilla and Tabitha, so can you watch the boys? They're done with school for the day."

Hadassah sighed internally. *So much for shutting myself away.* She couldn't leave Mom to wrangle three wild little boys while also making sure Matthew and Luke remained on task and teaching the girls. "Of course. We'll hang out in the living room."

Mom hustled over and gave her a quick peck on the check. "Thanks, sweetie. You're such a huge help."

Hadassah set the three boys up with a pile of jumbo Legos and blocks in the middle of the living room floor and plopped onto the couch with a laptop, the script pulled up on the screen.

She had only made it through three pages before Obadiah started crying because Isaiah knocked over his tower.

She struggled to maintain her patience over the next half hour as the boys continued to demand her attention for help with pieces not fitting together, sibling spats, and just admiring their constructions. Only fifteen pages into the script, she wanted to scream.

Hadassah could remember only one time she had actually snapped at her siblings. She'd been sixteen, studying for the SAT. At the time, she had dreamed of college—friends her own age, no siblings to care for, so many interesting things to learn. She didn't know what exactly she wanted to study, but she was ready for something new.

That day, Mom had gone to a doctor's appointment for baby number ten, leaving Hadassah and Yocheved with the kids. The current baby and toddler had been screaming, the preschoolers had gotten into the glitter, Matthew and Luke had broken a lamp, and Elizabeth was crying in frustration over a sewing machine malfunction that had destroyed hours of work.

Hadassah had slammed her practice workbook on the table and threw back her chair. "Would everyone, for once in your life, *shut up!*"

The entire family, minus the baby, froze, staring at her.

She slumped back into her chair and threw open her SAT workbook. "I swear that you all will be the reason I go to college in California or Florida or *anywhere* but here."

Slowly, Yocheved had walked toward Elizabeth and passed screaming baby Enoch off to the ten-year-old. "I need you to take the baby for a minute, Liz." Then she grabbed Hadassah's arm and dragged her into the bedroom they shared with Elizabeth.

Yocheved closed the door and faced Hadassah. "What was that?"

"I'm so sick of it." Tears brimmed. "I've been taking care of kids since I was in elementary school. I just want a break."

"I know it's hard sometimes." Yocheved cocked her head, brows knit. "Honestly, God has blessed us to have this opportunity. It's such good practice for when we're moms." She took Hadassah's hands. "Aren't you excited to have your own? Motherhood is God's greatest calling for women. We've been blessed as daughters to serve Mom as joyful helpers."

God's greatest calling. Was this God's plan for her? Was this her purpose—to care for children, like Jesus had? If so, moving anywhere else would be selfish.

"You're right." She'd straightened her spine. "I'm sorry. I'll apologize to the kids."

"I understand your frustration." Yocheved squeezed her hand. "Being a godly woman is hard, but we need to honor our parents and think of the whole family."

A year and a half later, Aaron and Yocheved were engaged. Leaving Hadassah with no choice but to stay, and no time for anything like a local college.

Now...Liz was old enough to step into the position.

Hadassah shook that thought away. No. The doors had closed for Hadassah. Clearly, God had called her to the care of children, to a long preparation for motherhood. She was so good at it, after all. Quiet, but firm. For Elizabeth, someone should give Liz that choice. To pursue her calling without worrying about the family. Hadassah would make sure Liz never ended up stuck.

Stuck like her.

Over the bickering of Enoch and Isaiah, a knock sounded at the door. Hadassah stood and went to open it.

On the other side stood Byron, hands in his pockets, a self-satisfied smirk twisting his lips. "Hello, Hadassah."

"Byron. What—what are you doing here?"

Behind her, something crashed, and Obadiah wailed.

Hadassah turned to see Isaiah standing over Obadiah's former block tower, foot still raised from kicking the structure down.

"Isaiah Elisha, that was not kind." Hadassah began to step toward them, ready to begin the usual rigamarole of the "we need to show love to our family" talk, guided apologies to the offended sibling, and working to right the wrong that was committed—in this case, helping Obie rebuild his tower.

Instead, Byron stepped forward. "You look frazzled. Allow me."

He strode toward the boys, expression stony. "Isaiah, sit in the corner. You're in time-out for five minutes to think about what you've done." He turned to Obadiah. "There's no sense in crying over blocks. You can stack them again just fine." He turned a stern gaze on all three boys. "You're going to play quietly, or there will be consequences. Understand?"

Eyes wide, the boys nodded. Isaiah slunk away to the corner and sat.

Byron returned to Hadassah and smiled. "There's that. It's nice how our families are so close like this. Now we can talk. What are you up to today?"

Hadassah gripped the door handle, struggling for words. Obadiah sat pale-faced, staring blankly at his blocks. Enoch watched Byron with mouth open. Meanwhile, Isaiah wiped what looked like a tear from his eye.

She clenched a fist, forcing her voice to remain steady. "I'm pretty busy today, actually. Right now I'm working on reading through the script while watching the boys."

"Oh, the script, excellent. Why don't I go over it with you?"

"There's no need for—"

"No worries." Byron cut her off and gave what he must have considered a charming grin. "It will be my pleasure. I figure as the stage manager, I'll have some useful insights."

She took a deep breath. That was true. She could use whatever help she could get. She'd never been in a real play before, after all.

"Okay. Thank you."

Hadassah closed the door and returned to the couch, opening the laptop. Byron sat beside her and leaned forward to peer at the screen.

"Ah. This part." He wrinkled his nose. "I think it's probably obvious that it's meant to bring sympathy for Emily. Nevertheless, I'm sure you can tell from something as on-the-nose as caring for the orphan boy."

"Right."

"Here..." He scrolled. "That scene really isn't important, so you can skip it."

Hadassah blinked. *Every* scene in a good play was important, every line of dialogue carefully crafted.

Disdain dripped from Byron's voice as he stopped scrolling. "Oh, this scene comes a little too early in the play, but it's an important character development moment for Emily. Well. Important might be a bit of an overstatement, as she doesn't really develop much."

Anger burned in Hadassah's gut. Griffith had worked hard on this play, yet Byron treated it like garbage. Wasn't he supposed to be supporting Griffith in his role as stage manager?

"It was so quiet, I thought I'd come check things out." Hadassah looked up to see Mom standing across the living room, smiling. "Byron, it's so good to see you."

"Mrs. Wright." Byron stood and nodded to her. "Always a pleasure."

Mom beamed at the boys, all sitting quietly. "Did you do this? They've been giving me a headache all day."

"It was nothing—I think they just appreciated some gentle guidance from a masculine authority figure." He chuckled. "You know how boys are."

"Thank you, Byron." Mom beamed at Hadassah. "I'm glad to see you two finally having a chance to talk."

"Unfortunately, I need to take Enoch and Isaiah to soccer practice." Hadassah stood.

"That's too bad." Byron cocked his head with a slight toss of his auburn locks. "Maybe we can spend time together this weekend?"

"Sorry, the older boys have a science convention. Good to see you, Byron." She waved to her brothers. "Come on boys, let's go get ready for practice."

Before Mom or Byron could say anything else, she escaped the room, two wide-eyed boys in tow.

Five minutes into the first rehearsal, Griffith wanted to leave.

The dramaturg Arthur had assured him that he would do well when he took over the first half of the rehearsal. He claimed that in past shows he would elucidate upon important items for actors to know about the context and characters of the plays in which he "drama-turged."

"In the previous theater I worked at, I even wore bloomers over my pants to help the kids in the production of Annie understand the garments of that era." Arthur had explained this over a pot of coffee when he and Griffith arrived at rehearsal thirty minutes early.

Griffith indeed had worked with dramaturgs before in past shows. They would always bring new life to the shows in which the actors took part. For instance, in Griffith's performance of *The Pirates of Penzance* in college, their own dramaturg let them know about how the musical's satire theme poked fun at the political institutions of its day.

Problem was Griffith's play had no production history, no political leanings, and no context to speak of.

As the whole cast sat in a circle on the stage, Arthur had informed them of his "interpretations" of the script.

"As you can see on page forty-six, Emily talks about how the post office is frantic this time of year. We can assume our author means to highlight the ineffectiveness of our government." He paced back and forth in the center of their blobbish formation of bodies. "On page sixty-seven, Oliver plays with a *red* ball."

He lifted up a finger, eyes twinkling.

"Now for those of us who have done literary analysis." He nodded at Byron. "We know that *red* represents *pain.* When Oliver plays with a *red* ball, he wants to show us about the *pain* of his childhood."

In truth, Griffith spotted Chekhov with a crimson squeaky ball when he wrote that scene and thought, "Why not? We'll throw that in."

Also, said "Oliver" in question had drooped in the circle. In fact, most of the kids had succumbed to a stupor during this boring tirade from Arthur.

Griffith shot to his feet.

"Yes, thank you, Mr. Arthur, for your wonderful insights. Looking at the time"—he motioned to the white clock at the back of the auditorium—"we really should be getting on to the next part of the rehearsal."

Arthur smoothed out a wrinkle on his mustard yellow shirt. "Really, Griffith, I still think we have ten minutes or so—"

"Yes, thank you. Everyone give Mr. Arthur a hand."

Griffith made a big display of clapping.

Half-hearted applause from all the actors followed. Wrinkles formed on Arthur's forehead when he exited stage left.

"Now." Griffith clapped his hands and winced at the enormity of his clapping. His large palms always sounded like thunder peals "I know it's unusual for a community theater to do a table work rehearsal."

He tried to make his voice go as high as possible, to contrast with Arthur's morose tones. Some kids a few feet away had jolted at the sound of his palms smacking together.

"For those who don't know what table work is, we basically look at the script and share with each other something we learned about our characters. After we do that, we'll read through the script together."

Thirty cast members had showed up for this rehearsal. Griffith emailed the non-speaking ensemble yesterday to let them know they didn't need to come. For everyone else, he sent off a message asking them to peruse the script before they arrived at rehearsal today.

"Does anyone want to go first? What did you learn about your characters?"

He grimaced at the question. With his luck, the actors would pull similar "insights" like Arthur did.

Everyone in the circle stilled.

Oh great, *no one* had read the play, had they?

Then, Hadassah's shaky arm lifted. Today she'd decided to wear what looked like a homemade button-up dress.

"Yes, Emily." He noticed some heads cock from about five of the child actors. "In rehearsals, I may often refer to you by your 'part' name rather than your real one. Anyway, Emily, go ahead."

"Well." Hadassah tucked a strand of hair behind her ear. Rose bloomed in her cheeks. "I think I may have learned something interesting about Emily when I read through the script last night." Her eyes widened. "I have no idea if it's right or not."

"Not to worry, *Emily,* there are no wrong answers."

Well, except for Arthur's "answers."

She sucked in a breath, exhaled.

"Okay, well, I noticed how Emily really struggles with her role as the director. Especially when a bunch of kids half-heartedly perform on stage. Because she wants to be up there acting, not directing."

Hadassah paused and bit her lip. Her fingers clutched her braid.

"She really wrestles with her calling. She knows that she feels the most joy when she acts, and she doesn't understand why she hasn't gotten the chance to, but—" Hadassah flickered through her hard-copy script. "I'm happy that at the end of the show, she gets a chance to end up on stage and do her calling. Right before curtain call. Huh."

She pressed a finger to her lips, as though deep in thought. "I hadn't thought about that, Griffith. Calling, curtain call. Did you do that intentionally?"

Did he? That sounded right, at least, more right than any of Arthur's elucidations.

Maybe his subconscious slipped that in, before he could notice anything. That happened sometimes when he wrote.

"Wow, Hada—I mean, Emily, those are great insights. Anyone else learn anything about their characters?"

Shoulders eased around the circle. Other hands rose as people shared. Leroy mentioned how his character seemed shy at first but at last gained confidence in his abilities when Emily encouraged him enough.

"These are amazing, guys." Griffith returned to his spot in the circle and reached for his papers. "I'd love for us to keep going, but we should probably get to reading the script." His eyes roved the auditorium. Parents of the children, who didn't audition for the show, had parked themselves in the chairs. "Before we run out of time."

They read.

Byron filled in the action beats and stage directions in the play.

Warmth spread throughout Griffith's ears as he heard the words, *his* words, spoken aloud for the first time. Red pen in hand, he marked up the sections of his own script for where he could improve sticky spots.

His lips twitched when the actors laughed at all the right parts, and some of the middle school boys shouted "ooo" whenever "Emily" delivered a zinger to a misbehaving child or condescending adult.

They reached the end of the play. Enthusiastic applause erupted from the circle.

Griffith's grin had spread so far that his mouth started to hurt. He glanced at the clock. Ten minutes remained in rehearsal.

"We have a little more time." He rose, and his knees cracked from sitting crisscross too long. "Why don't we do an acting exercise to finish up today's rehearsal? Everyone pair up with a partner."

A buzz vibrated in his pocket. He dug out his phone and squinted at the newest message from Lilian.

Lilian: Hey, I just remembered that decorating the lobby for last year's show was a bit of a mad rush. It may be best to start on it as early as possible. Any chance you can get decorations for that? The theater will reimburse you, of course.

Oh boy, yet another thing he'd have to add to the list. He already needed to roam the props loft to get an idea of what supplies the theater had for his show, and what set pieces he had left to procure.

Maybe he could squeeze decoration-shopping into the weekend.

He jolted back when he almost bumped into a figure in front of him.

Hadassah beamed, smile withering as she glanced over her shoulder in Byron's direction. "Hey, partner."

"Hey." He realized he'd stared at her a second too long and lifted his face to the rest of the group, who glanced at him expectantly. "This is a mirroring exercise. Choose an A and a B person. B, try to mirror all of A's actions. Like this." He angled his chin back at Hadassah. "You be A. Go ahead and move your arms or something."

Hadassah lifted her left arm. Griffith parroted her movement with his right.

"You get the picture. All right everyone, mirror."

"This was really fun today." Hadassah cocked her head and

lifted her right elbow. "It's not often that church productions let their actors go so in depth into the script. They usually just say, 'Be mad in this scene,' and so you're mad, but you don't know why."

Griffith chuckled and copied Hadassah's movement of lifting her leg. "I'm glad you liked it. Stories are far too important to be done haphazardly. I figured, let's do this thing right."

Hadassah frowned and reached for her dress pocket. Nice, she must've sewn those bad boys into the fabric.

Oh wait, this wasn't for the exercise. She'd unburied her phone and read a notification. All color drained from her cheeks. Once more, she flicked a glance at Byron. Had Griffith missed something? Did those two know each other?

Then Hadassah slipped her phone back into her pocket and pinched her nose. "Sorry, we can get back to the exercise."

"Something wrong?"

"Just." She lifted her hand, mime fashion, and waved it in a circle. "Something my mom wants me to do that I'm really not up for on Saturday."

Griffith impersonated her impression of a bird flapping. Maybe Hadassah's mom asked her to babysit the kids again. She did tow around about a million and one of them when she bumped into him at the library.

"Well, I am going decoration shopping during the weekend if you need an out. I could always use some good judgment. Like what you had earlier for the script insights."

"Actually." Color returned to her cheeks and her shoulders dropped two inches. "That would be perfect."

Chapter Six

HADASSAH STEPPED OUT OF THE MINIVAN in the parking lot of the Christmas tree farm and wrapped her coat more tightly around her.

Well, "Christmas tree farm" was a bit of a generous term. Every year, a tent popped up in one of the empty lots in town, and soon enough pine trees filled the lot, ready for Christmas. She and Griffith didn't have time for something fancy.

December cold nipped at her cheeks as she crossed the parking lot, heading for the tent that marked the entrance to "Carl's Christmas Tree Emporium."

When Mom texted her on Thursday to let her know that Dad had volunteered to take the boys to the science convention, her heart had dropped.

Mom: You can go with Byron on Saturday! Isn't that wonderful?

Part of her wanted to tell Mom the truth...but as kids, the adults had never listened to Yocheved when she complained about Byron. The golden boy could do no wrong. Why would Mom believe Hadassah now?

Luckily, Griffith had jumped in to save the day with a theater-related task that she, of course, had to attend.

She spotted Griffith's stocky form across the parking lot. She'd seen him playing basketball with his friends before—lanky Andy, tall Elijah, fine-boned Ryan, and then Griffith, built like a tank. He would make a good linebacker, though he was a little on the shorter side for football. Not the type people would expect on the stage, until he opened his mouth and fell into character.

Then—well, from the first time Hadassah had seen him give a

monologue, she knew he was destined for theater.

"Hey." He waved a gloved hand. "Ready to find some thespian foliage?"

"Trees that can recite Shakespeare only." She fell into step with him.

He grinned. "Thanks for coming along. To be honest, I don't have much of an eye for, well, decor."

"That makes two of us. Maybe together we'll make one design-savvy individual."

As they headed for the entrance, Hadassah checked the bounce in her step. Where had all of this energy—and all these quips—come from? Usually with people her own age, she felt herself turning inward, quieter, waiting for them to take the lead as Yocheved always had.

Or she said dumb, embarrassing things. Like when she'd gone on a date with Andy Jackson, and when he asked what she wanted with her future, she'd told him she wanted to have lots of kids. "At least six."

Though Andy remained friendly, they never went on another date.

Griffith waved in greeting to the owner of the "Emporium," a man in flannel with a thick mustache, when they entered the tent. Then Hadassah trailed Griffith into the rows of trees.

He planted his fists on his hips. "So. What makes a good foyer tree?"

Hadassah pictured the layout. "Tall and skinny, I think. We don't want to take up too much floor space, but we want people to be able to see the tree over the heads of the crowd."

"Good points." Griffith slowly rotated, scanning the trees. "I think the taller ones are toward the back."

"Just like picture day."

He chuckled. "Lead the way, tree expert."

She lifted her warm, heavy skirt, trying to keep from collecting any fallen needles with the hem. Pine irritated Obie's skin and could lead to itchy red bumps for the poor little guy.

Griffith pointed at a tiny, droopy sapling. "That would work if we were putting on a different play."

"Decorations would certainly be cheap with one big red bulb."

Griffith tromped around a tree with the girth of a reading lamp. "Maybe a little too skinny?"

"Poor guy must have missed Thanksgiving." Hadassah's forest green skirt flared in the wind, and she giggled. "Maybe I could be the tree." She spun to make her skirt poof out and put her hands over her head in her best tree imitation.

Griffith laughed. "Careful, there, Tree. You're going to crash into the other trees."

Hadassah stumbled to a stop with a giggle. It felt good not to be watching children run through the pines, worrying if they would topple the trees like dominoes. As she wobbled, she rested her hand on Griffith's offered arm. "Thanks."

A feminine voice drew her attention. "Oh, hey, Griffith."

A woman only a bit taller than Hadassah with honey-colored hair strolled hand in hand with none other than Andy of the embarrassing date.

Griffith's voice boomed with friendliness. "Hi, Caroline. Hey, Andy." He and Andy performed the ritual known as the "bro hug," clasping hands in a handshake while thumping one another on the back, before Griffith stepped away and gestured to Hadassah. "Do you all know each other?"

Hadassah could feel her cheeks burning even in the cold. "A little."

"Hadassah, right?" Caroline pulled her light gray peacoat closer as a breeze picked up. She looked more ready to walk the streets of New York than a so-called Michigan tree emporium. "We've run into each other here and there."

Despite Caroline's smile, Hadassah's skin felt too big, and she wanted to melt into the ground like Frosty the Snowman. Here it was, that awkwardness, the shyness that crept in every time she encountered new people—except on the stage.

"Nice to see you," Hadassah squeaked.

Caroline's eyes darted from Hadassah to Griffith, and her eyebrow twitched along with a sly smile. "Sorry to bother you two. I wouldn't want to interrupt anything."

Andy held back a smile and nudged her with his elbow. Meanwhile, Griffith's ears reddened. *He should really put on a hat with this chill.*

Griffith cleared his throat. "No worries, we're looking for a tree to decorate the theater's lobby."

"The big ones are back that way." Caroline pointed with one arm, wrapping the other through Andy's. "We just came from there, and they're way too large for either of our apartments, unless we want to live in a forest for a few weeks."

Andy chuckled. "Peaches and Sammy might like that."

"Okay, you can live in a tree and let the dogs become one with nature." Caroline turned her face up toward Andy, her nose wrinkled in amusement. "I won't be the one to explain your new pine needle carpet to your roommate."

From what Hadassah knew of Andy's worship leader roommate, Elijah, he might not mind.

Griffith laughed. "I think he and Liv might take revenge on you for letting it happen, Caroline, and get you two an even bigger tree."

While the three of them cracked jokes about who would prank who with obnoxiously large trees, Hadassah watched Caroline and Andy grin at each other, noticed the easy way their hands intertwined.

What would it be like to be that comfortable with someone?

Better yet—what would it be like for someone to look at her that way, not a frazzled glance and a quick thanks for taking care of the kids, but an attentive ear, someone willing to know what she thought, how she felt?

"Anyway, we'll let you go." Andy's eyes flicked from Griffith to Hadassah in almost the same way Caroline's had earlier. "I'll talk to you later about those flyers for the play, Griff."

"Sure thing." Griffith waved.

Hadassah managed to mumble a quiet, "Nice to see you."

As the crunching footsteps of the couple receded, Griffith cocked his head at Hadassah. "Are you all right?"

She focused on shaking pine needles from her hem. "Oh, yes, sorry. I was just thinking about making sure I don't track too much pine. My youngest brother, Obadiah, is allergic."

"Some people are allergic to Christmas trees?"

"Yeah, his skin gets red and irritated." She looked up to see Griffith's brow furrowed. "What's wrong?"

"We're going to have a lot of people in the lobby. I would hate for someone with an allergy to come into contact with the trees."

"Oh." She tucked her hands in her coat. "I hadn't thought of that. Maybe we can hang decorations from the walls and ceiling instead."

"That sounds good." He brushed his hands together. "I know it wasn't in the original plan, but would you like to come downtown with me to check out decorations in the shops?"

Her heart warmed. More time "occupied" with important tasks and unavailable to Byron? Griffith was speaking her language. "I'd love to."

If only she could look for Christmas decor forever.

Griffith chuckled as Hadassah held up a peacock-shaped ornament in front of her eye.

"Ah yes, Griffith, nothing screams 'Christmas play' quite like this one."

She set the "bird" back into the plastic bins they had in the all-things Christmas store in downtown Roseville. Griffith noticed how

Hadassah stared at her fingertips, as they had now received a fresh coat of purple glitter.

"Mr. Peacock certainly is a great contender for our lobby decorations. What about—" He reached into the bin and dug out a hamburger-shaped ornament. "What in the world? Who puts this on their Christmas tree?"

"*Obviously,* it was the fourth gift brought by the wise men. Gold, frankincense, myrrh, and a cheeseburger."

He dropped the bauble back into the box and laughed along with her. They'd made next to no progress in finding decor to bedeck the atrium. Not that that should've floated to the top of the list anyway.

Lilian has a habit of making a big deal out of small items.

For *The Importance of Being Earnest,* she employed Griffith with the task of painting the sets. However, she often halted his progress of coloring the buildings and stage floor by pointing to the "edifices" of the set-buildings and saying, "Oh, I think it would look pretty with vines. Do you think you could paint some vines right now?"

"Lilian." He'd pinched his nose, daubing some blue paint onto the skin. "I need to *paint* the building first before we can get in any little details."

"Oh, oh, right. Well, make sure you get some vines in there. Quickly as possible."

Would she do the same thing to his play? Make him focus on minute details and erase any time he had to work on the major ones?

He pinched the price tag attached to the burger. Yeesh, five dollars an ornament. The theater budget couldn't afford that.

"Too expensive?" Hadassah appeared to read his expression and set down a donut ornament. She wiped glitter off on her pants and gloved her fingers with some mittens from her pockets.

"We've been reusing the same Ben Nye makeup backstage for the greater portion of ten years. To be honest, we can barely afford to go anywhere to get *anything* for this play." He ought to have consulted the props loft—the island of misfit supplies of previous shows—before he went shopping.

He convinced himself that Hadassah needed to get out of an engagement. To appease Lilian that he accomplished one of the many "little" tasks she bombarded him with.

"Oh, wow." Hadassah clapped a hand to her mouth. The handmade sapphire scarf she wore today really brought out her eyes. "Now it makes sense why you asked the cast to bring our own makeup in the welcome packets. You really don't have much of a budget, do you?"

"Community theaters live in thrift stores and rummage sales. The only people who can afford the big stuff are the big guys. Even then, Broadway isn't what it used to be."

He winced at the words. More reasons to follow his parent's insistence that he drop everything and join them for mission work. "Plays are dying, Griffith," Mom had told him on a spotty FaceTime call. "Would God call you full-time to something like this when we and your brother are seeing lives changed every day?"

His phone hummed in his pocket. He pulled the device out and read the text from Ryan.

Ryan: You still shopping for trees?
Griffith: Downtown, actually. In the shops.

The message from Ryan appeared seconds later.

Ryan: Oh perfect! I'm actually in the area. Have something to deliver to you. Where are you at?

Griffith texted him the location.

"Well, if we can't afford anything..." Hadassah shoved her fingers into her coat pockets. The fabric on it looked frayed. How long had she had that thing? She did hail from a large family. Maybe they lived in thrift stores too. "How are we gonna decorate the lobby?"

Once they formulated a game plan, they charged into the outdoors. Street vendors lined the shops with tables full of hot chocolate, baked sweets, and pashmina scarves. Griffith spotted Hadassah casting a longing glance at a headscarf with golden threads woven into the fabric.

He fought the urge to reach for his wallet buried in his puffer jacket pockets. "We can scavenge the props loft for decorations, props, sets we can reuse. We also have plenty of generous people in the community who donate goods. I'll ask for Christmas decorations on our Facebook page later."

Thank goodness Hadassah had informed him about Obadiah's allergy to Christmas tree needles. He could only imagine Lilian's ire if someone broke out into hives on opening night.

"Speaking of Christmas decor, does your family have any traditions?" Hadassah weaved around a group of carollers stationed in front of an ice cream shop.

"We do. Or did."

He explained how in the Dominican Republic, most folks didn't place a Christmas tree in their homes. Instead they would position something known as Charamicos, wooden Christmas trees and balls, around the compound.

"We also had a Secret Santa thing of sorts. There, we called it Angelitos—little angels. How about you?"

Hadassah buried herself deeper into her turtleneck as she thought. "Well, we do have a really silly one. Have you heard of the pickle ornament tradition?"

Griffith glanced over his shoulder back at the all-things-Christmas store they'd just left. "You're making that up."

"I am *not*."

Clouds left her mouth as she laughed. She explained about how her family would hide a glass ornament, in the shape of a pickle, somewhere in the tree. On Christmas, after the family would read from the Christmas passage in Luke 2, the kids would attempt to find the "pickle." Whoever did had the opportunity to open the first present.

"It's a German tradition, I think. Oh!" A squeal erupted from her as she almost bumped into a man in an elf costume, who swung a bell. Griffith had to duck out of the way to avoid his teeth colliding with the lip of the instrument.

Instinct kicked in and Griffith swung an arm back to protect Hadassah. He dropped it moments later, as he recognized the figure in the costume.

"Derek?"

Elijah, another one of Griffith's friends, had invited Derek to one of their pick-up games of basketball. They had a chance to grab one of the courts during the fall. The greasy player shot all of five baskets and landed one—for the other team.

They did not invite him back.

"Yeah." Derek's voice cracked as the bell let out a high note. "They were running low on elves today because people didn't show up for their shifts. They called me in." He jerked his chin at the shop behind him, Toy Store-y.

Through the frosted windows, Griffith spotted a man in a Santa costume inside with a line trailing all the way to the door.

Derek sighed. "My girlfriend wouldn't come. She said, and I quote, 'If you make me wear one of those ridiculous costumes, I will personally see that you die in a painful way.' I think it's putting a rift in our relationship." He tapped his conical hat, which had jingle bells attached to it.

Griffith squinted once again at the warm glow from within the store. "Derek, are you the only elf here? Who's corralling the line?"

The queue snaked and bulged. He watched a kid try to cut in front of another one near a display full of stuffed animals.

Bells on Derek's shoulders tinkled when he lifted and dropped them. "No one. Why? Do you two wanna help?" His eyes brightened. "They pay thirteen an hour."

Cotton got caught in Griffith's throat when he swallowed. This place offered three dollars more per hour than She Brews. With him making nothing at the moment by spending all his time at the theater...

He eyed Hadassah. He couldn't ask her to do this, could—

"Sure, Derek. That sounds fun." Hadassah pulled at one of the tassels on her scarf. "I've been corralling kids my whole life, and..." Light dimmed in her pupils. "That's probably what I'll be doing for the rest of it, anyway." She sniffed and cleared her throat. "Why not?"

With a giddiness in his step, Derek led them to the back restrooms where they changed into shoddily-made felt costumes and conical hats. Hadassah burst out into laughter when Derek fitted Griffith into pear-shaped shoes that jingled with every step.

They flanked Santa and eased the line by going through and making the kids giggle. Griffith pretended to be very confused about the whole idea of Christmas, which caused a group of girls in puffy coats to scream, "No!" and explode into fits of tee-hees.

"What are these Christmas cookies that you speak of?" Griffith thumbed his chin.

"Christmas cookies for S-santa," one girl, with a missing front tooth, huffed out. "They're green and red and—"

"Do you *throw* them at Santa?" Griffith did a mock-pitch toward the rotund man in the large chair.

"No! He eats them!"

"After you throw them at him?"

"Nooooo!"

"Director Griffith?"

Griffith snapped his neck up when he spotted a group of children in well-worn clothing at the back of the room. Sure enough, Leroy stood next to a cluster of younger kids and the same woman

Griffith had seen at auditions, the woman who ran the foster home. Griffith waved to the group of girls and padded over to Leroy.

"Hey, Leroy. Great job at rehearsal the other day."

Leroy's cheeks darkened. He glanced at his wet boots. "Thanks. Umm, I'm actually glad you're here. I've been wanting to ask you something."

"Sure thing, bud, what is it?"

Leroy ran his fingers up and down the spikes on a stuffed dinosaur. "Why did you give me the part? Other people like Ty read it better. Was it because—?" He winced. "Because you were sorry for me?"

The line shifted forward a few inches. Leroy didn't move.

"Oh, bud, no." Griffith reached forward to clasp Leroy's shoulder and thought better of it. This culture wasn't as touchy as the D.R. Instead, Griffith dropped his arm. "I gave you the part because you understood the heaviness of it."

Leroy's nose wrinkled. Maybe he'd gotten a whiff of the muddy-slushy stench at the front doors. A few steps in, and he would've smelled the cinnamon the shopkeepers had brushed everything in. "What do you mean?"

"You have a lot of talent, *and* you understand the responsibility of getting a main part. For people like Ty, it's just another feather in their cap. Another thing to check off a list. I don't want someone like that leading my show—"

The bell to the shop dinged.

"—but you understand what I'm asking of you. I believe you're up for the task."

Leroy stared at the carpet, seemingly absorbing all of Griffith's words. Then he glanced up at him, pupils shining. "I hope I am."

"Griffith."

Once again, Griffith's chin snapped in the direction of the door.

Ryan held up a key ring, Griffith's. "Found this. You left them at my apartment when you stopped by earlier to drop off my kettle you borrowed." He gestured at his phone. "You haven't been answering yours."

"Sorry, been busy." He motioned at the line that snaked forward, this time, with Leroy joining it. "Thanks for bringing me my keys."

"That's not all." Ryan slapped the keyring into Griffith's open palm. "Since you haven't been answering your phone, your parents texted mine. Apparently they're at the airport waiting for a ride."

Warmth fled Griffith's cheeks.

"They're—they're in town? Already?"

"I guess it was supposed to be a surprise. They're staying with your aunt something-or-other. She got the times mixed up and is caught up at karate class. I would go pick up your parents, but." He gestured at his side. Griffith noticed the camera bag. "Senior pictures in twenty minutes. Some high school senior wants pictures by the Christmas trees downtown."

Griffith steadied himself, since the pear-shaped shoes threatened to give way.

Time to go pick up his parents.

Chapter Seven

HADASSAH SLUMPED INTO A CHILD-SIZED chair in the corner of the Sunday School classroom. After a quick glance around to make sure no one was watching, she slipped off her uncomfortable church shoes and wiggled her aching toes.

After attending the first service, she had spent the next two teaching Sunday School. Usually, she only taught one class a week, but the third-service teacher was out with a cold, so she'd volunteered.

On the plus side, that meant her family went home without her today—leaving her time to dawdle if she wanted, now that all the children had gone home.

"Knock-knock."

Hadassah looked up to see Yocheved standing in the doorway of the classroom. She jumped up. "What are you doing here?"

"Aaron is guest preaching next Sunday, so the pastor is showing him around this weekend. We would have attended with the family, but we just got here. We had to run out early after our second service."

Hadassah wrapped Yocheved in a hug. "I didn't think I'd see you again until Christmas."

"It was a last-minute thing." Yocheved gave her a squeeze. "There was going to be a different guest pastor, I guess, but he had to cancel." She looked down at Hadassah's feet and giggled. "Oh, are we on holy ground? I can take mine off too."

Hadassah snorted. "Just recovering from three services of church shoes." She gestured at the worn chunky black loafers. "Didn't they used to be yours? Or were they Mom's?"

"Who knows." Yocheved lifted her long corduroy skirt a few

inches and kicked off her footwear, similar in style to Hadassah's, but brown. "There. Good idea."

The two giggled, standing in their stocking feet next to the colorful paintings of Moses and Noah and other biblical figures adorning the classroom walls.

"Anyway, Aaron is going to be here for a while." Yocheved waggled her eyebrows. "I was wondering if you wanted to go get lunch with me."

Lunch with Yocheved instead of wrangling cranky post-Sunday School children? "Absolutely. The Roseville Grill?"

"Perfect. Can I ride with you?"

This time, Hadassah raised her eyebrows. "You trust me after the last time we drove together?"

Yocheved guffawed, a reminder of the carefree girl Hadassah had followed into plenty of scrapes. "I certainly hope you've gotten better at driving in the last five years."

Hadassah had been sixteen and new to her license, but she'd insisted on driving them to youth group herself. Problem was, February in Michigan meant lots of snow and ice, and Hadassah had plowed the family minivan through a ditch and right into a fresh snowbank. Luckily the van survived the ordeal with minimal damage, once Dad came to the rescue and pulled the vehicle free.

The two sisters hadn't had a solo driving adventure together since, and her siblings had teased Hadassah mercilessly for years.

Yet even this ordeal, as the two of them screamed through Hadassah's unintentional donut, brought a smile to her face. They had been more carefree then, before Yocheved became a proper pastor's wife, and Hadassah found herself in charge of eight kids.

Shoes back on, the sisters scurried through the cold parking lot and jumped into the minivan. Hadassah cranked the heater, which always smelled like something was burning. "Buckle up, partner. We'll try not to unsuccessfully impersonate a snow plow today."

Yocheved snorted. "Maybe that's your calling. Hadassah

Wright—snow-plow driver extraordinaire."

"At least give me a bulldozer. Or a steamroller. Those are cooler."

On the way to the diner, Hadassah flipped the radio to a Christmas station, and they sang along dramatically to the carols. Yocheved did all the voices for the characters of "Rudolph the Red-Nosed Reindeer" while Hadassah provided an echo.

The door jangled when they entered The Roseville Grill, and a waitress in 1950s garb pointed them to a booth with bouncy red seats. "My name's Candy, and I'll be your server. Just so you know, our special today is the Rose Burger, a cheeseburger topped with a rose made of bacon."

"Ooo, that for me please." Yocheved didn't even open the menu. "Can I do a side of onion rings? Oh, and for a drink, water and a hot decaf coffee."

"You got it, sweetie." The waitress scribbled on her notebook, then turned to Hadassah. "Are you ready, too, hon, or do you need a minute?"

The dreaded moment where she had to order and her social anxiety kicked into overdrive. Usually she studied the menu and practiced her order five times in her head before having to speak with the wait staff. "Oh, yes, the same thing for me."

"Alrighty. I'll be back with you ladies' coffee in a moment." The waitress swept away in a swirl of bright blue skirt and white ruffled apron.

Hadassah relaxed.

Yocheved chuckled. "Still copying me every time. You hate decaf."

"Not as much as I hate ordering." She leaned forward and cocked her head. "So. What's going on with you? You're...too peppy."

"What?" Yocheved fiddled with a ketchup packet. "It's the Christmas season. I've got Christmas spirit."

Hadassah watched Yocheved's gaze track a young family entering the diner, two little girls skipping behind their mother. Did Yocheved's eyes grow watery?

The waitress twirled by with their drinks, then spun away to help the other patrons during the post-church Sunday lunch rush.

"I mean, you don't have to tell me what's going on." Hadassah sipped her coffee and made a face. Decaf was a crime against humanity. "I'm all ears if you want to share."

Yocheved sighed, poking a straw through her water. "I went to the doctor on Friday." She swirled her ice. "Well. I went to the doctor again, I should say."

Hadassah's mouth went dry. She had a feeling where this was going.

Yocheved let out a long breath. "I mean, after this long, it's not really a surprise. I'm sure you remember my health issues when we were teens. Long story short..." Her lip trembled. "I can't have kids."

"Oh, Yocheved," Hadassah breathed. She reached across the table to grab her hand. "I'm so sorry."

Motherhood was all Yocheved had ever wanted. Hadassah had witnessed her dream about a husband and a family of her own for years, quietly listening to her sister's plans and hopes.

By what cruel twist of fate had God denied faithful, sweet Yocheved the one thing she wanted most?

She sniffed and swiped at her eyes, forcing a smile. "It's okay. Our God is a healer. We know He has a plan for everything."

Hadassah's heart clenched. It wasn't okay. Yocheved wasn't okay. She would let her sister move on, put on a brave face for now. She would be there when the smiling mask cracked, ready to support her.

Was God on a mission to squelch their dreams? Yocheved's desire for motherhood, Hadassah's yearning for arts and learning and theater? Were both of them destined never to fulfil their passions?

Not for the first time, Hadassah wondered with a sense of dread what on earth her future would hold.

"Pool noodles?"

Griffith furrowed his brows as Lilian dropped a ton of colorful tubes onto the foyer carpet.

Dust kicked up from them. Griffith shielded his nose and coughed. Yeesh, how long had they kept those things in the props loft?

Lilian arched her spine and wiped a sheen of sweat off her forehead with the back of her hand. Two flights of stairs led up to where they kept all the set pieces for shows. "You are practicing the candy cane scene today, right?"

Griffith eyed the group of children in the atrium. He'd instructed them to wait out here—where there was more space than on stage—to do a theater exercise before practice. Ty shoved another kid, who toppled over a chair stationed in the lobby.

"Yes?" Griffith forced his attention back to Lilian, who had emptied her pockets of other items she procured in the loft, including a compass and a Chinese fan. "The scene requires the kids to whack my character with plastic candy canes, not—" He gestured at the pool noodles.

Today, Lilian had decided Griffith needed to start scavenging for props and took it upon herself to march up and down the two flights to "take care" of it for him.

Unfortunately, she'd all but given the script a brief skim, so that meant she didn't know half of what Griffith needed for the show. Didn't stop her, though.

"There wasn't much time to search through *every* box." Tassels on Lilian's shawl flurried with dust motes. "We do have tons of couches and cabinets up there, you know. Anyway, I'll go look for more props and bring them down for your approval."

She disappeared into the door that led to the loft before Griffith could object.

He sighed and bent down to scoop up the pool noodles. Rushing into the auditorium, he deposited them on stage and returned to the lobby in time to watch Ty attempt to bludgeon another one of the actors with the compass Lilian had deposited.

Griffith slapped his palms together, and all the kids' spines jolted. "Ty, put that down."

With a sneer, Ty did so.

"Thank you. Now everyone gather around this chair." He motioned to a seat stationed by a high-top table.

Before shows, most folks congregated in this area. A concession stand, with its silver doors latched closed, often bursting with buttered popcorn and boxed candies on opening night. He could taste the sour sugar from one of his favorites.

"Now, we're going to do a practice exercise before we rehearse the candy cane scene."

During said scene, "James" would have to lead the "orphan kids" through some choreography for the show. The kids, fed up, decided to pull a prank on James. They would whack him with the candy canes instead.

Griffith made sure to email them that morning to let them know to tap him gently.

Of course, he hadn't anticipated using props this early into the blocking—teaching movement—rehearsals. Often, theaters didn't bring out real items for the actors to use until close to dress rehearsals.

Ty groaned. "These exercises are so boring, and pointless. Can't we just start practicing the show?"

A murmur of agreement rippled through two of the other boys. Great, it would be one of *those* days.

Griffith grit his teeth and mustered all his memories from his directing classes. What had the teacher said about dealing with child actors? Something about being gentle but firm?

"Ty, we'll practice as soon as we're warmed up. This is like what athletes do. You can't start playing until you get ready." Griffith's fingertips rattled against the seat. "Now for this exercise, I want you to pretend this isn't a chair. Each of you is going to tell me what this is—just say anything but a chair. This is going to work on your improvisational skills. Leroy." Griffith bobbed his chin at the boy. "Why don't you go first?"

Leroy approached the seat and stared at the upholstered buttons for a long while.

"It's a—a cave to shelter yourself from a snowstorm." He pointed to the "mouth" of the cave, the empty space between the legs of the chair.

"Great, okay, you." He motioned to an adult woman who wore large hoop earrings. "What is it?"

"Umm, a Christmas tree." She pretended to hang, what Griffith guessed, were ornaments around it.

"Creative, who's next?"

Five or so actors went with their suggestions, until Ty approached the chair and slumped into the cushions.

"It's a *seat*." Ty shoved his fist underneath his chin. "Can we be done now?"

Griffith rolled his eyes and asked another child to identify the chair, but this one also crossed his arms and stated, "Like Ty said, it's a seat. See? We didn't say the word chair."

Ugh, they didn't have time for this. Griffith ended the exercise and told the children to get on stage to learn blocking for their scene. Once they stampeded into the theater, Griffith motioned Zinnia to his side.

"I think blocking is going to take a bit longer with the kids. Any way you could get the adults started on some of their scenes?" He motioned to a packet of papers on the high-top table. "My notes are there."

Zinnia nodded. "No problem, boss."

Griffith bounded into the theater in time to almost collide with Byron. Why on earth had he planted himself right by the doors?

"Hey, director." Byron held up Griffith's copy of his notes he'd left on stage earlier, right next to the pool noodles.

Speaking of, the kids had begun to whack one another with them. Griffith barked at them to stop.

He turned his attention back to Byron. "Yes?"

"Since you're acting in today's scene, do you mind if I coach them on the blocking? I figure it might be a lot to do at once. I already looked over your notes."

Heat seethed in Griffith's fingertips. Why did both Byron and Lilian think that he couldn't handle multiple tasks? Coincidentally, as he thought this, Lilian stepped onto the stage with a bundle of paraphernalia in her arms. She motioned him over with the jerk of her chin.

"Griffith?" Byron prompted. "We don't have much time for blocking."

Griffith inhaled. "Fine, go ahead and get them started." He blew the breath out. "Make sure they're gentle when they whack me with those."

With that, Griffith charged up to Lilian as she deposited the various items into a pile. Griffith pinched a hat in the shape of a turkey and his lips sagged. "Lilian, I'm not sure what I'm going to be able to do with most of this in the show."

"These are only options. Figured I'd save you a trip."

Behind him, Byron gathered the children in a circle and instructed them on the various directions in the scene. How in the world did he get silence to wash over them like that? Moments before, they'd chased each other in circles.

"What about this one?" Lilian pulled Griffith's attention back to her as she held up a rubber mouse. "Maybe this could go in a scene somewhere."

Sure, if they hoped to scare someone with a rodent phobia in the audience.

"I'll take a look at these later." Griffith wagged his chin toward the clump of children. "Probably should get back to directing them."

Lilian wiped the soot off her leggings. "Fine, but walk with purpose. Don't run." She lifted a brow.

He knew exactly what she meant. Lilian would tell him this during past shows when he sprinted around like a beheaded chicken.

Saying it now implied she thought he looked frantic, out of control.

All the things she didn't want in a future director.

He dipped his head as a way of saying yes and forced himself to walk over to the kids, instead of jog.

"Griffith." Byron clapped the clipboard he held. "Just in time. I already walked them through what they needed to do in the scene. Shall we take it from the top?"

Griffith's jaw sank. Already? Blocking often took at least several minutes per scene. "O-okay. Sure." He collected the pool noodles in his arms and ambled to stage-left. He composed himself with an inhale, exhale, before he marched onto the stage for his starting cue. All the kids held their scripts, still not off-book yet. "Hey, kids," he recited the first line, "you ready to get started on today's rehearsal?"

Noncommittal "yeah" and "sure" sounded from the group.

"Now Miss Emily is running late, so she wanted me to get you started on the scene. You will hold these candy canes." He dropped the pool noodles at his feet. They made a thudding noise when they hit the ground. "You march around the theater with them. Got it?"

Confused nods from the kids. Leroy, in character for Oliver, stage-whispered to another kid, "I have a better idea." The "whisper" traveled around the group as Griffith's character handed each kid a "candy cane."

"Okay, looks like everyone has their candy cane. You ready?"

They smiled, eyes glinting.

"All right." Griffith pointed toward the audience. "Now march."

Instead, they thwacked him with the pool noodles. Hard.

"Ouch." Well, it *was* an actual line in the show. These puppies hurt. Like crazy. As though they'd slapped him with rods. Griffith held up his hands. "Okay, guys, stop."

They wouldn't.

"Stop."

Whack, whack, whack.

"Stop!"

Giggles erupted from the group.

Griffith rubbed the sores on his abdomen. "Guys, you're supposed to be gentle in this scene. Lightly tap me or *pretend* to hit me. Kind of like what actors do with stage punches."

Leroy wrinkled his nose and glowered at Byron, who stood in the center aisle with a disturbing smile on his face. "I thought Byron said—"

"Never mind what he said. I'm the director. I need you all to listen to what *I* say."

In the haze of lights, Griffith noticed Byron lift a brow, as if to say, *Not for long.*

Chapter Eight

No sign of Byron on Sunday or Monday. Thank goodness. Now she only had to make it through the rest of Tuesday.

Hadassah sat on a park bench, swinging her heels, content to let all five of her brothers get their energy out with a couple of soccer balls. December was far too cold for soccer, in her opinion, but without snow, the field remained clear, and the boys needed an outlet for their "zoomies." She preferred to get some fresh air, no matter how chilly, rather than coach Priscilla and Tabitha on grammar.

Obadiah dove along the ground to "save" the ball from going into an invisible goal. Hadassah winced as mud streaked his coat. Not that it mattered much—after being passed down from Isaiah to Enoch to Obadiah, the garment had plenty of stains.

She shivered and stood to make another lap around the field. Walking kept her warm. She'd circled about three times already.

With each step, memories peppered her thoughts.

When she had been about Priscilla's age, around nine or ten, Byron had been the same age as Matthew. Hadassah watched her thirteen-year-old brother peg one ball toward Luke, then tap the other to Obadiah. Matthew had reached the middle school gangly giraffe phase, all limbs and big feet, but he still managed to be gentle with his younger brothers—Luke didn't count, of course.

Byron had never been the sort to pull punches, with the Wright children or his own siblings. Once, he'd gotten mad at one of his little sisters during "P.E." and kicked a soccer ball straight into her face. It was written off as an accident, but Hadassah had seen the calculating glint in his eye.

Yocheved and Byron had always butted heads, both in classes and on the playground, as the two unofficial leaders of the local home school kids. Both had been too well-behaved to clash openly, but group projects, picking teams, and even deciding who to play with had always had a certain competitive edge.

Hadassah could remember a gap-toothed young Yocheved putting her hands on her hips and declaring, "Byron is a bully. We have to love him because God says so, but we're not friends with him."

Little Hadassah's eyes had gone wide at the idea of not being friends with someone. It didn't seem very nice. She didn't argue with her sister.

The adults hadn't agreed with Yocheved's view of Byron—he acted the perfect young gentleman around them. Gradually, as they grew into teens and Yocheved embraced her role as mother-in-training while the boys and girls began to divide into social circles by gender, Yocheved and Byron seldom interacted.

Unfortunately for Hadassah, she didn't experience the same.

In the present, adult Hadassah noticed dusk begin to creep over the horizon. She finished her lap around the field and waved to her brothers. "All right, boys. We should head home for dinner."

With the appetites of five black holes, they didn't need to be told twice.

In the car on the way home, she tried to focus on the road, but her thoughts drifted back to childhood.

Without Yocheved's aggressive presence to distract him, Byron's eyes often wandered to Hadassah. She would look up from doing homework or working on her sewing while waiting for her siblings and see him watching her from across the room. Whenever she caught him, he would respond with a casual smile, then walk away.

They never had a true conversation until the summer after she turned fourteen.

Hadassah had been sitting on the garden wall in the Youngs' backyard, watching her younger siblings play with the Young children and the kids of another home school family. Byron sauntered across the yard and hopped up onto the wall next to Hadassah.

He leaned back on his hands. "You looked lonely over here."

Hadassah fiddled with her skirt, keeping an eye on her siblings. Where was Yocheved when she needed her? "Oh. I'm fine."

"You're always so quiet." Byron pushed a hand through his thick hair, gaze fixed on her. "You're in high school now, right?"

"Yes." Her neck heated. Why was he talking to her? She glanced toward the house. All the adults were inside for an evening Bible study, leaving the older children to watch the younger ones.

"I'll be headed off to college soon." He tilted his head. "I'll miss you."

"Me?" she squeaked.

"Yeah." He slipped his hand over hers, stilling her fidgeting fingers.

Her heart pounded. Alarm bells rang. *Not right, not right.*

"I've noticed the way you've looked at me, all these years," he continued, as if he didn't notice how she'd gone completely still. "How you always seemed to be in the right place at the right time."

She had? Sure, they'd been in plenty of co-ops together, but there wasn't much she could do about that.

"I just wanted to say...I'll be gone for a long time. Getting degrees, all of that. When I come back, I'll be ready to take over my dad's business. I could use a wife to support the household." His eyes flicked over her in a way that made her cringe. "Someone mature, and beautiful, who's great with kids and domestic duties. There aren't many girls like that anymore." He squeezed her hand. "Wait for me, Hadassah?"

In the moment, she had frozen. She didn't know what to say first—"no, I'm fourteen," or, "I've never liked you," or maybe just a shout for Yocheved.

She didn't say anything.

He smiled and glanced toward the house. It had grown dark, and dusk made the playing children little more than blurred shadows. "I care about you, Hadassah."

Then, before she could register what he was doing, he grabbed her face and planted a kiss on her lips.

She reeled as he hopped down from the wall and waved. "Until we meet again."

Obadiah's giggles in the back seat returned her to the present. Her hands had tightened around the steering wheel until her knuckles went white. She relaxed her grip.

She'd never told Yocheved or her parents what Byron had said and done—why would she? He was gone, hopefully not to return any time soon...and she had been too embarrassed to recount the events.

When she entered the living room at home behind five sweaty, red-cheeked boys, she pulled up short, convinced she must be hallucinating.

There stood Byron, chatting with her mother.

Mom turned toward her and clapped her hands. "Oh, good, you're back. Just in time. Byron is here to take you out to dinner." Hadassah began to open her mouth, but before she could get any words out, Mom said, "Don't worry about the kids. Dad brought home a Disney movie, and we'll have a family movie night."

Her chest tightened. She had no excuse. The walls seemed to close in on her. "I...I'm wearing park clothes."

Byron offered a languid smile. "I think you look lovely. I'm happy to wait if you want to change."

She took a deep breath. *Change.* Maybe he had changed. She couldn't judge the man on what he'd been like as a teenager, could she? Maybe she was being unfair. "I'll be right back."

Her fingers trembled as she pulled on a warm skirt and blouse and ran a comb through her wind-tossed hair before braiding it tightly and wrapping it into a bun. She knew she looked drab—

exactly the appearance she was going for.

She emerged to find Byron shaking hands with Dad. "I'll have her home before nine, sir."

Dad's chest puffed. "I'm sure you will. You've grown into a respectable young man, Byron."

Gag me.

Byron opened the front door for her and made a sweeping gesture. "This way, milady."

He held the car door for her in a show of chivalry, but when he slammed it shut, the sound rattled in her bones like a death knell.

It isn't that bad. Give him a chance.

He slid behind the wheel and offered her a wide grin. "I'm so glad we could finally work this out."

"Er, yes."

He started the engine. "I have a nice place in mind. Nothing too fancy, but I want to make my intentions clear in this courtship."

"Courtship?" she choked out.

"Yes." He winked. "I know you've never forgotten our little promise all those years ago. I haven't either."

Never before had she regretted so profoundly that the three blind dates in her life had not landed her a boyfriend.

Byron wove through traffic. "I would have come back sooner, but I wanted to make sure I was financially stable, especially if I want to invest time in theater."

Theater. That, at least, she could get on board with.

Byron talked all the way to the restaurant, a popular Italian chain. He ordered for both of them, so Hadassah didn't have to say a word.

Over their appetizer of salad and breadsticks, Byron leaned forward. "I've told you so much about college, and my theater experience, and growing my father's company...I feel like we know each other the way we used to. I want to hear from you. What have you been up to?"

She hesitated. She wanted to tell him of exciting exploits or great achievements—prove she wasn't the same girl as seven years ago.

The problem being, she was. Nothing had changed.

"I've just been helping Mom with the kids." She noticed him straining to hear her and increased her volume. "Teaching co-ops and Sunday School. Doing skits when I can. Now, theater."

He swirled his breadstick in salad dressing. "You're a natural. It's a shame you don't have a better script to work with. For my plays, I'd be happy to cast you as my female leads. As long as it doesn't get in the way of your responsibilities, of course."

"That's very kind of you to say." She mustered her courage. "I like this script a lot."

He gave a dismissive chuckle. "Once you've read as many plays as I have, you learn to differentiate."

She focused on her salad. He could be right. After all, he had years of training and experience, and she had nothing.

Through the main course, he regaled her with tales of his previous performances and admiring professors. It seemed wherever Byron went, success followed.

By the time the check came, he smiled tenderly at her and took her hand before she could hide it beneath the table. "I love talking with you, Hadassah. I feel like you truly understand me—you're an excellent listener."

She forced a smile. "So I've been told."

She didn't think Byron could possibly come up with more to talk about, but he reminisced about childhood stories all the way home. However, his versions featured Hadassah as much more of an active participant than she remembered.

"You know, Yocheved was so hot-headed. I always thought our families should be united, but I knew she wasn't the right one." He took a left turn.

Hadassah's eyebrows shot up. Yocheved, hot-headed?

Extroverted, maybe, but always the perfect child.

"You..." He cast a glance at her. "You remind me of the woman in Proverbs 31. Quiet and meek, but hardworking and wise."

Hadassah didn't remember the "quiet and meek" part of the passage. She attempted to deflect the compliment. "I just try to follow God's call for me, as much as I can."

He beamed. "Exactly what I mean."

Great.

Hadassah couldn't exit the vehicle quickly enough when they arrived home. She beat Byron to the front door. "Thank you for dinner. I can see myself in."

Before he could protest, she slipped inside.

Mom jumped up from the darkened living room, piled with family watching an animated movie. "How was it?"

"Fine. I'm tired. I'm going to head to bed."

With that, she fled from questions.

Griffith handed his mother a mug full of steaming chai in his apartment.

The three of his family members squished together at the end of his bed. The room really wasn't much to look at—one full-sized bed, a small kitchenette, a tattered dresser he bought from Facebook marketplace, and a TV on a stand. The TV stand also hailed from Facebook marketplace. His father set his chipped cup down on a side table where Griffith had stationed a Charamico tree from his time in the D.R.

"Griffith." Hudson blew onto the contents of his cup. His brother always mentioned a phobia of sipping too-hot drinks and obliterating his taste buds. "You have a chance to work at She Brews with all this play stuff going on?"

Griffith stilled his fingertips on the ladle on the stove. Nutmeg clouded his senses.

Great, already five minutes into their visit at his apartment, and they'd begun their barrage of questions about finances. For the first three minutes, Griffith had given them a tour of the place—considering it was all of one room full of multi-colored stringed Christmas lights and dusty garlands he'd bought from the theater at a rummage sale.

He stirred the pot full of chai and clicked off the stove heater. "I'll be starting up some shifts soon after the play ends." He tried to make his voice shoot up a few notes. "I'm *really* enjoying my time at the theater."

In an automatic motion, he whisked the pot once more. Then he ladled liquid into a red ceramic cup and dropped into a chair at his high-top table.

Based on the winces from his family on the bed—they were uncomfortable in the confined space, no doubt. He looked at the chai to avoid their pained looks. Staring at them would only make him feel more embarrassed about his living situation. Time for a subject change.

"Hudson, how have things been at Village Ninety-Nine?"

Most of the Haitian Villages that resided in the Dominican Republic went by numbers at the compound. "Village Fifty-One," "Village Eighty-Three," and the newest one where Hudson had headed up mission's efforts, Ninety-Nine.

Hudson's shoulders dropped, face brightening. Griffith could feel the tension in the room melt like a snowflake on an eyelash.

"Really great. We've begun building a church. The kids..." He paused, spine straightening again. "Griffith, we could use someone like you at Ninety-Nine. Imagine what your skits could do."

Swirls of cinnamon floated to the top of Griffith's drink. He stared into the murky waters and dissolved into a memory.

Years ago, a tween Griffith had hidden himself in a concrete building in Village Eighty-Seven. His family had just moved to the D.R., and he hadn't anticipated the hugs, the friendliness, the touchiness.

Even back in Cub Scouts, he often buried himself in the corners of rooms during den meetings.

Camping trips meant he'd "accidentally" get lost in the woods during hikes—so he could perch on a rock under the shade of evergreens, alone.

A doctor who liked to hand Griffith stickers back in his elementary days labeled it as a social anxiety disorder. Blurs of his voice rang in Griffith's memory—"will fear social interactions with peers," "may isolate himself," "fear of embarrassment."

When they up and moved him to one of the most extroverted cultures in the world...

No, he could stay inside the cool shade of that building and stir a stick in a bucket full of gray concrete. God had built him like a construction worker, and so he'd do that work in silence.

"Grif." Hudson burst into the building. His polo stuck to him like a second skin in the humidity. Owing to the D.R.'s modest culture, he wore long shorts that went past his knees. "We have a problem."

Griffith spied a group of villagers and missionaries from the compound clustered near the building. He shrank into the shadows. "What?" His voice cracked.

"You know those high schoolers who were supposed to come here and help lead a VBS for the kids?"

Many schools in the States sent juniors and seniors to do a summer missions trip in the D.R. Children in the villages would often claim a "missionary" to give them piggyback rides and to play games that week. Sadly, they didn't stick around for longer than ten days, and so the kids would often discuss how they missed the friends they'd made.

A nod came from Griffith.

Hudson's elbow jutted out when he palmed his neck. "They decided to go to Village Fifty-One instead, a last-minute change. We need someone to entertain the kids with skits and dances."

Fire flushed Griffith's cheeks.

His gaze darted to the missionaries in the outside clump of people. "Is there any way one of them can do it, I'm—" He gestured to the bucket full of concrete.

"They're already leading the kids through Bible stories. Come on, Grif. You used to love doing skits for Mom back in the day."

Sure enough, Griffith and Hudson had put on many a puppet show for his mother back in the States. There was something immensely comforting about the shield of a puppet theater box.

Now he would have to venture out into the bright, cloudless sunshine to put on a skit for the kids.

"I'll do the dances." Hudson grabbed Griffith's arm. "Come on. Remember, they're covering the Bible story of the Israelites crossing the Red Sea. Do a skit involving that."

Griffith's thoughts raced.

He arched his back and tried to pull away, but for a slim-figured man, Hudson had an iron grip. Hudson plopped Griffith in front of the crowd and announced in Spanish that Griffith would tell them all a story.

Saliva got caught in Griffith's esophagus. He wobbled, caught his balance, and cleared his throat.

"The story of the Israelites in the desert," he said in the best Spanish he could muster. His parents had them take an extensive course for two years before they made the long-term trek to the D.R. It surprised Griffith how long it took his family to scrape together enough funds.

Children huddled around his ankles.

Oh boy, would Griffith have to do *all* the parts in this? The cloud and pillar of fire by which the Lord led the Israelites by night? The Egyptians? Moses?

"I need some volunteers."

The children bounced up and down with hands raised in the air. He tapped the fingertips of a handful and they rocketed to their feet and joined him by his side. Many clung to him in a hug. He assigned each of the parts.

"The Israelites had escaped the land of Egypt and made their way across the desert."

He told the entire skit in Spanish. Most of the villagers spoke a Haitian Creole, but they understood the secondary language.

A group of girls in long skirts pretended to trek across the "wilderness." Parents watched their children from the entrances of their makeshift huts.

"The Lord led them like a cloud during the day and a fire at night."

Billowing and crackling noises came from the boy who played the cloud and fire. He flapped his arms and spun in circles.

"Pharaoh was not happy."

A small boy in a basketball jersey playing Pharaoh firmed his jaw.

Light ignited in Griffith's chest. His spine eased. This wasn't so bad, being with people.

"He sent the Egyptians to go and get the Israelites."

The "Egyptians" chased the Israelites around the houses. After several minutes, Griffith had to call them back to the huddle.

"God told his prophet Moses." Griffith motioned to a boy in a striped t-shirt. "To raise his staff above the Red Sea."

Griffith gestured at the audience. "You are the Red Sea." Then he flailed his arms and made a whooshing sound. The crowd echoed him. Griffith's lips twitched.

"The sea split in two."

He instructed half the crowd to lean one way, and the other half in the opposite direction.

"The Israelites crossed the Red Sea." They did so. "When the Egyptians came..." He raised his voice, how he'd seen so many actors do in stage productions he watched back in the States. "The sea crashed on them!"

The crowd tangled the "Egyptians" with their arms. Giggles erupted from some of the "waves."

Applause rang from the children when the skit ended. A glorious glow had filled Griffith's chest. Was this—was this what he was supposed to do for the rest of his life? These skits?

"Moses" tugged on Griffith's shirt and motioned up. He wanted a piggyback ride.

"Sure thing." Griffith leaned down and heaved him up on his shoulders.

Hudson beamed at him from across the mass of people. "You're a natural," he told Griffith in English. "From now on, you're doing all the VBS skits."

Griffith released himself from the memory and stared at his family on his bed. Little had he known that that skit would ignite a passion for theater in him.

"Hey, Grif." Hudson sighed and cupped his drink in both hands. "I know you love community theater. Have you ever considered that maybe it was a calling for only a season? That maybe you are built for something greater, like our work in the villages?"

Griffith's jaw sank. Then closed. Words wouldn't come out.

I wish I knew the answer.

Chapter Nine

"We'll call that a wrap for the day and move on to the next scene."

Hadassah relaxed as Griffith released the actors from blocking. She descended the steps from the stage into the auditorium, where a gaggle of child actors climbed on the seats, sprawled on the floor, and generally made a significant amount of noise.

She saw Griffith's gaze dart from the children to the actors still on stage. Zinnia was busy helping take notes and call the correct actors to the stage for their scenes, and Griffith was tied up directing blocking, leaving the kids who weren't currently in a scene to their own devices.

Hadassah hesitated. Would Griffith mind if she stepped in?

If Byron were there, he would probably give the kids a stern talking to. Luckily, he had a family commitment this evening. Hadassah would rather the kids have an enjoyable theater experience, not one where they were forced to sit in silence.

Lucky for Hadassah as well—she hadn't seen Byron since their date last night, and she didn't know if she could face him again so soon. What if he asked her out again?

A child yelled across the theater, and she grimaced. No, she shouldn't intervene. She was only an actress—she had no place leading.

Motion caught her eye. In one of the rows, Leroy, or "Oliver," sat in a worn red seat, kicking his feet, gaze downcast. In the row in front of him, Ty leaned his arms against the back of the chair and smirked at Leroy. A smirk Hadassah recognized all too well.

As kids, Byron had often "helped" other students who were struggling in classes. The adults fawned over his giving spirit when he took the time to seek out kids who were struggling and offer homework aid.

Hadassah had overheard some of those conversations.

"Some people just aren't good at math," she heard Byron tell one boy, "but if you do these techniques, you should at least get a passing grade."

Always the introductory phrases to anything helpful.

"Oh, I would have thought that would be intuitive. Well..."

"I forget some people don't have the level of education I do. Anyway..."

"I mean, we can't all be good at school, but coming from someone who's always been a good student..."

Before Ty could open his mouth, Hadassah clapped her hands for attention. "Okay, theater kids, if you aren't in a scene, come to the back of the auditorium with me." She hesitated and glanced at Zinnia, who gave her a thumbs up. "Zinnia will come get you when you're needed."

Hadassah trailed children like a line of caffeinated ducklings down the center aisle. At the back of the theater, she directed them to form a circle, which turned into more of an amoeba. *Good enough.* "Okay, we're going to play a game that will help us with creativity and working together with others."

Ty raised his hand. "Excuse me." He dropped his arm. "I thought Griffith was in charge."

"He is, but he's busy right now. If you don't want to participate, you are free to sit there"—she pointed to a seat by the door—"and watch, but you won't be allowed to interrupt the people who do want to participate." She wouldn't allow him to sit and critique the other children if he refused to cooperate.

His nostrils flared, but he nodded.

"Good." She addressed the full group again. "We're going to play One Word Story. Together, we want to try to tell a story with a beginning, middle, and end that makes sense. But there's a catch."

She paused just long enough for several eyes to twinkle with interest. "Each person can only say one word at a time. We have to work together to tell a good story, just like in a play."

The Wright brood had played "the word game" many a time on long van rides or while waiting for their parents to wrap up lengthy conversations after church. Yocheved came up with the idea, and Hadassah later learned the game was often used as a theater warmup as well.

"Okay, the title of the story is 'The Mysterious Frog.'" Hadassah nodded across the circle. "Leroy, you can start us off, and we'll go to the left."

"The," Leroy said, which elicited a giggle from a few of the kids.

"Swamp," the child next to him added.

"Was."

"Stinky."

The circle burst into laughter, while the "stinky" boy grinned, proud of his contribution.

"Well, it looks like the frog lives in a *stinky* swamp." Hadassah pinched her nose and waved a hand in front of her face, drawing more giggles.

The story continued, sometimes confusing, but usually following the tale of a frog and his adventures, until the frog came across a stork.

"The."

"Stork."

"Was."

"*Hungry*," Leroy said with a grin.

Several children shrieked and giggled. "Oh, no, the froggy's in danger," a small girl chortled, bouncing on her toes.

Hadassah glanced at Ty. To her surprise, a smile splashed across the boy's face, and he laughed along with the others. It seemed that when the spotlight wasn't focused on him, and he didn't have anything to prove, Ty could relax and enjoy himself like any of the other children.

Zinnia strode down the aisle toward their group, and Hadassah went to meet her halfway. "Who do you need?"

"No one, right now." Zinnia stared at the kids, still continuing the story in a circle. "I didn't think that was possible with this group. Griffith was able to get through blocking in record time. I think I even heard him mutter that you must be the patron saint of children."

Her cheeks heated. "I have plenty of experience with them, is all."

"We're coming up on the big scene with all the kids on stage, but Griffith wants to break it up a few groups at a time before putting them all together." Zinnia glanced at her watch. "You're technically done for the night and can go home..."

"I'd be happy to stay." Hadassah smiled at another burst of giggles from the kids. Who knew what mischief the frog had gotten into? "I can keep them occupied." She nodded to a copy of the script balancing on a seatback. "I'll work on memorizing my lines while they're busy with activities."

"I won't argue with that at all." Zinnia motioned to a handful of kids and called their names from her clipboard. Then she flashed a smile at Hadassah. "Thank you."

No, thank you. Whenever Hadassah entered the theater, she never wanted to leave.

As Zinnia led the group away—a few complaining they wanted to know what would happen to the froggy—Hadassah noticed Griffith's gaze from across the theater. She waved, and he waved back.

Turning to the kids once more, Hadassah paused. She hadn't even thought to feel nervous talking to Zinnia, or taking charge of the kids in front of adults and a smattering of parents.

I don't know what it is about theater, but it makes me feel like a whole new person.

Or maybe, she felt free to be the person she already was.

"She should be here any minute." Leroy bobbled on his heels as Griffith waited with him by the door of the atrium.

Griffith vowed to wait for all the kids to get rides home before he would close up shop. He remembered days where his parents would take forever to arrive at den meetings. How he would watch the snowflakes cascade outside in deafening silence.

Behind Griffith, Hadassah flipped through her script and tapped a pen against the paper margins.

Always studious. He loved her for it. After all her help today, if Hadassah had told him in that moment she hoped to get a masters in theater or fine arts, he would've found a way to pay for schooling for her.

For now, he hoped she would settle for an offer of hot chocolate.

Especially since she promised to stay behind as well until all the kids had their guardians pick them up. This allowed for Zinnia to go home and film herself for an audition tape. "Not to worry, boss," she'd told Griffith right before she plunged into the frigid outdoors, "the shoot dates don't start until January. I'd never leave you in the lurch."

Good. Volunteers were as precious as diamonds in the theater.

"Any moment now." Leroy's breath fogged the glass doors.

The woman from the foster home hadn't attended many practices. She must've gotten caught up in the various activities of the kids in her care.

Griffith hobbled back and forth on his legs from standing too long. A buzz sounded from his pocket. He groaned when he spotted the sender—Lilian. What now?

Lilian: How are we on getting volunteers to help us during the show? Deck crew? Spot ops? Ushers?

Ice pummeled through his veins. He'd forgotten that often

directors did that too, found the volunteers for the shows. It always took a lot of begging. He remembered in college how a stage manager lied to him about the "ease" of responsibilities for deck crew, the people who moved sets during the show. "Oh, it'll be maybe a few hours of commitment."

One hundred hours later, he never wished to see another hay bale in his life, after sweeping the stage for *Oklahoma!*

He couldn't lowball anyone like that stage manager had. How would he get the volunteers?

Itchiness filled his fingers as he typed a message back.

Griffith: Not yet. I'll get on it after Leroy goes home.

After he had a chance to scavenge the props loft for any decor he could put in the lobby. Lilian had peppered his phone with texts about that earlier.

Whirring filled his skull. He needed to get his mind off this. He turned to Leroy. "You did a great job today. Seemed right at home on that stage."

"Home." Leroy breathed. He'd drawn a smiley face on the condensation on the pane. "That's what theater feels like. Home." He glanced at Griffith, ears red. "Sorry. It's just—I haven't had that feeling for a very, very long time."

His neck swerved back to the window.

"Oh. She's here. Thanks, Director Griffith, and Director Hadassah."

Hadassah's eyes widened. "Oh, I'm not—"

Before Leroy could hear her, he raced into a rush of wintry air. The door banged shut.

"Thanks for sticking around, *Director* Hadassah." Griffith gave her a stage-wink. "Sorry that you had to stay for so long—"

"Do you need help with anything else?"

Oh. He'd assumed she'd loitered behind for Leroy. Did she—

did she want to spend more time with him?

His chest warmed, but then froze as Griffith shook the thought away. *Nah, she's probably just a helpful person.*

"I'm about to take inventory in the props loft for Christmas decor."

"Wonderful." She bounced off a stool and placed her script on the vacant seat. "It'll make up for our unsuccessful Christmas tree hunt."

They wound up the two flights of stairs, kicking up sawdust. Everything in the props loft smelled like age and decay. Stained fabric on couches caught Griffith's eye first when he flicked on the light switch. Most of the sofas and chairs were on their last legs, literally.

After all, furniture went to the theater to die, as his college director had stated.

He led her to the "greenery" section, full of plastic vines, fake bushes, and trees. His gaze narrowed on the rows of Christmas trees and yards upon yards of garlands.

Had Lilian even *looked* up here? With the donations from the community, they would have no problem adorning the atrium in all things festive. Boxes upon plastic boxes of ornaments glistened in the hum of the fluorescent lights.

Speaking of Lilian, another message dinged from her.

Lilian: I'll get stagehands and spot ops on the theater volunteer Facebook page. Just keep this in mind for next time. Directors usually take care of this.

Great, she didn't trust him enough to find his crew.

Hadassah shrugged and almost kicked over a metal pot with her shoe. Directors in years past placed items in the most haphazard fashion up here. "Guess we looked in all the wrong places."

"Guess so. Thanks anyway for all your help. Here and earlier today."

Hadassah buckled her chin into her neck. "I have been told that I have a knack for kids."

"Leroy especially made huge strides today." One word echoed in Griffith's mind. *Home.* "I'm glad he's found a safe space here. It's too bad he doesn't feel like home is anywhere else."

Griffith understood that feeling.

When his family moved out of the country, off of the *continent,* he'd abandoned all sense of normalcy and permanency. Even when he found a temporary dwelling at college, he never really clicked with his peers. Had to adapt back to American customs.

Theater served as a replacement home to Griffith too.

When the spotlights illuminated the stage, an overwhelming sense of peace filled him, like an ounce of heaven came to greet him.

"Wish more parents would foster." Hadassah weaved around a labyrinth of cabinets. "Why don't you think that more people would provide a loving home to the Leroys of the world?"

His mind flashed back to his studio apartment. Could he even take care of a child in such a space? Even if he had the financial stability, wouldn't a kid prefer a large home and a parent who could whip up incredible home-cooked meals every evening? Besides, states required adopted or fostered kids to have their own bedroom, right? "Probably because they don't feel ready. Or their lives aren't perfect enough for them."

She craned her neck at him and wrinkled her nose. "If everyone thought that, no one would get adopted."

True.

He loved it when she shared her opinions, when he caught peeks of her effervescence crack through her shell. Why didn't she speak her mind more often?

"Anyway." Hadassah skidded to a halt, almost bonking her

forehead into a grandfather clock. By instinct, Griffith reached out a hand to catch her. "I am glad Leroy found some sort of home."

"Theater does that to people." They reached the stairwell, and Griffith clicked off the lights. "Gives a haven to the misfits, the homeless, the people who don't belong."

Just like him.

Chapter Ten

"Di-no-saurs. Di-no-saurs," Obadiah chanted.

"Shh, Obie." Hadassah put a finger to her lips. "Libraries are quiet places, remember?"

Hadassah led her gaggle of siblings toward the back of the library to the children's section. Isaiah sniffed loudly and wiped his nose on his sleeve. She bit back a sigh. "Isaiah, I gave you a pocket pack of tissues. Remember to use those for your nose."

Her siblings weren't misbehaving, and they visited the library every week, but for some reason, today every runny nose, every loud noise, every sibling argument made her want to scream.

She took a deep breath. Her grumpiness wasn't her siblings' fault. She couldn't take it out on them. Maybe the moodiness came from the cold, or her lack of proper sleep after staying late at the theater last night.

The memory of combing through the props loft with Griffith came to mind and a smile teased her lips. She could hang out with Griffith all day, talking about theater, or life, or cracking jokes.

"Hey, Hadassah."

She jumped and turned at the sound of Griffith's voice, almost as if her thoughts had summoned him. He strode down the row of shelves, a binder and a laptop under his arm.

"Hi, Griffith. I didn't expect to see you here." The kids darted away to the children's section, and she didn't stop them. She could see them from her location. "More things for the play?"

"Always." He gestured toward the back wall, where the library's printers were located. "Making copies of schedules for the parents. Some of them like physical papers."

"It seems like you're doing a lot of extra things besides

directing." She frowned, taking in the dark circles under his eyes.

He shrugged. "That's theater life. By the way, thank you again for working with the kids yesterday. I didn't know what I was going to do with them. Between this and our Christmas tree shopping, I owe you hot cocoa or something."

"It was no problem." She glanced at her siblings and counted. *One, two, three, four, five. Good.* "Let me know if you need help with anything else. I'd be happy to lend a hand with whatever needs to be done."

"Actually..." He scratched the back of his neck. "I could use a second opinion on ideas of how to keep the kids occupied during rehearsals and the show. Would you like to talk over a cup of hot cocoa? On me."

"I'd love to." She craned her neck to make sure Obadiah was still accounted for. Good, sitting on the floor with a book.

"Okay." He rocked on his feet. Was he nervous? "Are you busy tomorrow?"

"I'm sure I can move things around after I talk to my mom." She pulled out her phone. "Here, why don't I give you my number, and we can text about a time once I get it figured out?"

They swapped numbers, then Griffith resettled his binder and computer under his arm. "Let me know. I'll see you tomorrow!"

His jaunty steps toward the printer matched the lightness buoying her heart. Hot cocoa, theater, Griffith, and a break from the kids—tomorrow was looking up.

On her way to join her siblings in the children's section, her phone buzzed. Expecting Griffith, she pulled it out instantly.

Instead, an unfamiliar number blazoned across the screen.

Unknown Number: Hi, Hadassah. It's Byron. Your mom gave me your new number so we could communicate more easily. I would love to take you to lunch tomorrow.

Absolutely not. She switched messages and texted Mom.

Hadassah: What do we have planned tomorrow?

It took Mom several minutes to respond.

Mom: I need you to watch the littles while we're at the science fair Friday evening, but your afternoon is free ;)

Oh, no. Not the winky face. Luckily, she had a co-op class to teach in the morning. If Griffith could meet around lunch time...

Hadassah: Perfect, I have some theater things I need to do in the afternoon.

She switched out of her messages with Mom back into the one with Byron.

Hadassah: Sorry, Byron, I have commitments all day.

After shooting off a text to Griffith to confirm the time, she ignored her buzzing phone and the messages from Mom and Byron, content to read a book to Obadiah and look forward to her meeting with Griffith.

The next day after teaching co-op, she considered the clothes in her section of the closet. Should she stick with the cardigan and skirt she was wearing? Did she need something warmer? No, they'd be drinking hot cocoa inside.

What are you doing? When do you ever change halfway through a day?

Instead, she untangled her braid and brushed through her hair. Then, she re-wove the strands into two braids and twisted them around her head like a crown and pinned them.

She stared into the mirror for a moment. Huh. Maybe she should do pretty things with her hair more often.

She managed to dodge any questions on her way out the door. Before long, she pulled into the parking lot of She Brews—where else? Her scarf flapped in the breeze as she headed for the building.

Inside, scents of coffee, cocoa, and cinnamon swirled around her. She scanned the tables and found Griffith camped out at a corner booth, brow furrowed in concentration as he focused on what appeared to be notes and a copy of the script.

Her heart gave a little *thump, thump*. What was that about? She wove her way around tables, stools, and overstuffed chairs and slid into the booth across from Griffith. "Hi, there, stranger."

He startled, looking up. "Oh, Hadassah. I'm sorry I got so focused on my notes." His eyes traveled to her hair. "Wow, I didn't know you were a hair and makeup artist too. That's really pretty."

"Oh! Thanks." Her ears flamed. She cocked her head. "What are you working on?"

"Blocking for the kids." He pointed to a messy diagram. "We have one scene where all of them are on stage, so I'm trying to organize them so they don't look like..." He searched for a word.

"A Sunday School Christmas choir?"

"I was going to say 'a blob,' but I suppose they're pretty interchangeable."

She laughed. "I've always just been happy if none of them jumped off the steps and went running through the pews."

He set the papers aside and stood. "Hot cocoa? Or I can get you something else if you'd rather."

"Hot cocoa would be perfect."

"Great, I'll be right back with two hot chocolates."

She wished she had his confidence as he strolled up to the counter, chatted with the pink-haired barista, and retrieved the cocoa. A buzz from her phone distracted her.

Mom: When do you think you'll be home?

Hadassah sighed. Hopefully Mom wasn't scheming to set her up with Byron if she got back to the house early enough.

Hadassah: In plenty of time to watch the kids during the science fair, don't worry :)

"Do you like gingerbread?"

She looked up to see Griffith holding two mugs by their handles in one hand and a plate in the other. He slid all three onto the table, revealing broken brown pieces on the plate. "These gingerbread men broke, so Reina gave them to me since we can't sell them."

Hadassah dropped her phone back in her purse. "Thank you. I love gingerbread. I'd be happy to make sure they don't go to waste." She accepted her mug, the peppermint stick tinkling against the side as marshmallows bobbed.

"We're doing Reina a favor, after all." He chuckled, shuffled his papers, and stuck them in a folder. "Enough of that for now. I can pick your brain after our marshmallows melt, *Director* Hadassah."

She felt her cheeks heat. "I hope you didn't mind me working with the kids."

"Mind?" He blew on his cocoa. "With you overseeing the kids, I finally felt like I could focus on the adults. I didn't know you knew theater games."

"I don't, really. I do know children." She wove her fingers through the handle of her mug and stared down into the steam rising from the frothy liquid. "My mom has always said I was called to be a mother."

His brow wrinkled. "You don't sound...happy about that."

Why wasn't she? If she was so good at something, wasn't that what God wanted her to do? "How did you know?" she blurted.

"How did you know theater was your calling?"

"Well, sometimes I wonder about it, to be honest." He took a sip of hot cocoa. "Growing up on the mission field for a lot of my life...sometimes I wonder if I'm on the right path. If this is what God wants for me."

Hadassah blinked. The way Griffith's eyes lit up when he talked about theater, his obvious talent, the way his play had brought people like Leroy and herself out of their shells...even Griffith wondered? "I wouldn't have guessed." She ventured a sip of her hot chocolate, closed her eyes. "Wow. This is really good."

Yeah." Griffith sniffed his drink, sipped. "Maybe it could use some lavender. We could add that as a special menu item."

Hadassah couldn't hold in a chuckle. Being a barista, however, did *not* seem to be Griffith's calling.

"Honestly..." He swirled his peppermint stick. "I'm curious. How would *you* define calling?"

Her? Wasn't she the last person to ask? She chewed on a soft piece of gingerbread, thinking. "Hmm...I feel like calling is where your passions and the world's brokenness meet."

He stopped stirring his peppermint stick and tilted his head. "Could you...could you say that again?"

She focused on her lap, feeling her shoulders shrink inward. Had she said something dumb? "I mean...we're here for a reason, right? All of us are called to make the world a more beautiful place. To bring the kingdom of God. I have to believe if He made us passionate about something, it was for a reason. I think..." She lifted her gaze, meeting his stare. "I think calling is about following those passions in a way that glorifies God and makes this world even just a little better."

Teens laughed across the room, almost as if laughing at her. She ducked her head again. "Maybe. I don't really know, though."

"Hadassah, that was...that was beautiful." Griffith blinked. "I don't know if I've thought about it quite like that before. In a way that *doesn't* frame calling from the perspective of talent." He huffed a laugh. "No wonder you're such a good actress. That could be a monologue."

It was her turn to sit in stunned silence. Just because she was talented at something, that didn't mean she had to do it? "I don't know if I'm a good actress, but I do know that when I'm on stage, or even watching a play...something in my heart feels full."

A smile grew. "Yeah. Me too."

Maybe it wasn't only theater. Right now, sitting with Griffith, that warm feeling began to fill her heart.

Before she could think too hard about what that meant, she nodded to his stack of papers. "Ready to get down to theater business?"

"That's my favorite kind."

Nothing screamed "manly" quite like buffalo chicken dip and *Chariots of Fire*.

Or so claimed Ryan after his most recent breakup. He said the offender stated that *Chariots* "was a slow movie" and that she despised buffalo chicken dip, so Ryan promptly bid her adieu and called Griffith in for a movie night.

"Seems a little picky if you ask me, Ryan. Breaking up with a girl over movie choices."

Griffith prodded the reddish-orange contents in the crock pot with a chip. He slid the mixture into his mouth and said, "Mmm."

Then again, this did contain some nice cream cheese and a beautiful spicy kick.

No wonder Ryan felt the need to call it quits if she refused to give this dish a chance.

"I mean, there were other red flags." Ryan, on the couch of his apartment, clicked on the projector. Blue light illuminated his features. "After going on as many dates-gone-wrong as I have, you learn to discern the bad ones pretty quickly."

Zinnia had mentioned something earlier in rehearsal. That she'd tested about every dating app and Christian singles groups on Facebook.

"Everyone says there are a lot of fish in the sea." She'd wrinkled her nose over her clipboard. "There's a great deal of trash in our ocean as well."

Perhaps he could convince Ryan and Zinnia, the pickiest humans he knew, to grab some buffalo chicken dip together. That could match well...or end in a complete disaster.

Griffith clicked off the heater and scooped buffalo dip into two ceramic bowls. Then he bunched his fist against the top of the tortilla chip bag and loped over to the sofa. He slumped into his seat and handed Ryan his mound of dip.

The warmth that seeped from the bowl into Griffith's palm stirred memories of grabbing hot chocolate with Hadassah earlier. Their time together went far too fast. He wanted to listen to her voice forever, with how she spoke about calling and the theater.

As soon as he drove home, and right before he went to Ryan's apartment, he submitted his script to a handful of play festivals. He also sent his resume to a number of assistant directing jobs in some of the surrounding counties.

Who knew? If this opportunity with Lilian fell through, maybe he'd have another chance at a similar theater.

All thanks to Hadassah, who boosted his confidence...

"Dude." Ryan's upper teeth snapped into a chip. "That dopey smile is ruining man night."

Griffith prodded his chin to force his lips into a thin line. They curved upward as soon as he released. Ryan sighed and clicked the mute button, and the music on the title page of the movie ceased. Griffith hadn't noticed the melody until now.

"All right. Tell me about the date."

"Date? What date?"

He and Ryan seldom had chances to connect, let alone speak about Griffith's hot chocolate escapades.

Every moment Griffith spent out of rehearsal, his family had hijacked. They spent the greater half of yesterday, Thursday, winding their way through downtown shops. For Angelitos—the D.R.'s version of Secret Santa—Griffith had drawn his brother Hudson for the Secret Santa gift exchange they enjoyed doing on Christmas Eve.

"Come on, man. You've literally gone red." Ryan waggled his eyebrows. "Tell me about her."

"I don't know if you'd call it a date. More like thank-you hot cocoa for helping me in rehearsals."

He explained how Hadassah had aided him in the Christmas tree shopping, up in the props loft, and the other day with the kids in rehearsal. Ryan threw a palm up. By accident, he flicked a glob of buffalo dip toward the window curtains.

"Hold up. She went Christmas shopping with you *and* stayed behind to help you pick props *and* she grabbed hot chocolate. Did you pay for the drink?"

Griffith's chin buckled into his neck. He felt like a turtle whose face had caught on fire. "I mean, it was *thank-you* hot chocolate."

"You're meaning to tell me that you went on a date, and you didn't even know?"

A date?

His pulse quickened. He hadn't realized it had been a date; he figured it was just a get-together to discuss ideas.

Hadassah probably thought the same thing, right?

He reached into the bag of chips and poked a chunk of chicken in his bowl. "I think she was just trying to be nice."

"Describe her to me."

Oh, Griffith understood that gleam in Ryan's pupils. He got this way whenever he shared story ideas with Griffith. Would Ryan write Hadassah into one of his indie films? He eyed the screen. Then again, the world could use more movie characters like her—sweet, intelligent, a quiet but determined spirit.

As he recounted all her details, he felt his cheeks strain from how high his lips had traveled. Goodness, when had he last smiled this wide?

"A homeschool chick? Dude, you definitely went on a date. They don't spend time one-on-one with guys unless they're interested in something serious."

"Really?"

Griffith technically received a home school education in the D.R. Considering he seldom worked with any females his age who planned to stick around longer than a week for a short-term missions trip, he didn't venture much into the dating game.

Even in college, theater consumed most of his hours. Most thespians couldn't spare a moment to even grab coffee in between late-night rehearsals and classes the next day.

"Yeah. If you aren't serious about her, I'd set her straight now." Ryan arched a brow. "Considering you got that dopey smile..."

"Just play the movie, dude."

Griffith's thoughts hummed so loud that he didn't catch most of the opening scenes. He hadn't thought much about pursuing a significant other. Even though his mother often dropped hints about the long-term missionary girls who stopped by the compound, and Hudson put in a "good word" for him with some of the ladies at the missionary school he'd attended...

Memories melted back into the conversation he had with Hadassah in the props loft, when they spoke about fostering children.

He'd insisted so many parents didn't foster because they didn't feel ready. Didn't feel rich enough to provide a beautiful life for children.

"Well if everyone thought that, no one would get adopted."

Maybe he'd shoved away the idea of a girlfriend because so many turned their noses up at him when he said he worked part-time at a coffee shop. What man could raise a family on that and a dream that he'd one day break into the theater scene?

Had he sabotaged his chances in the past with ladies?

Ignored signs of flirting because he counted himself out of the race?

Speaking of race, one of the runners in the movie, Eric Liddell, was in the middle of an argument with his sister. She didn't want him to compete in the Olympics. Instead, he ought to join her in China for missions work.

Huh, familiar.

Eric agreed to join her in China, "I've got a lot of running to do first."

Griffith leaned forward, chip bowl discarded to his right. All of Eric's words washed over him like a high note song perfectly in a musical number.

"I believe that God made me for a purpose. For China. But he also made me fast. And when I run I feel His pleasure."

Goosebumps erupted on Griffith's arms.

Jitters filled his hands. He reached for the remote and clicked pause.

Ryan cocked his head. "You okay, bro?"

"When I run I feel His pleasure."

His pleasure, God's pleasure. Griffith embraced that feeling every time he roamed onto a stage.

"I—" Griffith leaned back into the couch and let the cushions absorb him. An overwhelming sense of peace swelled in his chest. "I never thought of it that way."

Chapter Eleven

THOUGH SATURDAY DAWNED AS THE COLDEST December day yet, nothing could dim the warm glow in Hadassah's heart.

She and Griffith had spent a long time yesterday chatting about theater and coming up with ideas for the kids that melded Griffith's knowledge of theater and Hadassah's practical insights into children. Her siblings had even been quiet and calm that evening, allowing Hadassah to work on memorizing lines.

She hummed to herself as she poured batter in a massive skillet for Saturday morning pancakes. Mom cracked a full carton and a half of eggs into a bowl to make scrambled eggs.

"You seem to be in a good mood this morning." Mom whisked the eggs with a splash of milk.

Hadassah shrugged. "Christmas spirit, I guess. Are we drawing names today?"

"Your Dad and I were thinking we could do that tomorrow late afternoon. Yocheved and Aaron would have a hard time making it over here today to get back in time for Saturday evening services."

Even living far away, Yocheved wasn't excluded from the family Christmas drawing, when every family member received a name of who they would be getting a gift for that year, kind of like a Secret Santa. Mom and Hadassah usually helped the younger ones pick out or create a gift for whoever they drew—no one wanted to get a pipe cleaner or a collection of acorns for Christmas from a well-intentioned but misguided four-year-old.

"That sounds good. I don't have anything for the play tomorrow, so I'm wide open after church."

As soon as the words left her mouth, she wished she could take them back. Mom tapped her whisk on the edge of the bowl. "It seems like you're always at the theater lately."

Hadassah flipped a pancake. That warm glow in her heart began to flicker. "Yes, well, we're pulling it together really quickly. That means packing a lot into a short period of time."

"I just don't want you to take on too much." Mom poured the bowl full of eggs into a large pan. "It seems like you haven't had much time for anything. Byron, for example. I've done my best to shuffle things around for you two to get together, but you're always busy."

"You really don't have to," Hadassah said quickly. "Move things around so we can get together, I mean."

Mom adjusted the burner for the eggs. "I know, but I want to. I want the best for you two. Where are you going to find another young man like Byron? Successful, financially stable, a good Christian man." She pointed at Hadassah with a spatula. "Those are especially hard to find these days. Not many people in your generation share our values."

Our values? Or your *values? I didn't know financial stability was considered a Christian virtue.* "I think I'm still waiting for the right one, Mom."

Mom sighed. "You're twenty-one, Hadassah. I married your father when I was eighteen. The older you get, the fewer options you have. Especially for mature, godly men who will support you and your children so you can raise them up in the way they should go."

Hadassah kept her mouth shut, turning another pancake.

"Where are you going to meet any eligible young men anyway? The theater?" Mom laughed.

Hadassah gripped the handle of the measuring cup as she poured more batter into the skillet. What did Mom want from her? One minute, Hadassah was spending too much time at the theater and should be more attentive to the family, and the next Mom wanted to marry her off and send her away. *Putting Liz in exactly the same position Yocheved left me in.* Sure, Hadassah didn't meet many guys her age—not like she would have if she went to college—but maybe that was for the best. Liz was too bright not to be allowed to choose her own path.

Just then, Elizabeth herself stepped into the kitchen. "Dad has the boys in the yard, and the girls are playing with dolls. Need any help?"

"In the yard?" Hadassah craned her neck to look out the window. Luke went streaking by in only a light jacket over his pajamas. "He didn't make them put on winter clothes, did he?"

Liz grimaced. "I don't think so."

"I'll go wrangle them into jackets and gloves." Hadassah handed Liz the spatula. "You're on pancake duty now."

She saluted. "Sir, yes, sir."

Mom laughed. "You two are the cutest."

Hadassah offered what she hoped was a convincing smile and left the kitchen to track down warm clothing.

The boys would probably be fine without coats or gloves for the short while before Mom called them in to breakfast, but dressing freezing siblings provided a good excuse to leave the awkward conversation about Hadassah's dwindling prospects.

A bundle of coats, gloves, and hats in her arms, Hadassah whistled to her brothers. "Time out! Clothes break."

She set the stack on a lawn chair while the boys swarmed around her, noses, cheeks, and ears red from cold. Matthew and Luke tossed a ball back and forth while wriggling into coats, too intent on play to fully cease.

Dad tucked a football under his arm, chuckling. "Always the practical one, Hadassah."

Someone has to be. Sometimes Dad felt like yet another kid.

The boys ran away whooping and hollering, back at it with a soccer ball and kickball. Instead of joining them, Dad remained near Hadassah, arching his back in a stretch. "Whew. I might be getting a little old for this."

"Were you a legendary football player back when you were growing up with the dinosaurs?" Hadassah teased.

He clapped a hand to his chest in mock offense. "You wound me." He chuckled, watching the boys. "It's good to see you here. You've been gone a lot lately."

Not Dad too. "A little more than usual, I guess."

"Out with Byron?"

She raised an eyebrow. "No, at the theater."

"Oh." His brow wrinkled. "I can't keep up with these things sometimes. Byron's a good kid. Man. You all grow up so fast."

"I've been really enjoying the theater." She attempted to redirect the conversation. "The play is coming up soon."

No luck. "You know, Dave Young has been talking about more expansion for his company. Obviously, the boys are too young now, but Dave said Byron would be willing to apprentice them in learning the business when they're older. I'd love to see my sons working for a good Christian business like that." He glanced at her. "Especially if they were learning under their brother-in-law."

Her eyes widened. There was Dad's reason, clear as day. If Byron and Hadassah ended up together, the boys would have an "in" to a competitive business world.

She could understand why Dad would worry about the boys— Dad didn't have the most lucrative job, but he did manage to put food on the table for their large family. Mom and Dad never discussed finances in front of the kids, but sometimes Hadassah wondered how they kept the family afloat. Hadassah had a sneaking suspicion that if a Young-Wright wedding did occur, the Youngs would be eager to foot the bill to provide the best wedding for their precious only son.

If Hadassah alienated the Youngs by rejecting Byron—would she cause a rift between both families? Would they be upset with not only her, but the rest of the Wrights as well? She hoped the parents were all better friends than that, but when it came to Byron...

"Dad." She struggled to keep her tone light. "We've been on one date."

"I know, I know." He gave an indulgent smile, as if he believed they were playing a fun game of pretending Hadassah wasn't madly in love with Byron. "I'll keep my lips sealed for now."

As Hadassah headed back inside, the warm glow from that morning faded to a dying ember.

The best way to start a crisp Sunday morning? Why, with a rejection slip, of course.

Griffith,

I really shouldn't be checking my emails over the weekend. As I'm sure you know, there's no rest for the wicked, or for theater folk. I wish I had better news in terms of the application you sent me when applying for the assistant stage manager position for Windsor Players.

Your enthusiasm practically jumps off the page. Seriously, though, you may want to tone it down on the exclamation points. The amount you use should be criminalized.

I do see you have a great education to back you up. We actually have a lovely woman working at the theater who also went to Calvin.

I'm sad to say that most places are looking for a lot more experience than what you've indicated in your resume. It's great that you have student directing credits and have acted in quite a few plays yourself—don't get me wrong—but I'm sad I don't see a whole lot of internship experience.

Unfortunately, most companies will be looking for several years of directing or assisting before they can take on someone. I would always be willing to offer an unpaid internship, but you'd mentioned being all the way out in Roseville, and that's quite the hike. Especially since we can't compensate you in any way—gas, food, etc. We just don't have it in the budget. Plays are a dying art, alas.

As I'm sure you know, theater still exists because of our volunteers. Considering you graduated college three years ago, I imagine you would like something full-time and paying. I did when I left Taylor University ten years back.

I don't ordinarily write emails this long, but you remind me a lot of myself. Keep plugging away, and hopefully, in a few years' time, you'll be able to puzzle piece well into a theater such as ours or one closer in your area.

Best,
Neil Brecht
Chief Executive & Artistic Director of Windsor Players

Griffith sighed and tugged a scarlet sweater over his head.

Chills ran up his spine from how close he'd placed his bed to the window. Chekhov snuggled next to Griffith's legs and thumped his tail against the mattress.

"Here we go with the experience thing again." Griffith scratched the "good" spot behind Chekhov's ears. Chekhov moaned and thwacked his tail harder. "How am I supposed to pay for my dog's lavish lifestyle if I can't seem to land a gig?"

Over the weekend, rejection slips had poured in from the various festivals and theaters—ones he'd applied to months before. None nearly as personal as Neil's message.

Had Griffith known, at University, that college really didn't do a whole lot for the life of a thespian, he would've dropped his degree, raced to the nearest theater, and asked if he could get an unpaid internship with them.

He couldn't do the volunteer thing, not now. Not with apartment bills and such.

Lilian would already run him dry with this play. If *In the Wings* flopped, hello sixty-hour weeks at She Brews, and no more theater.

Maybe that's for the best.

Someone with more experience like Byron would deserve the position more. Like the email said, he'd tried for three years straight to land something...how much longer could he go before he earned a full-time position?

Would he have to do the part-time thing his whole life and worry about paying the bills?

He shimmied into his khaki pants and raced out the door. His parents liked to show up to church early...half an hour, to be exact.

He near-slipped on a patch of ice by the entrance to the church, recovered, and bolted inside. A huddle had formed around three figures—*that figures.* Every time they returned home, a congregation of their own would gather around Griffith's parents to hear about their latest adventures in the D.R.

"—and you said your son Hudson did all that by August of this year?" A woman with a scarf still bundled up to her nose gasped.

Griffith's mom squeezed Hudson's shoulder and beamed at him. "We weren't certain if we'd be able to finish the construction project before the school year started, but this one"—another arm pinch—"stayed out all hours. Even missed his own birthday celebration because he was so busy finishing the schoolhouse."

Wows sounded from the crowd, all marshmallowed in their large coats and winter boots.

Griffith wiggled out of his well-worn coat and lifted it onto a wooden coat rack in the corner of the room. Maybe if he didn't make too much noise, he could slip away before...

"Oh, Griffith. Didn't see you there."

He turned and spotted his mother waving him over.

The bright eyes in the crowd dimmed upon his entrance. Most Sundays, he spent time at his friend Elijah's church—instead of the one that funded his parents' missions.

Not that he didn't love these brick walls full of the scents of powdered donuts and yellowed pages of books from the church library.

Nothing could beat how the church got into Christmas decorations. Wreaths bedecked in pinecones hung on every door. Several ladies, from Griffith's recollection of his earlier days at this place, would spend hours trimming the Christmas trees that glittered in the sanctuary.

Whenever Griffith went to this church without his family, everyone always carried an edge in their voice around him.

They would keep their greetings to one word, and he found himself parked in a pew by himself during sermons.

Griffith shuffled over and his mom's grip latched his shoulder. Tight. Maybe like she too had feared he would bolt at any second.

"I'm sure you all know my son, Griffith. He usually goes to The Vine, down the road."

This caused several nostrils to flare in the group. Small churches and megachurches tended to keep a steady dose of competition between them.

"He's the"—the lady in the scarf's voice dropped several notes, carrying a warning tone—"playwright, yes?"

Years before the pastor had gathered funds to send his family to the D.R., he mentioned something about why he didn't include skits in VBS. Said he thought theater was too manipulative on the emotions, as opposed to a well thought-out, logical sermon.

Pink spread on his mother's ears.

"Oh well, Grif does lots of other things too. He works as a barista at that wonderful local coffee shop She Brews."

More people concaved into their stomachs, with hunching shoulders, darkening expressions. She was losing her crowd.

"He has done so many other construction projects for us in the D.R."

Spines straightened.

Lights clicked on in their eyes.

Seemingly without a moment to lose, his mom launched into an explanation about how Griffith would often give up lunch and water breaks to mix concrete in buckets. She left out the part that he did this because people used to cause him anxiety, and lunch breaks involved eating peanut butter sandwiches in a crowd.

At least, he would cower before he started doing the skits with the kids.

Did his theater background embarrass her?

Griffith noticed how as his mother's story continued, members in the circle inched closer to him, gave him approving nods, patted him on the back when she recounted some of his more formidable construction projects.

"What can I say?" His mother sounded breathless. She's charged through the tale like a sprinter. "He was born to build."

"I'm glad you mentioned that."

The woman in the scarf lifted a gloved finger.

Griffith's mother cocked her head. "Why's that?"

"We have a wonderful elderly lady who is out to see her family for Christmas, in Ohio. We've been doing renovations on her house. Real fixer upper. She can't afford to have any work done on it."

The scarf lady sniffed. The doors to the foyer banged shut. Two parents and their kids unbundled themselves from their coats, seemed to spy the crowd, and joined the blobbing mass that surrounded Griffith's family.

"We're planning to do some of the heavy-lifting projects on Tuesday, December fourteenth. We may put up some drywall as well. There's a spot in her basement that desperately needs it. I don't suppose Griffith would be able to help us with that project that day?"

She directed the question at Griffith's mother.

Oh goodness, when would he find the time? Or energy? The play had taken so much out of him. Could he muster enough strength to lift cabinets and other heavier items of furniture?

Griffith flicked through the calendar in his mind for all his rehearsal days. He technically went to theater every day, but did they have—

"He'd love to do it." His mother squeezed him closer into a suffocating side hug. His ribs ached. "Nothing would make him happier than to serve the Lord."

"Wonderful." Even though her scarf hid her smile, Griffith could spot the crinkle in her cheeks. "Go to this address."

She scribbled on her bulletin with a red pen and handed him the sheet of green-colored paper. The church had gone festive for the holiday season.

Right as she passed him the sheet, he heard her whisper, "I'm glad to see you're putting those hands to good use."

Chapter Twelve

HADASSAH PLOPPED ONTO A PLASTIC FOLDOUT chair with a paper plate of cold casserole and lukewarm pulled pork. After ensuring the kids all got their meals and were sitting nicely at the foldout tables with their friends, her own food at the church potluck had grown cold.

Mom sat with Enoch and Obadiah, at least, watching over the two youngest while chatting with the other moms, most of them members of the home school group. Hadassah had no idea where Dad had gone off to—someone had mentioned knocking out a wall in the Sunday School classrooms for renovations, and a herd of dads had wandered off to give their input and take measurements.

Hadassah nudged Obadiah beside her as he began picking up cooked veggies with his fingers, and he begrudgingly took up a fork. On the other side of Obadiah, Enoch sat next to Mom, not-so-sneakily transferring all bits of vegetables from his plate to his mother's.

Finally, Hadassah could sit and eat in peace. After the chaos of Sunday morning and Sunday School, her shoulders began to relax. She took a bite of pulled pork.

The woman across from Mom leaned in toward the other ladies, lowering her voice. "I just couldn't believe it when Sarah told me."

Evidently I've walked in on some juicy drama. As juicy as home school drama could get, anyway. Maybe someone got caught reading *Harry Potter.*

She smiled to herself.

The woman—Mrs. Marlow, if Hadassah remembered correctly—continued with her story. "We all know Sarah's daughter, Jessica, right?" Heads nodded. "Well, she said I could share this with my prayer warriors—which is you ladies, of course."

Listening in, Hadassah searched her memory. Jessica Anderson had been a few years older than her, one of the other girls in one of her science classes.

The "prayer warriors" leaned in closer, intent on the information.

"Jessica has two children, both under five, you know? Sarah's pride and joy." Mrs. Marlow tapped her lips with a napkin. "Well, it looks like Jessica is planning to send them both to preschool because she wants to go back to working full time."

Gasps. Hadassah took a forceful bite of casserole.

Mom put a hand over her mouth. "Oh, how sad for such young children to be without their mother. Are they in financial trouble?"

Mrs. Marlow shook her head, gulping down a forkful of potatoes. "No. Jessica just wants to go back to *dancing*. I guess she was a ballerina and now she works at a dance studio."

A few moms grimaced at each other. "It's such a shame when mothers put money or careers over their children," one with poofy bangs said. "Has Sarah volunteered to watch the children?"

"Five days a week?" Mrs. Marlow snorted. "She's put in her time caring for little ones. Besides, I told her that might be exactly what Jessica is hoping for. I told Sarah to stay strong. When that girl realizes what she's doing to her children, sending them off to be cared for by overwhelmed teachers herding dirty, neglected kids all day, she'll see reason and forget this foolishness."

Dirty, neglected kids? Hadassah glanced at her brothers. Kids were always dirty. Did preschools really neglect children?

"Trying to take advantage of her poor mother." Mom shook her head. "What a shame. Maybe if Jessica had been called by the Lord to some kind of ministry..."

"What greater ministry is there than motherhood?" the poofy-bang mom asked. "The Bible makes it clear that child-rearing is our greatest calling. Anything else comes second."

Mom looked hesitant, but the other moms nodded.

Hadassah's brow furrowed. *Do you have a reference for that?* She focused on her plate. As far as she knew, the Bible said everyone's greatest calling was to follow Christ.

Casserole turned to ash in her mouth. If she pursued theater, even if she did become a wife and mother, what would these ladies say about her? What would other mothers *her* age say about her? Would she be a social pariah?

Byron's words rang in her head. *"For my plays, I'd be happy to cast you as my female lead. As long as it doesn't get in the way of your responsibilities, of course."*

She sighed. Maybe she'd gone about this all wrong. At least if she someday agreed to marry Byron, she could still act sometimes, still feel the joy coursing through her heart when she became another person entirely, gave her all into producing a work of art, saw the tears and smiles of the audience.

The moms turned to other topics, and Hadassah kept her attention on scanning the room, watching over her various siblings carousing with their friends.

As if summoned by her thoughts, her phone buzzed. She held it under the table and glanced at the screen.

Byron: Hi, Hadassah. We haven't had much of a chance to see each other outside of theater. Would you be interested in lunch on Tuesday?

She bit her lip, scanning the crowd while her mind turned. Maybe this was a sign to give him another chance.

Everyone else seemed to love Byron, after all. Why didn't she? Had childhood biases continued to influence her? Did shallow envy of his opportunities temper her view?

Lord, please give me an open mind.

"Mom." She waited for a break in conversation, keeping her

voice low. "Did you have plans for lunchtime on Tuesday?"

Mom tapped her chin. "Yocheved invited us to brunch, but not after that." Her eyes lit. "If you had somewhere you need to go, you could leave early."

"I don't think that will be necessary, but thank you." *Please don't ask where I'm going.*

Luckily, another woman drew Mom's attention with a question, leaving Hadassah to turn back to her phone.

Hadassah: Tuesday sounds good, if we can do a late lunch. What time were you thinking?

She took a deep breath. Maybe she was doing the right thing. Or maybe Byron was as odious as her subconscious insisted. If only she had a clear sign.

She did know one thing. No matter what happened in the future, she would give Griffith's play everything she had. Memorize every line, every gesture. Volunteer for anything he needed. Maybe, through this play, she could prove to her family she could do something other than care for children.

Maybe she could prove it to herself as well.

Griffith's chest deflated when he strolled into the auditorium. Every actor still held their script in their hands.

Well, every actor except for Hadassah, who had gotten her lines down pat by last rehearsal.

We're supposed to be off-book in two days.

He shook the thoughts away and planted a smile on his face as Zinnia led the actors through a warm up that involved stretches. Some of the scenes for today required more physical activity.

Actors always took a little extra time to memorize lines. Perhaps they would know most of the script by Wednesday.

Griffith's insides sagged a little more when he caught sight of Byron at the base of the stage.

Byron waved him over and then raked his fingers through his auburn tresses. Griffith forced himself to bound toward the stage manager, voice shooting up higher than he would've liked.

"Hi, Byron. Happy Monday."

"Monday, indeed." Byron gestured at the large circle of thespians on the stage. Zinnia instructed them to hold one foot behind their back and make the appendage stretch as far as it could go. "We're gonna have to split up this big group into two smaller ones. One in the foyer, one up on stage. Otherwise, we'll never get through the scenes."

Griffith chewed on his lip.

Ugh, that meant Byron would lead one of the groups. *Knowing him, he'll undo all my work with some of the actors.*

How could he argue, though? Lilian gave him half the time a director normally had to pull together a show.

Byron leaned against the stage and folded his arms. "I can take care of the kids in here. Anything I should know about what you want to see in the scenes they're practicing today?"

This sent Griffith's head cocking forty-five degrees to the right.

Did Byron—actually want *his* input on the scenes?

"I like what most of them are doing. Just make sure Leroy keeps playing up the subtle, shy angle. We're making really great strides with him."

One of the first things Griffith's instructors taught him in college was the danger of over-acting. Loud actors tended to stun audiences, sure, but they wouldn't ever evoke tears or true laughter.

On stage, Leroy dropped his foot and reached for the other one. How long would Zinnia lead them in this stretch?

"Got it. Will do." Byron saluted Griffith with two fingers.

"Wait, really?" Oh no, did he say that out loud? His fingers flew to his lips by reflex.

"Sure, Griffith. It's *your* vision. Stage managers are simply supposed to help execute that vision."

Huh, maybe Zinnia had a talk with him. She swore she would do so after every practice—but she also vowed to give said "talk" by grabbing a fistful of Byron's shirt and hoisting him up on a wall until he cried "uncle."

"Wow, Byron, I really appreciate it. You truly value theater." Up until this point, Griffith had been under the impression that Byron had simply thrown money at the fine arts—not intending to do anything with them beyond the age of thirty. Now...

Byron shrugged. "When you have a family like mine, who is convinced I'm just 'trying to get it out of my system,'"—he tossed up air quotes—"you take it seriously. To show them that you mean business." His expression darkened.

Something swelled in Griffith's rib cage. Hope, perhaps.

At last these two found something to share, families who disapproved. Maybe he'd read Byron all wrong.

"All right, Byron. You grab the kids on stage. I'll work with the adults in the foyer on dialogue coaching."

Byron clicked his tongue against his teeth—Griffith assumed to mean "roger"—and Griffith led the adult actors to the lobby. Halfway through one scene, he noticed how Hadassah had sunken into the same vocal patterns of past rehearsals.

Actors tended to this, one of his drama instructors had once mentioned in class.

"Once they have their lines memorized, they might get stuck in saying the dialogue the same way, every time. Remind them that it's important to mix it up, and be present in the moment. No *one* performance should be exactly the same."

Griffith threw his palms up and Hadassah stopped, choking on a word. Her eyes widened.

"Did I do something wrong—?"

"No, no. I'm going to have you do a weird exercise for me, okay?"

She chuckled, spine relaxing. "Okay."

"I'm going to have you emphasize every other syllable. You've been saying the lines the same way, and this exercise will help you to break that habit."

She tilted her ear to her shoulder and scrunched her eyebrows. "Okay?"

"Like this." He cleared his throat. "MY how THE snow OUTside IS fall-ING." He spread-eagled his arms. "Just like that. Every other syllable."

He glanced out the window. Indeed, flurries cascaded onto the blacktop. Maybe they'd have their first white Christmas in years.

Hadassah bobbled her chin. "Okay, I think I've got it." She drew in a deep breath and shut her eyes. Then her eyelids flew open and the scene began. "OH, James HOW you LOOK so HAND-some TO-night—"

The lines continued. Griffith glanced over his shoulder in the direction of the auditorium. He watched Byron stop a scene and motion Leroy down stage—the part of the stage closest to the front row seats. Griffith forced himself to relax and look away.

He'll follow your directions. To make sure Leroy keeps doing the subtle angle. Byron said he valued your vision.

He tuned back into Hadassah's monologue.

"AND how I wish YOU could SEE me UP there—"

"Okay, Hadassah, talk normal."

"—and realize that I've finally found home, on stage." Hadassah clutched at her throat, face radiant. She bounced up and down. "Oh, you're right, Griffith. Because of that exercise, it did sound different this time. I was so worried that the monologue was starting to come out the same."

The adults continued their scene work until Griffith stole a glance at the time on his phone. Shoot, five minutes left. How did time escape so fast when he did lines with Hadassah?

"Okey-hhdokey, everyone." He slapped his palms together and

winced at the sheer amount of decibels that echoed from the clap. "Let's go inside the auditorium and see how the kids are doing. After that, everyone can head home."

He threw open the doors to the theater, in time to catch a line from Leroy.

"I HATE IT HERE! THIS IS THE WORST PLAY IN THE HISTORY OF PLAYS AND YOU CAN'T MAKE ME DO ONE MORE SCENE."

The line had, in fact, come from Griffith's play. Act II, Scene Seven, to be exact. The screeching, the balling of the fists, the veins popping out of Leroy's neck from the utter power behind the yell— all of those things Griffith tried to *avoid*.

Byron undid all of his work in one practice.

"Scene." Byron, wedged in a corner seat close to the stage, clapped. "Great work, guys. Make sure to bring a notebook next time to rehearsal so you can write down anytime I give you notes."

Heat bubbled in Griffith's cheeks. He found that he, too, had rolled his hands into softball-sized balls.

"All right, everyone." This time, Griffith's voice came out loud on purpose. "You can head home. Make sure to have your lines memorized by Wednesday. We'll be off book then."

Yikes, as his words bounced off the walls, he heard the tone boomerang back. Terse, seething.

All the actors hunched into their sweaters, perhaps turtling themselves as protection from Mr. Scary Director.

Griffith squeezed his eyelids shut and counted to ten. In college, people would take a gander at his massive size and clutch their purses and bags a little closer. Some went as far as to race across streets to walk on sidewalks opposite of him.

Big men frightened people.

Griffith exhaled and spoke much quieter. "You all did a great job. Keep up the amazing work."

People untucked themselves from their turtlenecks when he said this and bounded out of the auditorium. Griffith waited until all the actors had disappeared before he charged toward the front row.

"Byron." A growl lodged in his throat. He swallowed it. *Easy, big guy.* "What happened? I thought I told you to make sure Leroy played up the subtle angle."

"He did. Well, at first—"

Byron leaned back into the seat and placed his hands behind his head. How did he look so relaxed?

"—but he was too quiet. Couldn't hear him past the fourth row. Yelling was the only way we were going to hear him in the back. People pay good money for those tickets, you know."

Griffith's fingers twitched. He forced them to still. "What about preserving the director's vision?"

"Sure, when the director is *experienced* it's important that we do what he or she wants. Until then..." Lights from overhead twinkled in Byron's pupils. "Everyone has to be open to adjustments."

Chapter Thirteen

"Remember, seatbelts stay on until the vehicle comes to a *complete* stop." Hadassah gave her siblings a stern look in the rear-view mirror.

Behind her, eight kids bobbed their heads. Elizabeth grabbed Obadiah's hand. "I've got Obie."

Hadassah returned her eyes to the road, hands at ten and two as the van rumbled down the country lane. The vehicle could use some new shock absorbers, evidenced by the children bouncing in the back. As long as she could avoid any of them leaping out of a moving vehicle this time, she'd call it a win.

Mom had awoken with a splitting headache and the sniffles, so Hadassah volunteered to take the brood to visit Yocheved without her. The hour and a half drive would have been a breeze on her own, but with Obie shouting the ABCs, Enoch needing a bathroom break twenty minutes in, Matthew and Luke playing finger football and nearly hitting her in the head with the paper "ball," and Priscilla and Tabitha singing Disney songs...ninety minutes felt like several hours.

They pulled into the drive of Yocheved's home, a cottage-like structure that reminded Hadassah of a gingerbread house. The eaves dripped with Christmas lights shaped like icicles, and a manger scene sat next to the sidewalk, complete with a sheep, a cow, and a donkey. Hadassah smiled. Adorable and very Yocheved.

The second Hadassah put the van in park—and luckily not a moment before—the brood spilled out the doors. While Hadassah turned off the engine and locked up, Obie ran to pet the animals in the manger scene, shouting, "Sheeeep!" as Liz chased after him, and Priscilla and Tabitha raced to be the first to ring the doorbell.

Yocheved opened the door beaming. Her gaze met Hadassah's most likely frazzled expression, and she laughed. "Come on in, everyone. You've had a long drive."

"I have to go potty," Enoch announced, zooming through the door.

Hadassah made a head count as the crowd bumbled through the doorway. Liz carried Obie on her hip, grunting out, "Sorry, bud, you can see the sheep again later."

Inside, Yocheved directed the kids to the kitchen sink and the bathroom. "I bet you guys are hungry. Wash up and we can get started. I thought it would be fun to decorate our own Christmas pancakes—kind of like Christmas cookies."

Priscilla and Tabitha squealed. Even Liz broke into a grin, admitting, "Okay, that's pretty cool."

Colorful paper plates with Santas and reindeer sat on the dining room table and a foldout table pushed up against the end, forming ten spots. In the middle, plates of pancakes in the shapes of Christmas trees, stars, and gingerbread men wafted steam, interspersed with bowls of sliced fruits, sprinkles, crushed peppermint, whipped cream, and two different kinds of syrup.

"I have an egg bake staying warm in the oven." Yocheved winked at Hadassah. "Some protein to fend off the sugar highs."

Hadassah laughed. "This is awesome." She hugged her sister. "When Mom said you invited us to Christmas brunch, I didn't expect just how Christmas-y it would be."

Yocheved gave her a squeeze. "I don't get to do much of this sort of thing with just me and Aaron. I've been looking forward to this since Thanksgiving."

The sparkle of delight in Yocheved's eyes, the energy as she directed the kids to the table and poured water, milk, or orange juice into their plastic cups...

Yocheved loved kids, and keeping house, and mothering children of all ages.

Somehow, some way, she is destined to be a mother.

The siblings laughed, decorated, and chowed down. Matthew used whipped cream to stick a raspberry to his nose and started singing "Rudolph the Red-Nosed Reindeer." Elizabeth's pancakes were a work of art. Yocheved's egg bake was everything Hadassah could have dreamed. Warmth bloomed in her heart as she watched her siblings, and worries of calling and future and Byron began to melt away.

Byron. Stress came flooding back. Right. They had a date today for a late lunch.

After brunch, Yocheved directed the kids to the living room, where a stack of games and puzzles sat on the coffee table. "I got a new game I've been hoping someone will try out. Here, let me show you."

While Yocheved explained the rules of the kid-friendly activity—something about sticking cards to your head and trying to guess the food, animal, or object—Hadassah began clearing the table and carrying leftovers to the counter to be stored in containers.

Hadassah made it halfway through rinsing out the cups and putting them in the dishwasher before Yocheved bounced back into the kitchen. "Thanks for doing that. You didn't have to."

"It's no problem." Hadassah found herself infected with Yocheved's grin. "You made it easy with the paper plates."

"Weren't they cute?" Yocheved retrieved plastic containers for the leftovers. "I wouldn't use them all the time, but for a special Christmas brunch, I couldn't resist." She popped the lid off a square container. "I started collecting fun things for kids as soon as Aaron and I got married, honestly, but then..." She sobered. "I haven't really had a use for them."

Hadassah's heart squeezed. Her thoughts turned to the kids in the play, the theater games they had enjoyed. They would adore Yocheved. Especially kids like Leroy.

"Hey." She paused, dirty forks in hand. "Have you thought about fostering?"

Yocheved chewed her lip. "Actually...we went through the process to get approved, and we did. Get approved, that is."

When she didn't continue, Hadassah glanced up from the dishwasher and cocked her head. "What happened?"

Yocheved twisted a dishrag between her hands. "I..." She glanced at their siblings. "I chickened out."

"What?" Hadassah turned to face her sister. "What do you mean?"

She sighed. "What if I make a bad mom?" Tears glittered in her eyes, and she blinked rapidly. "What if that's why God hasn't let me have kids? Because He doesn't think I'll do a good job?"

"Oh, Yocheved." Hadassah wrapped her in a hug. "You're so good with kids. None of us can be perfect at anything, but if anyone is equipped and gifted, it's you." She pulled away, resting her hands on Yocheved's shoulders. "Just because it isn't turning out the way you thought it would doesn't mean God is saying no. Maybe it means that He has a different and even better plan."

It doesn't mean God is saying no. Did she take those words to heart herself? When college plans fell through and her theater dreams seemed to collapse?

Yocheved's breath shuddered, and she wiped a finger beneath her eyes. "You think so?"

"I know one thing. God doesn't ask us to be perfect. He asks us to be faithful. That's something I know you will be." A smile lifted her lips as images rose in her mind of a younger Yocheved's eyes scrunched closed, hands clasped as she talked to God each night before bed. "You've prayed for your future husband and future kids as long as I can remember. They're covered in prayer." She took a deep breath. "I know fostering can be hard, but I can't think of anyone God would be more delighted to use to love these kids than you."

Yocheved hugged her again. "Thank you," she whispered. She released Hadassah, wiping away a stray tear. "I'll talk to Aaron. He said he's happy to start taking in kids, but he's willing to wait as long as I need."

"He's a good guy."

"He really is." Yocheved tilted her head. "Speaking of guys. You have a date soon? With *Byron*?"

Hadassah returned to the sink to avoid eye contact. "It's been a long time since you last saw him."

"Thank goodness for that." She grimaced. "I would like it to stay that way."

"Mom and Dad really like him."

Yocheved scowled. "They always have."

"Trust me for now?" A tall order, seeing as she didn't trust her own decisions at the moment. "I won't do anything crazy just because they want me to."

"I trust you." As a ruckus of shouting broke out in the living room and Yocheved headed toward the commotion, she added, "It's Byron I don't trust."

After today, Griffith never wanted to see another sink again.

Hunched in the kitchen of the elderly woman's house—the lady whose name he couldn't remember—he unscrewed one of the pipes underneath the sink and pinched his nose with his free hand. He learned five minutes into the job that the sense of smell played a distinct disadvantage when it came to cleaning out the tubes underneath a sink.

Why did my parents sign me up for this?

Much as he loved helping members of his parents' congregation, he'd all but forgotten they'd volunteered him to help until he got a text from his mom this morning.

Mom: Don't forget to stop by the address below to help with household projects. The volunteers will start at nine this morning.

I'll send a screenshot of the location so you can plug it into your GPS.

He'd read the text at half past nine. He stumbled out of bed, pulled on a worn pair of jeans with several slashes of paint on the fabric—his "set-painting pants" as he called them—and defrosted his car.

Making it to the squat house, albeit a little late, he got his first job assignment, fixing the garbage disposal in the sink. The woman claimed the machinery made sputtering noises any time she ran it. Before she left town, according to the members of the congregation, she ate out for a week because her sink wouldn't work.

"Can't afford a plumber." A man in a brown winter coat told Griffith when he entered the house. "Here's to hoping you're handy with a wrench."

By good fortune, Griffith had plenty of experience. That came with the territory of the theater itself. Back in college he would learn random skills on the fly. Memories washed over him of all the assignments he'd received in his Bachelor of Arts days.

"We lost a spot-op today. Griffith, the show starts in fifteen. Think you can learn it?"

"Hey, so here's an electric screwdriver. I'm gonna need you to put together an operational coach for our production of Cinderella. Any way you can do it in a few hours?"

"Hey, Grif, the sink in the green room is flooding. Go fix it while I run lines with some of the characters."

Thus began his amateur career in plumbing.

Rice grains fell out of the pipe into a bucket Griffith had set next to himself. He tried not to peer into the watery contents in the vessel. That would churn his stomach.

As he got to scrubbing out the pipe, he forced himself to focus his mind elsewhere.

At first, his ears landed on the sound next to the kitchen. Two men scraped the drywall and exchanged conversations about the latest football game between the Wolverines and some other team.

Then they picked up the sound of a radio stationed near the elderly woman's Christmas tree. "Have a Holly Jolly Christmas" crooned out of the speakers.

Next to the tree—all glitzed with handmade ornaments, perhaps from her grandchildren—tarps sprawled on the family room carpet. Two men slapped paint on the walls, their broad streaks stoppered by blue tape when they reached the edges of the walls.

Huh, I wonder when I need to start painting the sets.

The moment the thought hit Griffith, he grimaced. The thought of everything he had to do at theater twisted his intestines in knots even more than the "sink finds" in the bucket beside him.

After the disastrous rehearsal on Monday, his director shot him a text of "to-dos" for the next meeting, Wednesday. He'd hoped to get on the first item on the list today—selecting colored gels for the stage lights—until his message from his mother woke him up this morning.

At least he had a chance to work with Leroy a few minutes after and undo the damage inflicted by Byron. With Hadassah volunteering to hang back and do scenes with Leroy, they at least heard his old self creep through the lines.

God bless that woman.

He twisted a rubber washer onto a pipe under the sink and tried to ignore the blush creeping up his cheeks at the thought of her.

Thankfully, the woman who owned this home liked to keep her house lighting dimmed, except for the colorful string lights on the tree, so none of the men working would notice the rose that Griffith felt bloom on his face.

He jiggled a new pipe back into place. Before he got started on the sink, he had made a quick run to a hardware store to grab spare parts.

Even with Hadassah and Zinnia's help, there's no saying if Byron won't keep trying to interfere.

Hence why, on Monday night, he sent an email to the cast. A pointed one, far bolder than Griffith would've done in the past. Desperate times...

Hey, Amazing Cast!

It feels like yesterday we were at auditions. I know we've had such a short time to pull off this show, but you're all making wonderful strides, and I can't help but swell with pride.

With that said, sometimes old habits can creep in, so I wanted to issue a few reminders before our rehearsal on Wednesday.

Reminder One*—Be off book by Wednesday. I know you haven't had much time with the script, but our performance date is looming. If you forget, you can call "Line," but really try to forge your way through the scene if you can't recall what happens next. We've done lots of ad-libbing exercises, so you should be able to improvise if you get stuck.*

Reminder Two*—Remember that although our stage managers and crew are absolutely awesome, I am the one with the director's vision. If someone gives you new instructions for what to do in a scene, make sure to check with me beforehand.*

Reminder Three*—Please have fun :)*

See you on Wednesday. Memorize those lines and make me proud!

Director Griffith

He hoped Byron would catch the hint from the email and back off.

Screwing the last pipe into place, he sighed, lifted himself from the ground, and arched his back. *No one should sit hunched over for that long like that.*

"Well." A feminine voice beside him caused him to snap forward. "Let's hear how the disposal is running."

Griffith didn't recognize her. Dark curls framed a pale face, and as she set down a crock pot on the kitchen counter, he noticed a baby bump protrude from her navy long-sleeve shirt.

He eyed the food. Realization dawned. One of the men had mentioned his wife would bring food. Spicy chili scents overpowered the stench of the kitchen.

"Umm, sure." Griffith flicked on the tap and toggled the switch for the disposal. The machine let out a well-oiled groan.

"Wow." The woman wiped her forehead with the back of her glove. Despite the below-freezing temperatures outside, she must've struggled to lug the heavy dish from the car to the kitchen. "You really have a knack for this sort of thing."

A voice piped up from the drywall sanding crew. "No wonder his parents want him on the mission field. With a handyman like that, you could build entire villages."

Heat prickled Griffith's skin.

He stared at his boots and then back at the woman.

Maybe a subject change. "Need any help getting more food out of the car? Don't want to make you overwork with the—" He gestured at her stomach and his ears flamed. What if she wasn't pregnant?

She grinned and cupped the bottom of her belly. Her hands caressed the bump.

"Not a problem. Some of my ladies are bringing in dishes."

Sure enough, the front door banged open seconds later. Women cradled dishes in oven-mitted hands. A distinct scent of cornbread wafted from one. They set their burdens down and met with their husbands in the family room area. Everyone laid down their tools and began chattering.

The woman hadn't yet left the kitchen. Her husband must've been the one upstairs fixing the toilet. Someone would have to alert him about the break for food.

"So, umm." Griffith hadn't conversed with many people outside of the theater and the coffee shop. "Boy or girl?"

"Girl." The woman beamed, eyes sparkling. "It'll be our third."

Griffith blew out a long breath. This woman couldn't be past her mid-twenties. "Wow. That's a lot to take care of. Do you stay home?"

Most of the wives in the family room did boast of being stay-at-home mothers.

She nodded. "Most rewarding job in the world."

"I'll bet. Did you always want to do that?"

Many Christian girls he'd run into in his college days said they'd dreamed of having two or four little ones running around the house.

She smirked. "Actually, no. I was a middle school teacher and was sad to say goodbye to all the kids. Had to leave mid-year. I was scared I wasn't up for the job. Grew up in a pretty rough household."

Griffith frowned as she flipped off the lid of the crock pot and stirred a spoon into the chili. He spotted beans and sweet corn.

"You still love what you do, even though you were sad to go?"

"For sure. I realized along the way that sometimes we mix up career and calling." She tapped the spoon against the rim of the pot. "They aren't always the same thing. Although I wasn't into the idea of being a stay-at-home mom at first, I wouldn't trade it for the world now."

She went behind Griffith to unwrap the cornbread dish.

As the foil crinkled, one thought consumed Griffith.

Even though I don't feel excited about missions' work, will I be one day? The bubbling chili didn't answer him.

Chapter Fourteen

HADASSAH CLIMBED INTO THE MINIVAN AND took a deep breath. *Here goes nothing.*

After driving her siblings home from Yocheved's house and dropping them off, she had immediately turned around to drive the smaller vehicle to her date with Byron.

Her heart pounded in her chest. Was this how dates were supposed to feel? This nervous energy? Maybe these were the butterflies she'd heard about.

Why did they feel so uncomfortable?

She pulled out of the driveway. Byron had offered to pick her up, but she'd declined. Maybe so she could flee if necessary.

They had agreed to meet near downtown. He apparently had a romantic adventure planned. Not exactly the lunch date she'd expected, but with the magic of Christmas in the air, how bad could it be? Her mind traveled back to her time looking at Christmas trees and in little shops with Griffith. Her heart warmed. That had been fun. This should be similar, right?

She found a parking spot near a fish and chips restaurant decked out with the Union Jack and red and blue Christmas garlands. Before she even finished pulling into a spot, she saw Byron striding across the small parking lot toward her.

As she exited the vehicle and hit the lock button, Byron reached her with a grin, his bright red scarf flapping behind him. "What are the odds we would find the same place to park? You look lovely."

She did? She hadn't bothered to change from her forest green sweater, gray wool skirt, and clompy boots that she'd donned this morning with only warmth in mind. With her coat on top of that, she probably looked like a fuzzy marshmallow. "Thanks."

He offered his elbow like a Victorian gentleman. "Should we embark on our adventure?"

"Sure." She clasped her hands in front of her, pretending to miss his gesture. "Lead the way."

He gave her a wink, elbow still proffered. "I appreciate your modesty, Hadassah, but you need not be so cautious. I have only the most honorable of intentions in this courtship."

Her face heated. That hadn't been what she'd meant to convey. At all. Best not to give any weird impressions. She linked her gloved hand through his arm.

"Off we go." He took off in a jaunty stroll.

Garlands wrapped the light poles and hung across the street from one side to another downtown, red ornaments bobbing on the lines. Lights sparkled in shop windows. Hadassah noticed her clenched jaw and stiff muscles and attempted to relax. *You're overreacting.*

So what if he wanted to walk with arms linked? What was the big deal?

Her mind flashed back to that unexpected kiss all those years ago. He was young and foolish then. Besides, it was just a kiss. She'd hoped that she would share her first kiss with the man she someday fell in love with, but that was an unrealistic childish dream.

If she married Byron...well, it would still be true, wouldn't it?

"I love the Christmas season. Celebrating the birth of our Lord." Byron glanced down at her, eyes alight. "What's better than...well, you'll see."

They reached the town square, blocked off from vehicular traffic. String lights hung from the bare trees. At night, she imagined they would highlight the Christmas deer, the Santa and his sleigh, and the manger scene tucked beneath a spreading tree.

Near a gazebo, an unfamiliar man with a shock of messy blond hair waved at Byron. "Hey, brother!"

Byron waved back. "Good to see you. I hope we're not late."

"Not at all."

As they approached, Hadassah saw three more people, two guys and a girl, all wearing long-sleeved t-shirts that proclaimed, "Jesus is the reason for the season." They held what looked like...pamphlets.

Oh no.

"I really appreciate you volunteering, brother." The blond-haired man clasped Byron's hand in a handshake, then smiled at Hadassah. "This must be your girlfriend. Hey, I'm Carter."

Girlfriend? She released Byron's arm to shake hands. "Hi." Her voice came out in a squeak.

Carter gestured to the volunteers. "We have a couple more t-shirts for you guys. We're just trying to remind people what Christmas is all about."

Hadassah caught a glimpse of the front of one of the pamphlets. It read, "Is there a Christ in your Christmas?"

Please no. Please.

She was all for remembering the reason for the season and sharing that with others. But stopping busy strangers and shoving pamphlets at people who didn't want them? Striking up conversations with people she didn't know?

Without even trying, Byron had ensured this would be the worst date ever.

At Carter's behest, she shed her coat and wriggled into an oversized t-shirt that hung nearly to her knees and smelled like she hadn't been the first—or even the second—person to wear the garment. Even with a bulky sweater underneath, she was swimming in fabric. She began rolling up the sleeves.

"That was the smallest size we had in storage," Carter said apologetically.

Byron chuckled, pulling on a shirt that fit him far better. "I think it's cute."

She barely mustered a smile.

Carter handed them a stack of pamphlets and gestured across the street. "We'll have you two on that corner. Let us know if you need more pamphlets."

"Roger that." Byron took Hadassah's arm. "Hopefully we'll be back for more soon."

The pep in Byron's step only seemed to increase as they crossed the street. "I just love giving back to the community and serving the Lord. Don't you?"

She nodded. Yes, she did enjoy both of those things. But not like this.

How would he know that? He probably thought with her love of the stage, she would be outgoing. In that way, this was thoughtful, and showed he really did care about the community.

Unless that's exactly what he's hoping I'll think.

She shooed away the uncharitable thought. She had no reason to assume such things.

As soon as they reached the corner, Byron pasted on a massive smile. "Merry Christmas! Can I interest you in some free literature?"

Surprisingly, people did stop to chat, asking about what organization he represented, what they were doing, even thanking him for the pamphlets.

"It's nice to see young people with their priorities straight," an elderly man said, tipping his flat cap.

Every time Hadassah attempted to say something, it came out as a half-whispered, "Um, pamphlet? Would you...paper? Okay." A man gave her an annoyed look, and she shrank into herself, wishing the pavement would swallow her.

Byron flashed her his charismatic pamphlet-smile. "Just like in the theater, Hadassah, you need to project so people can hear you."

"Right." She took a deep breath, pinning her sights on a woman with an armful of Christmas gift bags coming toward them. As the woman approached, she practiced her speech in her head. *Merry Christmas! Would you like to learn more about the reason for the season?* No, that was tacky. *This paper is all about Jesus.* Too simple. What should she say?

When the woman was three feet away, Hadassah shouted all in one breath, "WOULD YOU LIKE PAPER JESUS?"

The woman stared. Hadassah stared back.

"Merry Christmas," Hadassah squeaked, then turned and fled.

She didn't know where she was going, power-walking with her head down. Back to the van, maybe, to drive home and hide. She still had the shirt, and pamphlets. She needed to give them back. She needed to...

Overwhelmed, she ducked into an alley of sorts between two little shops, leaning against the wall to catch her breath.

"Hadassah? Hadassah!" Footsteps pounded behind her. Byron rounded the corner, concern etched in his brow. "Why did you yell at that woman?"

She buried her face in her hands. "I didn't mean to. I'm...I'm not very good at this sort of thing."

"Are you still shy, like when we were kids?"

She removed her hands and hugged herself, staring at him. Was it not obvious?

"I thought you got over that, considering you participate in the theater now." He dropped his stack of pamphlets into his pocket and took her arms. "I believe in you. I know it can be scary. I get jitters too, sometimes. But when it's for the Lord, it just...floats away."

She clenched her jaw, blinking back tears. Why did his comfort only make her feel worse? "I...I think I'm going to go home now, Byron. Mom wasn't feeling great. She probably needs me to help with the kids."

"Oh. Of course. I'll walk you to your car." He took the crumpled pamphlets she still clutched. "I'll bring all this back for you. We can do the second part of our outing another day. I'll tell the others that you didn't feel well."

"Thank you." He seemed to be taking it surprisingly well.

That wink made another appearance. "Don't worry. I won't spill your little secret. We can work on this shyness."

His words stabbed her heart. Great. He was ashamed of her. No wonder he wanted to send her home—he needed to save face in front of his evangelism buddies. Her head drooped.

"Aw, Hadassah." He pulled her into a hug. "Don't worry. I'm here for you. I care about you no matter what, okay? I'm not the type of guy who gets bothered by these things."

She nodded, managing to detangle herself. She pulled off the "reason for the season" shirt and handed it to him. "I can walk myself back. Thanks. For everything."

She brushed past him before he could protest and power-walked all the way back to the parking lot, stopping by the gazebo for her coat on the way.

For once, he didn't follow.

"Line."

Griffith groaned as Leroy cupped his hand to his mouth to call this into the audience. With his other arm, Leroy gripped Chekhov's leash as the dog took a sudden interest in sniffing the cast members' shoes.

Lilian had insisted Griffith bring the dog to practice more to get used to the stage. He'd hoped they could've done it on a day where the actors hadn't *just* gotten off-book.

In the dim auditorium lights, Griffith spotted Zinnia's lips sag. Today she wore an oversized sweatshirt, leggings, and fuzzy socks. She perched her ankles on the back of a chair in the row in front of her.

"'No.'" Zinnia uncapped a pen and scribbled in a script in her lap.

Before rehearsal, Griffith texted her and asked if she'd mark all the places actors forgot lines. By the end of today, she would have marred the entire sheet in scarlet ink.

"Come on." Leroy tugged Chekhov in his direction. The dog ignored him and moved on to Hadassah's skirt. "Please give me my line."

Zinnia sheathed her writing utensil. "As I said, your line is 'No.' Honestly, this is the fifth time you've asked me for help in this scene. Remember what Griffith said in his email." She tapped her temple with the pen. "Improvise if you get stuck." She gestured at the rest of the cast on stage. "Help him out if you remember what he's supposed to say, guys."

The sound of scissors gliding through wrapping paper echoed at the back of the auditorium. Lilian claimed she'd multitask today by wrapping presents for her family and watching today's rehearsal. She paused, mid-cut, and glared at the stage.

Griffith swallowed. *A bad sign.*

"How do we do that?" a kid cast member in mittens asked Zinnia. Byron traversed in and out of the costume shop today to start fitting a few people into smaller outfit pieces.

"The email also says to defer to Griffith with all decisions for what happens on stage." Zinnia winked at Griffith, who responded with a grateful nod. "I'll leave that up to him."

"Thank you, Zin."

Griffith clapped his hands and motioned for those on stage to huddle up.

"Now, if anyone forgets a line, someone else should cue them. Here, uh." He scanned the crowd and landed on a certain beauty. "Hadassah, mind being my example?"

Byron rushed on stage with a pom winter hat in hand. He shoved it on Hadassah's head, whose face had gone redder than the fabric cap. Byron glanced at Griffith for approval.

"Yes, that looks nice. Thanks, Byron. Mind grabbing scarves for the kiddos?"

Byron nodded—not without an eyeroll—and bounded off the stage.

Hadassah pulled the brim of the hat off her eyes. "I can do an example, Grif."

"Perfect. Now let's say at the top of the scene Hadassah forgets her line which is, 'Oh, James, I'm so happy to see you.' What are a few ways we can prompt her to remember her line?"

No hands shot up. One kid's finger ventured a dangerous journey up his nose into his cranium. The sound of Lilian cutting tape on a dispenser and the stage crew on the catwalk hanging lights took up the next few seconds.

Griffith sighed.

"Maybe." He kept his voice high. "I can say something like, 'I'm so happy to see you. Are *you* happy to see me?' Then Hadassah may remember her line. Got it?"

Some hesitant nods passed around the circle.

"Wonderful, now let's take it from Leroy's most recent line. 'No.'"

"No."

Griffith's spine eased. Hopefully they could keep the scene on track for now. He followed up with his next line. "What do you mean, 'No,' Oliver? I thought you were excited for the Christmas play."

"I am, it's just—" Leroy paused, mouth agape. He swallowed. Started again. "It's just—"

Here came another awkward silence. Great, Leroy forgot again.

Come on Leroy. Say, "It's just. I don't know if I believe I can do it."

Another two seconds of painful, prickling silence.

"Don't you believe you can do it, Oliver?" Griffith prompted.

Leroy's lip trembled. He firmed his jaw, eyes flitting from Griffith to Zinnia and back to Griffith. Then he opened his mouth again.

"Line."

"All right." Lilian's voice boomed in the back. "Everyone take five and go over your lines in the lobby." She lifted herself from a pile of half-swathed gifts. "You." A dangerous finger pointed at Griffith. "Upstairs. Tech booth. Now."

Griffith glanced at Chekhov, whose tail wound in circles. The dog would need to go for a walk soon.

Hadassah met his eyes and grabbed the leash from Leroy. "I'll handle it. Go." Her chin pointed in the direction of the door that led to the tech booth.

"Thanks."

With a leap, he bounded off the stage and up the ramp. Even though his insides soured at the thought of the lecture Lilian had primed for him, she would be even angrier with him if he kept her waiting.

He thumped up the staircase and almost crashed into her in the booth.

Unfazed, seemingly, she held up some of the blue gels he'd selected to put in the lights. The ones the crew weren't currently putting up on the catwalk.

"You've chosen these for the show?"

Even though she'd bedecked herself in an oversized "ugly" Christmas sweater today—complete with an LED light-up Rudolph nose—he watched her tiny frame slump. A certain sign of disappointment.

"Sure, some of the scenes are a bit sadder, moodier. Blue would go well with those."

She pinched her nose. "Griffith, it's a Christmas show. People are expecting holly-jolly and happiness. Not some noir film."

"There are happy lights too. Like the ones those guys are hanging up."

He gestured at a man who straddled a beam on the catwalk. The stage crew member panted. Some of those lights weighed more than a bench press.

"His grip is slippery." Lilian motioned at the man. "Go help him. Those lights cost thousands of dollars."

Yikes.

Griffith rushed out of the booth and toward the catwalk. He remembered from his college days the unease of hanging up lights several tens of feet above where the audience would sit. If someone didn't screw the clamp down hard enough, they not only risked thousands of dollars in investment—but some serious injuries to the patrons below.

He reached the catwalk and parked beside the man. Instinct took over and he gripped the clamp attached to the light.

"Thanks." The other man smelled strongly of gingerbread. "Phew. This is the scariest part of my job."

"Speaking of scary—"

Griffith's shoulders hitched at the sound of Lilian's voice behind him.

"—today's rehearsal certainly was. No one knows their lines except for Hadassah."

"We did give them a tight deadline." Griffith held the light steady on a metal bar on the catwalk as the other man tightened the screw. "Maybe we could do what some of my directors have done. Have portions of the script on prop pieces."

Once, he participated in a community theater that vowed to put on a production of *Beauty and the Beast* in forty-eight hours, as a social media fundraiser for the theater. The ASM had printed plenty of excerpts from the script on stage for when characters forgot. Most of the audience members didn't detect the words printed on prop pieces such as candelabras and books.

"Hmm."

Even though he couldn't see Lilian, he imagined she stroked her chin with her finger. Her "thinking face."

"Doable. We still have miles to go in other areas."

The stage crew member finished cinching the bolt and nodded at Griffith to let go. He did so, and the light wobbled. Panic seized his veins. He gripped the light in time for it to unclamp from the catwalk.

Caught. Right before it could fall.

He rose to his feet, lifted the light, and returned it to the catwalk carpet, cradling the equipment.

"*This*, Griffith."

Griffith glanced up at Lilian.

"This is what I'm afraid of."

"All the other lights are secure. I think I let go of this one too early. Maybe if we—"

"No, not the light." She balled her fists and scrunched her eyelids. "Griffith, I'm worried about my investment in you. I'm wondering if I should've—" Her gaze roved to the stage. Byron, on the platform, wrapped scarves around the necks of some kids who hung behind to practice lines. "—invested in someone else."

His arms sunk and he set down the light.

"I don't know what else to do, Lilian. I've done everything you've asked. The play has kids, a dog, a large cast. I can make accommodations for the lines. I can only do so much with what I've been given."

Lilian hugged her elbows and kept her gaze on the stage. Rudolph's nose rose and dropped in a sigh.

"There is one more thing you could do that may draw an audience, and help salvage this play."

A mixture of dread and hope swirled in his gut. "What?"

"Add a kiss at the end. It feels empty without it. Practice with Hadassah at next rehearsal."

A kiss? Hadassah seemed like a reserved type. Even if she felt comfortable with that, would she be okay with this being sprung on her at the last minute?

Lilian lifted a brow. "That stage needs painting. See to it that you're helping with that at the next rehearsal. Heaven knows we're scrambling for volunteers as it is."

Without another word, she left the catwalk, the carpet silencing her steps on the way out.

Chapter Fifteen

A GUST OF COLD AIR PUSHED Hadassah in the direction of the theater, ushering her toward warmth. Both the warmth of a heated building, and of a certain director who waited inside.

After the disastrous date with Byron on Tuesday, she hadn't seen him until Wednesday evening rehearsal, where he shoved a stinky red hat on her head. Romantic.

After rehearsal, Byron had walked her to her vehicle. The winter wind nipped her nose and made her eyes water.

"You're excellent on the stage." Byron swung his arms, seemingly unbothered by the cold. "I really do wish you had a better script—and cast—to work with." He shot her a smirk. "Maybe someday we'll play the leads together. I think you would enjoy having real chemistry with the male lead. Griffith does fine, but..." He shrugged. "There's definitely a certain difference in acting caliber, you know?"

She did not know. As far as she was concerned, Griffith had a natural talent. Even better than his directing, his acting seemed like an extension of his being, the way he slipped into character, embodied the parts. But she didn't have any training in theater. What would she know? She'd never seen Byron act, after all.

She stopped at the minivan. "This is me."

Instead of leaving, he faced her, expression serious. "Hadassah...I sense some worry. I just want you to know, I'm here for the long haul." A slight smile played across his lips. "Bad dates, awkward moments, busy schedules...none of that matters to me. I care about you."

Her heart thumped a rapid staccato. Her fingers trembled, but she didn't think it was because of the cold.

"I've sensed our connection since we were kids. Almost like God was pushing us together. I'm not one to argue with God."

She sensed a response was needed. What? Her brain blanked. She couldn't have him thinking she didn't listen to the Lord. "Me neither."

The spark in his eyes told her that was the right answer—which meant it was the wrong answer. Very wrong. He brushed stray hairs away from her face and tucked them behind her ear with cold fingers. "I knew you felt it too."

Did God really tell him to pursue her? Many people in her life seemed to think she and Byron were perfect for each other—was she somehow missing the cue? *Why don't I feel something toward him? Maybe that's what these jitters are?*

He leaned forward, and those jitters increased. His hand cupped her neck, fingers icy against her skin, sending a shiver down her spine. He must feel her pulse racing.

Apparently, he interpreted that as a good thing. His lips met hers and she froze. Her mind went blank. She heard the wind whipping, felt the cold metal of the van behind her.

Then it was over. He rested his forehead against hers. "See you tomorrow?"

Her voice shook. "I...I uh, have to check my schedule."

"No worries." He kissed her forehead and pulled away. "Text me."

"O...okay."

Then he walked away, leaving her shivering next to the minivan.

Not what I want to be remembering and thinking about today. Pushing through the doors of the theater, Hadassah yanked her mind back to the present. Time to focus on painting sets and Griffith's humor—anything but Byron.

She hadn't, in fact, had anything on her schedule for today. No excuse to get out of seeing Byron again. So she'd asked Griffith if he needed help with any tasks for the theater. Lo and behold, he planned to spend the evening painting sets—and could use as much help as he could get.

"Griffith?" Her voice echoed in the foyer. A few Christmas decorations hung from the ceiling and over the doors, not the full ensemble, but a good start.

Lilian poked her head out of the ticket office and hooked a thumb toward the auditorium. "In there. Are you painting?"

Hadassah bobbed her head.

"Good. He could use some help." She ducked back into the office.

Inside the auditorium, a broad-shouldered form on stage dipped a roller in paint and spread it across the set piece of what appeared to be a fake shop. Hadassah made her way toward the front of the auditorium, dodging random set pieces near the stage.

"Hey. How can I help?"

Griffith turned, wiping a hand on his paint-covered pants—even though he was also wearing a disposable smock. Judging by the amount of colors on the jeans, they had been used for multiple plays.

He broke into a grin. "Hey, Hadassah. Glad you could make it." He gestured to the set piece. "How are your art skills? We could use windows painted on."

"Rudimentary, at best, but I think I can paint rectangles." She ascended the stairs to the stage. "Are there extra smocks?"

An hour later, her smock was splattered in paint, but two large windows had materialized on the fake shop front. She'd even managed to add Christmas boxes inside. Her perspective was a little off, but she didn't think the audience would mind too much.

Griffith wiped his brow, smearing a bit of paint on his temple. "Wow, that looks great. You're a natural." He nodded toward the auditorium. "A lot of people end up painting too small for the audience to see when they first start making sets."

Her heart warmed. She had, in fact, tried to focus on what the audience would see. "It wasn't too hard."

"Well, you seem to have a knack for all things theater." He knelt and used a tool to pry the lid off another paint can. "You up for painting some 'wood'?"

He showed her how to use a paintbrush to make a wood grain texture. They worked side by side, Griffith humming a show tune under his breath, almost as if he didn't realize he was making the sound aloud.

"*Fiddler on the Roof?*"

His cheeks pinked. "Yeah. Plenty of catchy songs in it."

"I love that one too." Hadassah summoned her deepest singing voice, wrinkling her brow in what she hoped to be a manly expression. "'If I were a rich man...'" She gave her best impression of Tevye's dance, shaking her arms.

Griffith's eyes widened, and he burst into booming laughter.

Encouraged, she launched into the milkman's impression of the poultry in his yard if he were a wealthy man. Griffith doubled over laughing.

She gave a final drawn out note and then took a bow. *What has gotten into me?* She giggled. "Someday, I want to try musical theater."

"Someday, *I* want you to try musical theater." He wiped a tear from his eye.

She picked up her paintbrush once more. "Hopefully." She couldn't meet his gaze. "My family...they have other plans for me."

"Ah." He slapped his paintbrush against the wall, creating a long streak of wood grain. "Are they still giving you a hard time?"

"Not...precisely." They hadn't *really* discouraged her from theater, after all, besides complaining of her absences. They had just encouraged her toward Byron.

He sighed. "My family hasn't been a huge fan of all this either. Especially lately."

She frowned. Poor Griffith. His calling was so clear. Why

couldn't his family see that? "Some people don't understand how the arts can be a calling. I really like that your play speaks to that." She dabbed her brush in more paint. "The theater call...stage call..." She snapped her fingers. "Curtain call! Like at the end of a play, when the actors all take a bow."

She smirked at her own pun. In theater, the end of a play was followed by a curtain call, when all of the cast took turns coming out to bow for the audience while the people applauded. Often, audience members would even stand, shout, or whistle their approval. The audience's delight made all the long hours feel worth it.

Hold on. *Curtain Call.* Griffith's play was all about the calling to the stage. *In the Wings* was a good title, but did it really capture the main takeaway? Was the play really about waiting in the wings, or was it about finding one's calling?

No, she shouldn't suggest changing the name. She shouldn't interfere. This was his play, after all. After Byron's behavior...the last thing she wanted to do was overstep someone's boundaries.

"Curtain call." Griffith chuckled. Then his brow knit in thought. "Huh. Curtain call."

She hesitated. "Um. You can totally ignore this. I don't want to say too much. It might not even be possible, or you might not like this idea, but..."

"What is it?" He tilted his head. "I'm always open to ideas from you."

She could almost hear what he didn't say. *"Just not from Byron."* She didn't blame him. At all. Not after how condescending Byron was whenever talking about or to Griffith.

She took a deep breath. "What if you changed the title to *Curtain Call*? That's what the play is really about, right? Finding your calling?"

He sat back on his heels. "That's it." His sponge dropped into the paint. "That's our title. *Curtain Call.*"

If I had the money for a wedding, I'd marry that woman right here, right now.

Okay...maybe that was a little extreme. Hadassah had cracked something in his chest. Like an ornament that had secret lights inside, now bursting forth at full capacity.

Sure, changing the title of the play wouldn't boost any ticket sales. The link to buy admission to the show had gone up days ago—and Lilian wouldn't hint if patrons had purchased an adequate amount to keep Griffith in the theater.

Somehow *Curtain Call* put Griffith at ease.

Like it was the answer to a question he'd been asking for a very long time.

"Grif." Hadassah stifled a snigger by placing a finger to her nose. "You forgot to put paint on the *sponge.*"

He looked down and found his hand inches deep into the paint bucket. They'd begun to work on adding "bricks" to the buildings on the set. They did this by slabbing paint on one side of a sponge and pressing into the "building" edifice.

Except he'd forgotten to grab the sponge this dip, and so his fingers decided to take a bath in the ruddy-hued liquid.

"Whoops." He yanked his hand out and dabbed each side on the tarps that lay on the stage.

Hadassah giggled. "You probably want to wash that off."

"Right-o."

Once he'd dried enough of the liquid off his palms—by smearing the disposable smock he wore—he rose and ambled off the stage. As he did so, the door to the back of the auditorium banged open. Lilian grasped two buckets full of paintbrushes as she entered.

"Lilian." He dashed over to her, best he could while eyeing his hand for any loose, falling paint drops. "Hadassah had the most wonderful idea for a play title change. *Curtain Call.* What do you think?"

She didn't answer him until she dropped the buckets on stage.

Then she turned to him and tucked strands of loose hair behind her ear.

"I mean, it's your play, Griffith. I won't tell you what to do."

He frowned. Hadn't she been doing *exactly* that since the beginning of the process?

"Maybe you want to hear about the reasons for why we think it could be a great title."

"To be honest, I don't."

Oh.

She shrugged. "People don't tend to pay attention to the names of plays they don't know. If we suddenly changed *The Sound of Music* to *The Sound of Money* they would notice, but not here." A smirk crossed her face.

"You don't think it would be a problem if we changed the name, then? I knew the title I gave you for the deadline before auditions just wasn't it. You know?"

"The biggest issue you're going to run into is that we need to print programs. Like, yesterday. What if your designer has already created the graphics for the show?"

Hope wilted in his chest.

Andy had volunteered to create the illustrations for the playbills—as a favor to Griffith for when Griffith helped him with his book release. Griffith had given Andy a deadline for two days prior. With his lagging behind on emails, he bet Andy's design sat waiting for him, somewhere buried under a hundred messages.

Paint dried on his fingertips.

Right, clean first. Check emails after.

He shoved the back door to the auditorium, with his non-tainted hand, and sped to the restroom. Five minutes under warm water finally chipped the last of the red. He unfurled a few paper towels, wiped down, then checked his inbox.

Beams of light exploded in his chest again.

Thankfully, Andy hadn't sent anything yet.

Without a moment to lose, he dialed Andy's number and palmed the sink, waiting for the dialing to stop.

Four rings later, Andy picked up.

"Hey, sorry, dude. Is this about the program? I know I've gotten way behind on that. Mr. Knox has been emailing us about once a day for our next book project, and with family celebrations and such—"

"Andy, please tell me you haven't finished the design for the play yet."

"Well, I was putting on the final touches. Why?"

Griffith breathed. Would he cause Andy a headache and a half for switching the title at the last minute? If only Lilian hadn't pushed Griffith to come up with a name for the play so fast, maybe he could've spent more time pondering this.

"I have a possible title change." Griffith grimaced. "I don't want it to be a hassle."

Nothing sounded from the other side of the line.

A sink nearby dribbled water.

"Andy?"

"Oh, sorry, had to put it on mute. My dogs were barking up a storm. Lots of packages getting delivered this time of year. Yeah, no problem, dude. As long as I don't have to change the main design, only the title. What is it?"

"*Curtain Call.*"

"Nice. Give me five minutes, all right? I'll have it in your inbox. Sammy, no. Sammy, we don't rip into presents." A muffled growl and bark came through the receiver. "Gotta go, bye."

The line clicked.

Griffith stared at the mirror.

Did something...did something just go right for the first time in the history of this play?

Ten minutes later, the email arrived from Andy.

Some emotion he couldn't identify swelled in his insides when he peeked at the design. The silhouette of a woman, a single spotlight, an open curtain. His director back in college had once said, "We act to translate emotions that are beyond words, beyond description."

He tested the flavors of this feeling. Longing, joy, hope. Yes, all of those, and more.

In between the curtains, the block lettering read, *Curtain Call*.

Taking fifteen minutes away from his set painting duties, he pulled out his laptop in the lobby and posted social media announcements to a number of theater Facebook groups about the new name, along with changing the information on the theater's website. He also sent a quick email to the cast.

Hey, Everyone!

I know I've thrown a few surprises your way, but this one I'm really excited about. We're changing the name of the play from In the Wings *to* Curtain Call.

Don't worry if your family or friends have already bought tickets. We'll accept any tickets with the name In the Wings *on them too.*

I'm always pushing for us to be real, to be honest. I thought I'd share why this is so important to me.

To be candid, everyone, I've been struggling with my calling.

I want to believe hard that it's theater, but it seems like I've encountered many obstacles on the way to that that I've begun to doubt myself. Sounds a lot like what happens in our play, right? LOL.

In the same way the director in the play hears a distinct call to the stage, I feel right at home when that spotlight goes on.

Maybe you feel the same way too.

Please go ahead and share the new graphic on any social media, and thank you for allowing me to be transparent with you, as you are transparent with the audience every time you grace the stage.

Director Griffith

When he clicked the laptop lid shut, he heard the swish of skirts. Hadassah held up paint-spattered hands.

"It's spreading." She wriggled her fingers. "The paint got you and now it's got me."

Griffith laughed. "Oh, no."

"Anyway." She jerked her head in the direction of the restroom. "Lilian said you needed to work with me on something. She mentioned a change at the end of the play."

Griffith's eyebrows drew together. What could she—?

Images from the catwalk glimmered across his vision. Right, *that* change.

"Oh, she, umm." His cheeks flamed. "Wants us to kiss."

Hadassah froze, mid-step on the way to the restroom. She whirled around, face pale. "She-she does?" She winced. "A-a kiss? I've never done a stage kiss before."

He should've anticipated this.

He remembered how his pulse throbbed in his fingertips the first time he had to practice a stage kiss in rehearsal. Unlucky for him, the director decided to "get it out of the way" during the first practice. Griffith knew little else about the actress he kissed that day, other than that she lived in a dorm called "Veenstra" and that she didn't believe in breath mints.

"Do you"—Hadassah wrung her hands—"do you think she wants us to practice right here, right now?"

The answer was probably yes, but with how much Hadassah shook, she looked ready to shatter into a thousand pieces.

"No, no, don't worry about it. We can always practice that at later rehearsals. Worst case, there are ways to 'fake' doing it."

She exhaled so long that she hunched into her stomach, relief clearly etched onto her visage. "There are?"

"For sure. Tons of ways that we can make it look real, but it doesn't actually happen. Lips won't touch. We only do it for real if you feel ready."

Hadassah bunched her skirts in her hands then released the fabric.

"Thank you, Griffith." She blinked away a sheen in her eyes.

I wonder why she's so scared? Not that it mattered. He'd met plenty of people at college in the theater program who asked to be exempted from more romantic stage directions.

Everyone had a reason, and it was only their business if they felt ready to tell it or not.

A buzz erupted from Hadassah's bag. She dug inside and pulled out her phone. Even though she kept her lips sealed, Griffith could hear the audible groan from her nostrils.

Babysitting duty again, I'll bet.

She chewed on her lip. "Ugh, not on a Friday too."

"Have something Friday you need to get out of?"

"You could say that." Hadassah shoved her device into her satchel, even though it kept vibrating.

"I could use some help posting fliers downtown for the show. On *Friday*. Think you know of anyone who might be able to assist me?"

She flashed a grin. "You know what? I think I can come up with at least one person."

Chapter Sixteen

Telling Byron she had plans on Thursday only delayed the inevitable by one day.

Immediately after Griffith had brought up the stage kiss, her phone buzzed with a text from Byron.

Byron: It was too bad you were busy today. How does tomorrow sound?

Luckily, Griffith had saved her with a task—a theater task. She couldn't possibly say no to that, after all.

Hadassah: Sorry, I'm booked all day.

Friday dawned cold but sunny. After ferrying her siblings to classes and helping Mom with household chores, Hadassah finally put on a festive sweater, twisted her hair in a braided bun, and set out.

Griffith met her at a parking deck near the downtown area. She found him at the entrance, waiting by the automatic ticket booth. He waved, a stack of flyers peeking out from a messenger bag draped over his shoulder. His gaze went to her sweater and he laughed. "Great minds, as they say."

She giggled. He too wore a festive Christmas garment, reindeer leaping across the tapestry of red and green. "It seemed to fit the occasion." She straightened her sweater. "We need to represent the play."

"My thoughts exactly." He patted the messenger bag. "I was thinking we could start on one side of Main Street, work our way through the shops there, then come back up the other side."

"Efficient. I like it."

Pennants fluttered in the breeze, and Christmas music drifted from shops. They fell into a pattern—together, they would scout shops for bulletin boards, then Griffith would ask the staff if they could post the flyer for the play, and Hadassah would hang it up. Because, as they learned after the first encounter, Griffith could not hang the flyers straight for the life of him, any more than Hadassah could muster the courage to talk to shopkeepers.

"Are you sure it's okay if I don't ask people?" Hadassah clutched a stack of flyers to her chest. "We could cover more ground if we split up."

Griffith held the door to a candy shop open for her. "We can if you want to. If it makes you uncomfortable, I'm perfectly happy to keep going with this system."

Warmth filled her chest. After her disastrous date with Byron a few days ago, she didn't want to talk to strangers again anytime soon. "I like this system."

From boutiques to coffee shops to a cowboy-themed restaurant—an interesting choice for Michigan—they popped into stores, on the lookout for bulletin boards or tables where they could leave flyers. Even light poles got the special sign-treatment.

"Public property is fair game—except for mailboxes, which are illegal to post anything on." Griffith stuck a sign to a post.

"Do you know that from experience?" Hadassah smoothed the flyer, using a layer of tape to protect it from the elements.

He laughed. "Fortunately, no. It's just always wise to look into local laws before hanging flyers."

Noted. She wouldn't have thought to check. "What about sticking one *in* the mailbox for the postman to see? With appropriate postage, of course."

"Innovative." He chuckled. "Too bad I don't have any stamps."

They made their way down one side of the street and began a

loop around the square, suggesting more and more ridiculous places to hang flyers the whole way.

"On people walking by. Moving advertisement."

Hadassah nodded, maintaining a serious expression. "Good. Or, hear me out, we give them to pigeons, who then drop them from the sky above the city."

"Ah." Griffith wrinkled his nose. "I don't know. I mean, it's a good thought, but wouldn't dragons be better?"

Hadassah slapped a hand to her forehead. "Of course. Why didn't I think of that?" She held up a finger. "Wait. You know how pigeons are…messy? Imagine a flock of dragons."

Griffith cracked first with a guffaw. "You clearly spend a lot of time with children."

"Gotta be practical about these things." Giggling, she noticed a couple walk by carrying an open tub of colorful morsels, munching as they strolled. Popcorn—her favorite snack. The smell of caramel, butter, and kettle corn wafted from the tub in an intoxicating aroma. "Ooo. That looks yummy."

Griffith followed her gaze. "Mmm, yeah. I know that shop. It's really good. When we reach that stop on our route, I'll have to buy you a bag. Any flavor you want."

Her mouth watered. "Can we share it before I go home? The boys will scarf it down before I hardly get a taste."

"Absolutely." He chuckled. "I remember when my brother and I were tween boys. Nothing can fill the gaping void of the boy-stomach." He patted his own abdomen. "Don't worry, the shop's smallest size is still a good-sized bag—we'll make sure you have some all to yourself."

She clasped her hands, tempted to skip down the sidewalk. A Christmas-filled day, a break from babysitting and Byron, joking with Griffith, and now the world's best snack food. "Be careful what you promise. Coming from a big family, food is my love language. I can pack in the popcorn."

Instead of laughing, as people usually did when she made such statements and they looked at her small stature, he nodded solemnly. "I believe it."

She noticed they had slowed, standing close together to converse, flyers forgotten for the moment. The humorous twinkle in his eye reflected the Christmas lights in storefront windows.

Hadassah opened her mouth, about to say something—she didn't know what—when a familiar voice behind them spoke.

"Well Hadassah, when your mom said you had gone off with Griffith, I was hoping she'd misunderstood."

She whirled.

Byron stood behind them, arms crossed. "I like the matching sweaters, by the way. A nice touch."

Oh no.

"Byron." Her voice shrank to that of a mouse. "What are you doing here?"

He bobbed his head toward the surrounding shops. "A bit of Christmas shopping. The real question is, what are *you* doing here?"

Unease registered on Griffith's face, but he gave a friendly smile and held up the flyers. "We're hanging up posters for the play. Do you—do you want any?"

Byron's interrogative stare turned to a hard glare when his eyes darted to Griffith. "No, thank you." His gaze fixed on Hadassah once more. "I thought you said you couldn't see me today because you were busy."

"I...uh..." Her fingers trembled, her cheeks and ears burning in embarrassment. Caught. Caught avoiding him. What would he think of her and Griffith? Griffith had innocently offered a theater task, but Byron might not see it that way.

"I stopped by your house to deliver cookies from my mom and sisters." He flicked a piece of lint from his sleeve. "Your mother didn't know anything other than that you would be downtown with Griffith. She *guessed* it was probably on theater business."

"I..." Her mind raced. She hadn't done anything wrong. Words stalled in her brain. It screamed only one thing—*run.*

"I have to go. I think my mom needs me." She shot Griffith an apologetic glance, Byron a cringing one. "Thank you both."

Then she turned and power walked away with as much dignity as she could muster.

Harsh winter wind bit Griffith's cheeks as Hadassah dashed away.

He'd made a mistake. A horrible, horrible error.

How often had he misinterpreted Hadassah's volunteering as interest in him? She was just being her kind self. Why couldn't he see that before?

Byron kept his gaze fixed on Hadassah as she disappeared into the blur of a crowd that surged onto Main Street. Then he turned to Griffith, jaw firm. "Grif, why don't we talk somewhere less busy?"

There was nothing to talk about, right?

Griffith thought back to his college days, when his roommate accidentally went out on a date with a girl...who had a boyfriend. She failed to inform his roommate of this.

The boyfriend didn't take his "explanations" all that well and decked him behind their dorm. Griffith's roommate nursed a broken nose and bruised eye for a long time.

Even though he and Hadassah were not technically on a date...

He could see why Byron thought so.

And Griffith really needed his nose to be *not* broken for the play.

Okay, Griffith, we'll slowly explain to him that this is all a misunderstanding.

Customers from the nearby stores surged past them like a river of people.

The handbell players stationed in the middle of the street blocked off by orange barrels began a quick rendition of "Carol of the Bells." Each bell plunk and ring caused Griffith's heart to pound even faster.

Byron had spotted him and Hadassah together in the square—when the two of them supposedly had a date scheduled.

Speaking of Byron, he dodged shoppers and their bags and planted himself beside a streetlamp. A sign dangling from it advertised Carols on Christmas—a popular Roseville event that took place in the town square on the evening of December 25.

Cotton filled Griffith's throat as he loped over to Byron. If Byron really was dating Hadassah—Griffith committed a serious faux pax. Best to start apologizing and hope he could put out the raging fire that appeared to flicker in Byron's eyes.

"Byron." Even though the journey had been a few yards, he was somehow out of breath. "It's not what you think." He flapped the flyers in his hands. "She was trying to help out with the play. Like Zinnia—"

A hand shot up from Byron.

"I don't want to hear some monologue you've rehearsed in your head a dozen times for when you got caught, Griffith." He shoved the gloved hand into his jeans pocket. "I'm very perceptive. Nothing gets past me."

Dragon's breath trailed from Byron's mouth. So much for putting out fires.

Griffith stepped back a few feet in case Byron felt like swinging his arms soon. "Look, we're friends. You know, Hadassah. She loves to help whenever she ca—"

"That's not the issue. The issue is you *know* Hadassah. Or at least really want to. You see, Griffith, I can't allow that to happen. Not while I'm courting her." His brow arched. "You are aware of the rules of courtship, yes?"

Courting?

They're that serious?

Images from rehearsals reeled in Griffith's mind. Had he missed any signs? Why didn't Hadassah and Byron show any instances of physical affection—hand holding at the very least?

Now that he thought of it, Hadassah had come from a shyer sort. Maybe she didn't enjoy physical touch that much. No wonder she balked at the idea of a stage kiss.

"I can see that you don't. Allow me to explain the rules of courtship."

Heat flushed through Griffith's face and fingertips. He couldn't interrupt now. Not while trying to make amends.

And if he learned anything from his family in the D.R., even if you had nothing to apologize for, you ended up sorry anyway.

He recalled an instance of one day when he'd gotten tired of concrete mixing. He set down his concrete bucket and went out with the kids to perform more skits.

Hudson stopped him, mid-journey, with a frown.

"What are you doing?" Hudson had asked.

When Griffith explained, he shook his head. "Absolutely not. You're on concrete duty. Apologize and get back to it."

Then, Griffith didn't have anything to apologize for.

But he said sorry anyway.

Because if he hadn't, he would've earned quite the lecture from his mother. Skits would have to wait until later that day.

Byron's sharp voice drew him back. "Rule number one. A courtship is an arrangement in which you are intending to marry the maiden you are courting. It's far more committed than mere dating."

He sneered at the last word.

Wails from the bells behind them pealed louder.

"Rule number two. If someone attempts to break up the courtship, it's the equivalent of getting a girl to cheat on her fiancé. We wouldn't want that, would we?"

Indignation prickled like ants on his skin.

He would *never*. A friend in college discovered her mom had cheated on her dad. And the face he saw on that friend that day... No, he could never be that person.

"Byron, that wasn't what I was doing. We're just playing parts in a—"

"Rule number three, if someone has the audacity to intervene in a courtship, you will do whatever it takes to protect the fair maiden and your honor. Chivalry 101."

Griffith shuffled back further, boots landing on a sheet of ice on the sidewalk.

What did that mean? Would Byron deck him right here?

Byron appeared to read the question dangling on his lips. "If you don't ease back and leave Hadassah alone, there will be consequences. I promise." He spun on his heel and stalked away, red scarf flailing in the wind. The handbell music ceased.

Several moments later, Griffith registered what had transpired.

Cold fingertips gripped the flyers. He shivered and glimpsed the rest of the stores he and Hadassah hadn't touched on this strip. Part of him wanted to bolt home and bury himself in his room, to allow the deep shame to consume him.

The other half of him knew he had to finish posting these notices. Perhaps someone would see the advertisement and buy a last-minute ticket.

With a deep exhale, he charged into the nearest storefront, a popcorn shop by the name of "This Place Is Popping." Strong aromas of butter, cheese, and cooking oil greeted him as he entered. A line snaked to the counter, and behind it, a sign displayed forty-nine flavors of popcorn the establishment offered.

One time, when his family had returned from a brief hiatus from missions, they'd balked at the idea of a store dedicated solely to the movie-time snack. After a bite of their cinnamon roll flavor, Griffith had gotten hooked.

The memory of the taste soured in his stomach.

He bet Hadassah would've liked this place too. Hadn't he even offered to get her a bag of whatever flavor she wanted, moments before they ran into Byron?

I came on way too strong. He should've known. For a beauty like her, no wonder Byron had already swooped her up.

Clearing the thoughts away with a good shake of the head, Griffith approached the worker in a pinstriped shirt at the counter and held up a flyer.

"Hey, I'm from the local theater. We're putting on a play and I was wondering—"

"Griffith?"

Even though his ears had numbed from the below-freezing temperatures outside, he couldn't mistake his mother's voice. He whirled around and spotted his family at the tail end of the line that almost reached the door. Forcing a grin, despite how he felt, he held up one finger to indicate he'd be there in a moment. He slapped an advertisement on the counter and jabbed a thumb over his shoulder. "Gotta go. If you hang that up in your window, we'd be so grateful."

Unable to hear the response of the worker, due to the din of the conversation in the shop, he strode over to his folks.

"What are you all doing here? I thought you were leery of this place."

"Last-minute shopping." His mother lifted her arms, laden with bags. "We know how much you love the cinnamon-flavored one...well, I don't want to give away one of your Christmas gifts." Her hair was wet from freshly melted snow. "I'm so glad we ran into you. We've been trying to get hold of you all day."

They had?

He did put his phone on silent, hoping to dedicate most of his concentration on the conversation with Hadassah. If only he'd known...

"Yeah? Are you all doing okay?"

"We will be when you join us for gingerbread house making." His father feigned interest in a popcorn container on a shelf, nestled near the door. The store advertised a price of thirty dollars for it. "It's tradition, remember?"

Shame curdled in his gut.

First Hadassah and now this. So swept up in all the last-minute play arrangements, he'd forgotten about the annual holiday activity.

His mother pulled off her gloves with her teeth. She stood directly under a blasting heater. "Now why don't you go drive to your apartment and we'll meet you there?" She winked and sheathed her hand coverings into her coat pockets. "Don't want you seeing me buy one of your presents."

He nodded and plowed into the streets and toward the parking deck where he'd left his car.

Thank goodness his family arrived home ten minutes after he had, so he didn't have to soak in his thoughts. Because they seemed to run on a loop.

Hadassah—Byron—Courting—Threats—Embarrassment—Repeat—

His mother carried several trays of gingerbread parts. She must've baked them before their shopping trip, because the cookies didn't singe his fingers. Griffith and Hudson grabbed two icing bags and piped the siding of the house.

"You should be a natural at this, Griffith." His mother fed frosting onto a gingerbread man. Two eyes and a smile materialized moments later. "You seem to have a knack for house projects. Everyone said you did a stellar job on fixing the sink and helping with the drywall."

After he'd gotten the sink to work, they had him finish sanding down the wall. They claimed he should quit his day job and start his own home improvement business.

"Could make a fortune and give some of that money back to the church," one of the men had said over mouthfuls of chili. "Or a good cause like your parents' missions."

Guilt choked him.

Had he been irresponsible by taking low-paying to no-paying jobs? If he wouldn't join his parents in the D.R., couldn't he help them out by getting a more lucrative occupation and paying their yearly expenses?

Especially after all they'd done for him?

Once he finished covering one side of the house in white frosting, he observed a glow from his phone. Lilian had sent a group text to himself, Zinnia...and Byron.

Lilian: Including everyone in this, so we make sure it happens.

What did that mean? Did she not trust him to follow through on something?

Another message blinked.

Lilian: We need to practice the stage kiss tomorrow, so it doesn't look awkward on the night of the show.

His lungs punctured. It took him several moments to regain oxygen. Byron received the same text. What would he do, especially after he'd warned Griffith to stay away from Hadassah? Or could he tell that it was only a stage kiss and nothing more?

Before he could ask any further questions, he heard a snap. He glanced down and watched the side of the gingerbread house crumble in his hands.

Chapter Seventeen

TECH WEEK. DEATH WEEK. THE WEEK to be feared.

Hadassah had never participated in a full-on play before, but she had heard tales of the horrors of the final week before a play's production. Known as tech week, during this time, the technical elements of the play were nailed down and rehearsed. That meant rehearsing with lights, props, set pieces...the whole shebang. With so many things to perfect, the days were notoriously long and the nights infamously late.

But she would take death week over the death stares Byron had been giving Griffith. Even with the way her feet ached and her eyes burned from stage lights.

Byron sighed and gestured to the deck crew. "That piece goes stage right, not stage left. We can do this, people. *Stage* right means from the perspective of on *stage*." He closed his eyes and rubbed between his eyebrows.

Six hours in and Hadassah was beginning to understand why thespians considered tech week the worst. Several more days of this would definitely wear her out. Hopefully they would finish today in time for her to pick up her younger sisters from a cookie decorating party.

Griffith took his place next to her in the middle of the stage as the lighting crew adjusted the spotlights. The costumes weren't quite ready, so he and Hadassah wore their normal clothing. The lights danced over them. On. Off. Move. On. Off. She didn't know what happened up in the tech booth, but they appeared to be struggling.

A screech rang through the speakers, and everyone covered their ears. A few of the kids in the wings shrieked. "My bad!" a voice from above called.

"Yes, it was," Zinnia's voice echoed, then, more muffled, "Are you playing videogames on the side? We don't even have sound for this scene, guys."

Hadassah stifled a snicker.

Griffith sighed but also cracked a smile. "Zinnia will whip them into shape."

A smile remained on her face, until she glanced to stage right, where Byron watched with lowered brows. The levity vanished.

Her attention returned to Griffith, who shifted uncomfortably and cleared his throat, taking a small step away. Her heart squeezed.

After she'd darted off yesterday, leaving Byron and Griffith together—probably a poor choice in retrospect—she hadn't seen either of them in person until rehearsal. Byron made up for that with plenty of texts.

Byron: I'm sorry we couldn't have talked more before you had to go. Wanted to make sure you know I was not upset with you in any way. I am a bit unsure why you told me you were busy, however.

When she received the text, Hadassah had clenched her teeth and shoved her phone back in her pocket. She looked at Mom, who stirred a pot of spaghetti noodles beside her. "Why did you tell Byron I was with Griffith?"

Mom tapped the spoon on the edge of the pot and set the utensil aside, reaching for a colander. "He asked where you were." She grasped the handle of the pot. "It was so sweet of him to bring over those cookies. Isn't it nice having him around again?"

"Yeah." Hadassah gripped the bread knife and hacked through a loaf of garlic bread with more gusto than was warranted.

Mom probably hadn't thought of the repercussions of telling Byron that Hadassah had gone off to do something with another man. Because it *shouldn't* be an issue.

Even as dense as Byron could sometimes be, he unfortunately still seemed to have picked up on the fact that Griffith held a higher place in her regard than Byron.

After she, Mom, and Liz set dinner on the table for the hungry brood, Hadassah rattled off a quick message.

Hadassah: Sorry I had to run off so fast. When I said I was busy, I meant hanging up flyers for the theater.

She ignored her buzzing phone during dinner and while washing the dishes. Finally, she pulled the device back out to look at the messages, spread out over the past forty-five minutes.

Byron: I wish you had told me the truth.

Byron: To be clear, I trust you, Hadassah. I know you're an upstanding woman, filled with integrity, but I worry about you.

Byron: I know you haven't had much experience with the way the world works outside of the home. I understand and respect that. Having traveled and gone to college, I've seen and learned things that make me concerned about you spending time with a man unsupervised.

Hadassah snorted at that. If meeting in a public location surrounded by other people meant "unsupervised," she had spent plenty of time unsupervised with Byron the past couple of weeks. What did that make their...moment...in the parking lot? When she had frozen, and he'd kissed her?

Byron: I think Griffith is getting a bit too close to you. No other women are putting as much time into the play as you, except perhaps Zinnia. I suspect Griffith is asking for help more than he actually needs. That causes me to ask why.

Byron: I know your loyalty is not in question. I know the proper avenues of courtship are important to you. I worry about Griffith's intentions. I would advise you to interact with him as little as possible.

She leaned against the kitchen counter and took a deep breath. Slowly, she typed out an answer.

Hadassah: Sorry for the delayed response. I was busy with my family. I appreciate your concern, but I want to assure you that Griffith is an upstanding guy. He's also the director, and the co-lead in this show, so we'll probably have to spend quite a bit of time interacting.

She wanted to type more—maybe something along the lines of "don't worry, Griffith isn't interested in me that way." Her heart gave a strange sinking feeling at that thought.

What if Griffith *did* like her?

She felt comfortable around him. They could talk, laugh, even encourage one another. She never felt any pressure from Griffith. He did offer to spend time with her in order to help her escape from responsibilities—also known as Byron. He didn't *need* her to help with things like flyers. She thought he simply enjoyed her company and wanted to help her out. What if he did have other motives?

Beneath the sound of her brothers hooting over a board game, the drum of her heartbeat pounded harder in her chest. What if Griffith started acting like Byron? Would she lose her friend?

Byron: I understand that you'll have to interact with him for the rest of this show, unfortunately. Sometimes we get stuck with people we don't like for certain shows—it's part of theater. Just be careful. I can't help being suspicious of why he added a stage kiss after he knew you would be the female lead, and not before.

Lilian had added the kiss, not Griffith.

He didn't fight against it, though, did he?

Regardless, she couldn't let Byron keep casting aspersions on Griffith.

Hadassah: I don't think you need to worry. Lilian added the kiss, not Griffith, and she kind of insisted on it. I'll be careful.

The glare of the spotlight pulled Hadassah back to the present.

Another two hours passed of lights flashing on and off, actors running through scenes with props, the deck crew pushing around sets.

"All right, folks." Griffith glanced at Lilian, watching from the fourth row of seats and shuffling papers in her lap. "Let's work on the final scene and then take a break. I think our dinner brigade is starting to trickle in."

Hadassah's stomach growled. She looked forward to the meal break before another few hours of work.

The final scene...butterflies erupted. That was the kiss part.

She moved into position, along with Griffith, Leroy, and the other actors present for the scene. She took a deep breath, focused, and descended into character.

"We did it. I can't believe we did it!" She clasped her hands and stepped forward with a twirl, landing just right so her hand ended up in Griffith's.

The lines flowed from her tongue, and Griffith matched her energy. She found herself wearing a genuine smile. As he looked at her, Griffith's eyes sparkled in a way that didn't make her feel like it was only an act.

Her heart sped. Her mind flashed to Byron, the cold, frigid fingers on her neck...

She never wanted to feel that way about Griffith. The scared, trembling feeling, the frozen shock.

Griffith leaned closer but waited for her to initiate.

Her heart pounding, she panicked—and hugged him instead.

He hugged her back and released, so smoothly finishing the line meant to follow the kiss that the imaginary audience would probably never know something hadn't gone to plan. She saw the confusion in his eyes.

Her cheeks burned with shame. She had messed up the scene. That meant they would probably run the part again. She would mess it up, again. In front of the whole cast and crew. Past Griffith, her gaze met Byron's, and her heart ricocheted in her ribcage. His fists were clenched, as if he could hardly stand to see her even hug Griffith. Like Byron already owned her, had claimed her with the kisses she wished she had rejected.

I can't, I can't, I can't.

"Sorry-I-have-to-go-I-have-to-get-the-kids-sorry-bye." The words spilled out in one uninterrupted breath.

Then her legs were moving across the stage, carrying her down the steps, away, far away, out into the cold, out into the minivan.

She was driving away before she noticed the half-frozen tears dampening her cheeks.

"For the first time in the history of theater, someone has left a tech week rehearsal early," Zinnia informed Griffith.

Griffith leaned back as Zinnia reached over him to snatch a paper plate off of the makeshift food table in the lobby.

"The End Times are nigh, Griffith."

He snorted. She could say that again. As soon as Hadassah stormed out of the auditorium, Zinnia volunteered to fill in for the vacant part. They might need a substitute by the time the show rolled around if Hadassah couldn't follow through on that stage kiss.

Maybe that's for the better.

Byron had, after all, threatened Griffith to keep his hands off. Something soured his insides at the thought of Zinnia taking Hadassah's place.

Much as he appreciated Zinnia, she didn't fill his belly with the same warmth when he stood counter to Hadassah on stage. When he glanced into those beautiful eyes...

Didn't have the same "stage chemistry," as his college director would call it.

He shook the thoughts away and reached for a paper plate of his own. Mothers of cast members volunteered to cook them dinner for a break in between scenes. Darkness outside the lobby windows—pierced by streetlamp light—showed several more of them bringing in silver trays, covered in foil. The cast had plowed through the first batch.

Griffith set down his plate and held the door open for them. A blast of cold air stung his cheeks. Once the women entered and set up their dishes on stands—canned ethanol heaters beneath the trays—Griffith thanked them and retrieved his plate.

He grabbed a spoon and dug into a heap of steaming penne, covered in pasta sauce.

"Thanks for filling in anyway, Zin." Griffith had almost forgotten about their conversation before he let the women in.

"Better me than Byron." She grabbed a canister of parmesan and caused an avalanche of cheese to hit her dish. Did she even have any spaghetti underneath all of that dusting? "Speaking of." She glanced over her shoulder in the direction of a fake fireplace in the lobby.

Perched on a chair, Byron was in deep conversation with a man in an ombre blue sweater.

It took Griffith a few seconds to register where he'd seen this man last—one of the deck crew members who moved around the sets during the rehearsal. Byron, under Griffith's direction earlier that day, had coached them through when they'd transition furniture and set pieces in between scenes.

"What do you think he's up to?" Zinnia clamped the tongs in her hands. Then she pinched the salad with the kitchen tool.

Tomatoes, cucumbers, and lettuce hit her Styrofoam bowl.

"With our luck, nothing good."

They found an open spot on the floor near posters of past shows. A woman in a wedding dress, from the advertisement for a previous production of *Mama Mia!*, grinned at him.

Griffith didn't smile back. He skewered a crouton with a plastic fork.

Zinnia split open a packet of Italian dressing and drenched her salad in it. "If looks could kill... Lilian didn't seem too happy about the kiss scene, eh?"

The burn of her glare stayed imprinted in Griffith's vision every time he blinked.

He poked a noodle with his fork and shoved the pasta into his mouth. Tomato sauce burned on his tongue. Just how high had they set the food heaters' temperature?

Griffith swallowed. "I don't know what to do about it. It wasn't in the original script, and honestly, Hadassah seems super hesitant."

With a hyper-serious relationship with Byron, no wonder.

Speaking of, Byron had vacated his spot on the chair and moved to another deck crew member, who had stationed herself by a Christmas tree in the lobby. Oh man, he was *definitely* up to something.

"I know." Zinnia's voice pulled him back. She poked a straw into her juice pouch that had a "strawberry-kiwi" label. Clearly, the cast moms had gotten used to preparing meals for kids.

He sucked on his own container, a juice with a "cherry" flavoring.

"With how Hadassah has been acting about physical touch." Zinnia plunked her empty juice container on the ground. "You'd think she's been traumatized by a bad relationship."

Griffith choked on his liquid.

Several coughs later, he cleared his now-raw throat.

"Wait, what? Really?"

Had she experienced a rocky relationship prior to this play?

Zinnia nodded, eyes dropping to her feet. She set down her fork. "Same thing happened to my sister. She was a super cuddly and kissy type. Until her boyfriend, junior year of college. Horrible guy." Her cheeks reddened. "After that, well, it took her a solid month before she'd even hold hands with her next boyfriend."

Huh, he'd always assumed Hadassah was just shy about that sort of thing.

That could explain a great deal about why she paled so much when he mentioned the stage kiss. "Do you really think that's what's happening here, Zin?"

"Well." She picked up her fork. "Hadassah has committed to everything else on the stage. More than most of the cast. Don't you think she would do so with the kiss—unless there's some sort of aversion to that sort of thing?"

He rolled his fists, hands shaking.

How could Lilian *make* Hadassah do this if she had qualms with it—whether she chose to share about her past or not?

Zinnia reached out and pressed fingertips to Griffith's arm, steadying him until they stopped quaking.

"Hey, we'll work on her tomorrow about faking it. I'll help." She crunched on a tomato. "We won't force her to do anything that would remind her of something bad, I promise."

His shoulders relaxed. How long had he kept his jaw clenched? He released it and his teeth ached.

"Speaking of help." Zinnia set down her salad fork and crunched into a snickerdoodle cookie. The moms had wrapped assorted baked goodies in plastic bags, tied up with red and green strings. "Any chance, after rehearsal, you could aid us in finishing some of the costumes? Volunteers are way down this year."

"Sure thing."

College taught him to work a sewing machine, and ten stitches to his finger later, taught him to also keep his hands far away from the juddering needle.

The rest of the rehearsal went the best that it could. Leroy knew most of his lines by now, but used some prop pieces with his script written on them for a few moments. Actors tended to pull everything off at the last minute, after all. Zinnia played Hadassah's part well, tripping only on a line here or there. A true stage manager as always, Zinnia knew the script better than anyone in the theater—even the playwright himself.

After Griffith gave the cast notes and sent them home, he met Zinnia in the costume area. A room full of z-racks, dust, and hangers had buzzed to life with the sound of several machines running.

Griffith made sure to wear sturdy shoes in here, as pins and needles littered the linoleum floor.

He planted himself in a chair near Zinnia's and began to work on a garment set before him. He pressed his foot against the pedal of the sewing machine, and it chittered to life.

Zinnia paused her sewing and motioned at Griffith's fabric. "For Hadassah's skirt in the final scene."

A glow from a TV interrupted her last words. One of the volunteers scrolled through past episodes of *Project Runway* on a streaming service. They clicked on one that had a stunning red-carpet dress on the photo introducing the episode.

"Also, speaking of Hadassah." Zinnia pulled a pin out of her garment and stuck it between her molars. "Wanna tell me what happened between you two? What's with all the awkward tension?"

Griffith forced his attention downward, quick enough to notice he'd stuck himself with a needle. He sucked his teeth, hissed, and then put the finger in his mouth to stop the bleeding.

"Something, umm, happened when she helped me put up flyers."

In between the drumming of their machines, he explained about their run-in with Byron in the town square. Zinnia's nose wrinkled so much, she'd given him a full view of her nostrils. Not exactly the sight he'd hoped for at eleven-something at night. Or really any time of day, for that matter.

"Hadassah and Byron together?" Her nose relaxed. "Nuh, uh. That definitely can't be real."

A strange hope lifted Griffith's ribcage. Why?

He tried to choke down the feeling. "Byron's insisting that they've been courting."

"Dude, she scurries away from him every chance she can get. I would know. I'm the stage manager—well, ASM—I observe everything. If you ask me"—she pulled a bouquet of pins from her mouth and poked them into a pincushion on her wrist—"if anyone has caused her trauma, it's him."

"B-but he claimed they were courting."

A dizziness pounded his temples. Zinnia *did* like to exaggerate from time to time. Maybe she'd gotten caught up in her own conspiracy theory. Until Hadassah confirmed or denied her relationship with Byron, he could do nothing.

"Trust me, hon." Zinnia stilled her machine. "I've had plenty of guys say to me, 'God told me to marry you.' Until the Lord himself tells me, I'm going to think their sources are faulty. Byron's probably are too."

Before Griffith could finish registering her words, or the numbness that filled his arms, a rap at the door stole his attention. His family, all wrapped up in their best Christmas sweaters, glowered at him. All brightness and joy had vanished from their faces.

"Griffith." His mother said his name slowly, drawing out each letter. In the days of his youth, a punishment would follow her saying it in such a way. "Have you thrown your phone into a river? Why can we never get hold of you?"

"I—uh." His throat had gone dry.

His mother gestured at her sweater, bedecked in silhouettes of white reindeer pulling Santa's sleigh. "Family Christmas photos, right after your rehearsal. You're two hours late."

"Sorry, rehearsal went long and." He gestured at the sewing machines. "They needed help down here. We're short on volunteers."

A deep sigh weighed down the shoulders of everyone in his family.

"Griffith." His mother started again. "Sweetheart, I've tried my best to stay out of this, but this." She gestured at the array of clothing racks. A petticoat from a dress next to her threatened to swallow her hips. "All the hours, the lack of pay, I'm just worried you're throwing your life away."

He glanced at Zinnia for help, but she'd shrunk into her seat—kept her eyes on some hand-stitching.

Even she knew when not to overstep personal conversations.

Griffith turned back to his family. "There's a lot riding on this show. If it all works out, my hours—my pay. Everything's gonna be more reasonable. Everything's gonna be worth it."

Maybe he said it to convince them.

Or maybe to convince himself.

His mother exhaled. "Hmph. Doesn't *that* sound familiar?"

Shame coursed up his neck. He hung his head. How often had he said, "One more play and the director will recognize me," or, "One more hour of volunteering and they'll add me to the paid staff?"

His family inched out the door, but his mother popped her head back in. "I hope it was worth it—neglecting your family."

With that, they disappeared.

Chapter Eighteen

Griffith had declared Sunday a day of rest for the cast—but Hadassah almost wished he hadn't. She far preferred the drama on stage to the drama playing out in her own life. Even if she had embarrassed herself in front of the entire cast and crew.

Even if her break earned a, "Glad we finally get to see you. Seems like you're always at the theater" from Mom.

The big white van pulled into the Youngs' circular drive. Sitting squashed between Elizabeth and a bouncing Obadiah in one of the back seats, Hadassah felt sick to her stomach. She wished Yocheved were still here, one of the kids squished in the back, giving her a reassuring smile. Yocheved couldn't make it to this after-church luncheon with all of her responsibilities as a pastor's wife.

As long as she could remember, the Youngs and Wrights had taken turns hosting a lunch the Sunday before Christmas. She'd enjoyed the get-togethers while Byron was away—his sisters were sweet, she liked Mr. and Mrs. Young, and the siblings got along well—but today, she wanted to melt through the seat and join the slush on the side of the road.

"We're here," Mom chirped. "Remember, boys, we chew with our mouths closed."

"I'll keep that in mind." Dad chuckled at his own joke.

The family spilled out the doors of the van, the younger ones capering up the steps to the Youngs' sprawling front porch, bedecked with Christmas lights. A manger scene and a Santa and sleigh decorated the yard.

Mrs. Young opened the door with a wide smile. "Fancy seeing you all here. Come in, come in."

The Wrights filed into the wide open-concept foyer. Stairs led to the second story, with a dining room to the left, and a spacious kitchen toward the back. Elizabeth and the two older Young girls immediately set to chatting, while Priscilla and Tabitha darted off upstairs with the two younger girls to play.

"Just for a little while, girls," Mom called. "We'll be having lunch soon."

Hadassah scanned the crowd for the face she most dreaded seeing. No Byron. Had she gotten lucky?

"There we go." She turned at the voice behind her. Byron stepped out of the dining room, brushing his hands together. "I started a nice fire in the living room for us."

"Thank you, son." Mr. Young clapped a hand on his shoulder. "Aren't you handy to have around?"

It's a gas fireplace. How handy to have Byron around to push a button. Thank goodness no one could hear her thoughts aloud.

Byron's attention turned to her. Even though most of the Youngs and Wrights wore Christmas sweaters or shirts, he wore a dark green well-tailored sweater over an oxford shirt. In a "Holly Jolly" long-sleeved shirt featuring pom poms herself, Hadassah was of course considerably more stylish.

He stepped forward and took her hand. "Hadassah. It's good to see you." He brushed his lips against the back of her hand like a Victorian suitor.

Hadassah's eyes darted around the room. *Did anyone else see that?* The parents seemed too wrapped up in their own conversation. Only Elizabeth and the two older Young girls giggled to each other, as if Byron's actions were romantic instead of incredibly uncomfortable.

Byron's gaze also went to their parents. "I wanted to check on you." He kept his voice low. "Are you okay after last night?"

Her cheeks burned. "Yeah. I'm okay now."

She had managed to get her tears under control by the time she reached home the night before. Why did she panic about a stage kiss?

Not even a real kiss? It was clearly no big deal to Griffith, so it shouldn't be to her either.

Byron squeezed her hand. "I'm glad to hear it." He tilted his head, an expression of concern furrowing his brow. "I know it must be difficult to perform a stage kiss with Griffith in this awkward situation. I'll keep my eye on him."

Fire burned in her veins. *Griffith doesn't need anyone to keep an eye on him.* He had been nothing but kind to her. Maybe if someone had kept an eye on Byron...

"Anyone up for appetizers?" Mrs. Young's voice rang through. "I have snacks set out in the breakfast nook."

Byron smiled at her. "Care for some hors d'oeuvres?"

She trailed the group to the kitchen.

Mr. Young waved them over. "Byron. We were just talking about the play you two are working on."

"Isn't it nice you get to spend more time together?" Mom beamed at them.

Fantastic.

Byron gave an easy smile and slipped his hand into Hadassah's. Right in front of their parents. She stiffened. "It feels like a God thing, honestly. It's so nice to have a shared passion." Byron looked down at her.

She tried for a smile, but she imagined she only achieved a grimace.

"It's so wonderful to see our kids connecting." Mrs. Young placed a hand to her heart, glancing at Mom. "As best friends with kids, you speculate about matches, of course, and you can hope, but you can't control these things."

You all certainly tried.

Mrs. Young's marinated mozzarella balls with tomato and basil usually had Hadassah's mouth watering, but today they tasted like cardboard. Hadassah tried to focus on the appetizers as conversation swirled around her. Dad and Byron laughed about something. Liz and the Young girls chattered a mile a minute. Mom bustled with unusual energy in the kitchen alongside Mrs. Young. *Our families adore each other.*

She tried to picture a wedding to Byron. Wrights on one side of the aisle, Youngs on the other. Yocheved would be her matron of honor, of course. Everyone having a wonderful time at the reception, all knowing one another. Christmases and Thanksgivings all together. Would it be so bad?

Who knew if another man would support her involvement with theater? She suspected Mom only tolerated her long absences because Byron was there, too. If she remained single, she might not have these opportunities. Or a husband might be like many of the home school families she had met, wary of the moral implications of performing in front of an audience and bringing attention to oneself. Byron was certainly used to her large family. He probably wouldn't mind if she often helped Mom, making sure Liz wasn't left alone to share the same fate—no college, no dreams.

What about Griffith?

What about him? She shook away the thought. Griffith wasn't relevant to the debate. Other than the fact he might lose his position in the theater to Byron—but that wasn't something she could influence one way or another.

"Hadassah." Mom waved to her from the kitchen. "Would you help us glaze these dinner rolls with butter?"

"Sure." She wove her way to the spacious kitchen and took the bowl of melted butter and the basting brush. The bowl clacked against the granite countertop as she brushed the golden liquid over the domed bread, glad for something to occupy her hands.

"It's good to have her around," Mom confided in Mrs. Young. "It seems like she's always at the theater."

Hadassah pressed her lips in a thin line. *I haven't shirked any duties.*

Movement caught her attention, and she watched Dad and

Byron wander away into the other room, a serious expression on Byron's face. Her eyes narrowed. *That can't be good.*

Mrs. Young giggled while stirring gravy on the stove. *Giggled.* "I don't mean to pry, Hadassah dear, but my son is closed-lipped as it comes about things of this nature. He's a very private young man, but..." She glanced at Mom, and they shared a conspiratorial smirk. "Well, you're just so perfect for each other, and we must know. Are you expecting a proposal soon?"

Hadassah froze with the brush hovering over the rolls. "Wha...what? It's been less than a month."

"Oh, but you've known each other your entire lives." Mom patted her shoulder. "I can see from the way you get so frazzled whenever you talk about him. You're head over heels."

She clenched the basting brush. Did Mom really know her so little? Or did Hadassah not understand herself? The fear and butterflies might be what falling in love were like—how would she know? "Regardless of how long we've known each other, we've only been out a few times."

Mrs. Young turned off the burner and leaned against the counter, a dreamy look on her face. "I knew after our first date that Dave was the one. Two months later, when he got down on one knee, and we kissed for the very first time..." She sighed. "Soul mates."

Mom waved a dish towel at her. "No need to be scandalous." She smiled at Hadassah. "I agree. When you know, you know."

If Mom thought mentioning a kiss upon engagement was scandalous, what would she think if she knew Hadassah and Byron had kissed already? More than once?

Maybe that's another reason I should just go with it. I wanted my first kiss to be for my husband. That can still be true. With luck, she could even stretch out the engagement for as long as possible, to spend time adjusting to the idea. Clearly everyone else thought she and Byron were perfect for each other. Everyone loved Byron— except Yocheved. Perhaps she was missing something.

Okay, Byron. I'll keep giving it a chance.

But if they were meant for each other, why did her chest tighten and her eyes mist at the thought?

On "*Dark* Night," Griffith taught the dramaturg Arthur how to work the spot-*light*—ironic.

Dark Night, as described by his college theater professor, was a day dedicated to no rehearsals. Actors could get a well-earned break during tech week, and often, during dress rehearsals.

Although Lilian had advised against wasting any more practice time, Griffith knew from the weariness in the faces in the cast, from the purple shadows underneath their eyes, that many lacked sleep because of their commitment to theater.

His insides burned.

How often had the same happened with him and his family? Imprints of their last encounter, in the costume shop, seared into his memory.

Often husbands, who had wives who went into acting, called themselves "theater widowers" during performance seasons. After all, their spouse may never make an appearance at home except for the early hours of the morning when the whole house had vanished into a slumber.

Did Griffith do that to his family? Theater-widow them?

He choked the guilt down as Arthur stink-eyed the spotlight. The lighting fixture reminded Griffith of a rotating tank turret. It was certainly heavy enough to be one.

"So." Arthur gripped the handles attached to the spotlight. The theater owned two of these monstrosities. "I aim the spotlight and then turn it on? Why don't these darn things have crosshairs? Targets you can see through so you know exactly where the light will shine?"

That question...Griffith had often wondered the same thing.

Perhaps more advanced theaters would have a target in which

the spot-op could aim the spotlight with precise accuracy.

For stages struggling for funds like theirs, they'd have to settle for an older model, which meant "flying blind."

"You have to do your best guesswork. Which is why it's important to turn on the light slowly. That way, if you miss the actor completely, you can dim the brightness and adjust where you aim."

Squinting, Arthur directed the spotlight toward the left side of the stage. Then he flipped the toggle to turn the light on.

Sure enough, the beams didn't even reach the stage. He highlighted the first row of seats.

"That's when you'd dim the light." Griffith pressed a lever that faded the shafts of light. "Adjust where you point it." He did so. "Then you turn the brightness up. Go ahead and practice."

Arthur muttered under his breath, interspersing each word with a grunt or groan. Griffith decided not to argue. Desperate for any volunteers he could get, he almost fell out of his bed this morning when he received an email from Arthur offering to aid with "whatever, whenever."

Griffith slipped into the tech booth—right next to the mounted spotlight—and pulled up the lighting cues for his show. Now he could run through those to make sure everything looked just right before dress rehearsal.

A master script sat right next to the keyboard where he'd click the lighting cues. Zinnia's loopy writing filled every page.

Thankfulness glimmered inside him.

If all else failed, his ASM kept detailed notes of everything— every cue, every sound byte, every stage direction. If Griffith had a heart attack, Zinnia would take over, no problem. If only he'd been able to make her the main stage manager, instead of the one cloistered in the lighting booth during the show.

He tapped the key labeled "Go" on the board. During shows, the ASM would call out cues. For instance, "Lighting cue forty-six on standby...Go." Whenever the "Go" sounded, the person manning the keyboard would click the button, changing how the lights appeared on stage.

Four finger-clicks into the cues, Griffith heard a hum from his phone.

He pulled the device out of his pocket, and a message from an unfamiliar number burned his eyes.

Unknown Sender: Hi, I don't know if you have my number. This is Ava. I was told to let you know I won't be doing deck crew for the show. I am hoping to get a ticket. I've been enjoying rehearsals. This play is honestly one of the best I've seen at this theater. Thanks for understanding!

Griffith's heart sank. A deck crew member gone? When they'd already operated with a skeleton crew? He squeezed his eyes shut and forced himself to imagine the reasons why she'd drop the commitment all of a sudden.

Maybe she has a family emergency. Or health issues herself. I may be able to help move her sets during the show.

He sucked in a breath and continued to run through the cues.

Two minutes later, another handful of messages torpedoed his phone.

Unknown Sender: Bridget. You may not have my number. Anyway, I'm sure you already know this, but I won't be able to do light cues in the booth. Good luck with the show! Can't wait to get involved in the future.

Unknown Sender: Deck crew member Lincoln reporting for duty. Well, not reporting. Since I'm leaving. I hope you all "break a leg," and I'm sure the performance will be great.

Unknown Sender: Levi, here. I know you were supposed to train ushers tomorrow, but I was told you had plenty. So I guess I'm dropping out.

Once Griffith overcame the initial shock and lead-filling-his-chest sensation from all the texts, he peered at the last one.

"'I was told you had plenty'?" Griffith rubbed his eyes and then re-checked the messages to ensure he read right. "Who did that?"

He prattled out a message to the last Unknown Sender, Levi, and then saved his contact in his phone. The Good Lord knew he didn't have enough time to get down the numbers of everyone in the cast and crew, not with doing theater activities during all hours.

Griffith: Hey, Levi! I'm so sorry I never got to meet you in person. Could you let me know who told you that we had too many ushers?

Three dots filled the screen. Then the next text from Levi—

Levi: I think it was from the general theater email. So I'm not sure if there's a sender name. I can screenshot the message.

Griffith: No need. I have access to the email. Just give me one moment to pull it up...

He clicked on an app on his phone that had an envelope shape on the front, then logged into the theater email. Once he tapped the sent box, his stomach dropped.

Over a dozen messages with the same subject littered the screen. "Too Many Volunteers Signed Up to Help the Show." Each email contained a brief paragraph about how the theater had many gracious members of the community sign up to help. Therefore, they no longer needed the services of XYZ crew members. They should message Director Griffith to let him know they would drop out, so he could mark their absence accordingly in his records. No signature accompanied each email.

Only three people have access to this email account. Lilian—who hemorrhaged volunteers for this play—Griffith, and Byron. Lilian gave Byron access to the email to help Griffith screen messages the actors accidentally sent to the general theater inbox instead of Griffith's personal one.

Byron did this. Who else?

He must've primed them when he chatted with them in rehearsals *and* sent out emails to them. That way it seemed more like official theater business.

I've been backing off when it comes to Hadassah. So why did he do this?

Maybe this was payback for all the times Byron sensed the two of them—Hadassah and Griffith—had romantic tension with one another.

He sent a quick text to Levi, and the others, begging them to come back. Saying, "There's been a mistake. We actually could use more volunteers." Not all replied as Griffith clicked through light cues, but the ones who did said they unfortunately made plans during rehearsal dates.

"Are we going for a strobe light effect?" Zinnia's voice pulled Griffith away from the computer. "You're clicking that button so fast, I swear I'm going to get a heart attack from how fast the lights are going." Her smile slipped into a pursed lip when she appeared to catch his expression. "What's wrong?"

He showed her the texts, the emails. Explained who had access to the general theater inbox.

Zinnia pinched her nose. "I have no words. Well, I do. Not appropriate ones to say in a theater that often has children inside it."

Griffith slumped into his rolling chair. The seat collided with the painted brick wall behind him. "I don't know what to do."

Zinnia stared at her feet. Then at his phone. "Gimme it."

"Why?" He still handed over the device. Best not test a sharp tone like the one she spoke with.

"Password. I need four digits to get inside."

There was a pause.

"Griffith."

"One, two, three, four."

She arched a brow. "Really?"

"I'm not proud of it, okay? My phone is very hack-able."

Her nails clacked against the screen as she typed out the password. Then her fingers went rapid-fire as he heard the click of text messages and the whoosh when they got sent.

"Are you trying to message the crew members who quit? Because I tried that and—"

"Nope. Texting all your favorite contacts. Is Ryan someone important?"

Arthur, behind Zinnia, curled his fist and waved it at the spotlight. So the dramaturg hadn't made much progress.

"Okay, done." Zinnia dropped the phone in Griffith's lap. "We're meeting with Ryan and Andy at She Brews in ten." She slung her purse over her shoulder. It had slipped down her arm. "Get your coat."

The next ten minutes passed in a blur. Before Griffith knew it, he was scrunched in a comfy couch with Andy and Ryan on the other side of the table. Zinnia explained the situation to them as Griffith took sips of peppermint-flavored hot cocoa.

"Let me get this straight." Ryan had shrunk in his chair. Something told Griffith that Zinnia's intimidating voice and demeanor had gotten to his roommate. "Your stage manager—Byron—is trying to jeopardize the show, and booted all your volunteers?"

Griffith flicked some whipped cream off his upper lip. "Exactly. I don't know what to do and am not totally sure how getting wintry drinks is going to help us fix this." After all, Griffith couldn't expect to direct and act and move sets and click lighting cues and hand out programs and, and, and...

"Hot cocoa cures all, dude." Andy blew into the rim of his cup. "I don't think you have to worry, Grif."

But...he did? Did Andy not grasp the gravity of the situation?

Andy nodded, seeming to pick up on the doubt that pricked Griffith between the eyebrows. "We'll do what you did for me and Caroline when we released that book. Get all of our friends to fill the slots you need." He pulled out a sketchbook and tore a page. "Usually use these for illustrations, but I figure it works for creating a list as well." He clicked the end of a pen against a table. A red tip sprung to life, poised with ink.

Hope lit a fire in Griffith's chest. So this is what it was like...to be on the receiving end of love, of help.

"Okay, Griffith." Andy pressed the pen against the sheet of paper. "What positions do you need filled? We won't leave until we have one person for every spot on this list."

Chapter Nineteen

ZINNIA HELD A TAPE MEASURE TO Hadassah's hem, brow furrowed in concentration. "The last person who wore this dress was quite a bit taller than you."

"That's not hard to be." Hadassah held very still. The skirt trailed on the ground, much too big for her. Rehearsal hadn't officially started yet, but many of the cast and crew bustled backstage, prepping costumes and sets, rehearsing lines, practicing stage makeup, and...yup, those kids seemed to be messing with makeup and prosthetics to transform one another into wrinkled, elderly denizens. *Not* their roles in the play.

Zinnia chuckled and scribbled measurements on a scrap of paper. "In costuming, it seems like the previous wearer was always a giraffe or a mouse, no in between. I've done some interesting alterations on low-budget sets."

Right, Zinnia was in the film industry. When she wasn't working her day job at Helping Hope Publishing, of course. Theater, publishing, film...was there anything Zinnia didn't do?

"How do you do it?" Hadassah blurted. When Zinnia looked up, Hadassah's face heated. "You know—just decide to work in the arts, and then go for it?"

The ASM grabbed a pin cushion. "A lot of audacity, a dose of ambition, and a heavy helping of not caring what people think, I guess." Her expression softened. "That's not really what you're asking, is it?"

Hadassah bit her lip as Zinnia pushed pins into her hem. "My family keeps making comments about acting." If Byron wasn't also at the theater, how much grief would they have given her about the situation?

"Ah. Families." Zinnia grimaced, precariously balancing a pin between her teeth. She plucked the pin out and stuck the sharp end into the skirt. "I've definitely put a rift in some relationships by insisting on following my own path, and in pursuing it since. Still trying to make up for some of the snarkiness to my coworker, Caroline."

The name sounded familiar. Ah, yes. Andy's girlfriend, the author. "I don't want to cause rifts with anyone."

"I don't think you will." The pins pushed in and out. Hadassah feared for her ankles. "The arts also bring people together. Like you and Griffith, for example."

Hadassah resisted the urge to shift uncomfortably. "Yeah. We, uh, don't talk a whole lot anymore."

Zinnia shot her an assessing glance. "Byron issues?"

"Kind of." She let her breath out in a whoosh. Might as well be honest. She scanned the room to make sure neither Byron nor Griffith were near. Only the kids still messing with stage makeup. One of them had transformed into a lopsided tiger. "My parents want me to be with Byron."

"Gross." Zinnia halted. "Sorry. If you like him, that is. If not, not sorry."

Hadassah snorted, then broke into giggles. "You sound like my sister." She sobered. "It seems like the only way I can stay in theater."

"Oh, no. No no no." Zinnia wagged a finger, long, bright red acrylic nail blinding. "We do not seduce, date, or marry to advance in the arts. That's one of my main rules for myself." She pointed at Hadassah. "Trust me. Been there, done that. The dating, anyway. It's not worth it."

Zinnia plucked another pin from the pin cushion. "Your mental and emotional health is way too important to date people you don't click with." She laughed. "Did you know Griffith and I went on a couple dates a while back? He's a great guy, but we did not vibe.

We're way better off as friends." She stabbed another needle. "I worried it would cause a problem with our theater relationship at first, but if anything, it gave us more respect for each other. We're better friends than ever."

"I...don't think that would work with Byron."

"Have to agree." She snorted. "That's because Griffith is a quality dude and Byron is an...well. He's not."

Giggles broke out from the kids. Zinnia looked their way and scowled. "Hey, you five! Where are you supposed to be? Put the makeup away and go there."

The children dashed off.

"Anyway." Zinnia stood. "Glad to hear you're not actually a Byron fan. Griffith felt really bad because he thought you were together and he just hadn't realized, but I had my suspicions."

"Wait. Griffith thinks I'm with Byron?"

"Oh yeah. Byron gave him a lecture." Zinnia closed up the sewing kit. "You can take the dress off now."

Blood boiled in her veins. Byron gave Griffith a lecture? Griffith didn't deserve that—he hadn't done anything wrong. "I need to talk to Griffith." She glanced in the direction of the stage. "After all this. He's a little busy."

"Agreed. Especially after some of the shenanigans Byron has pulled." Zinnia grasped the handle of the kit. "You want my advice? Dump Byron. When you've been called to something, God tends to make a way, and not a way that ends up compromising who you are." Zinnia glanced around. "I don't want to say too much, for Griffith's sake, but Byron has been up to no good."

No good? Had he done something to Griffith?

Before Hadassah could ask, a cheerful voice interrupted. "Hey there, sister."

She turned to see none other than Yocheved standing in the doorway wearing a cozy Christmas sweater and lugging a large picnic basket. Leroy tailed her with a jug of milk in each hand.

"Yocheved. What are you doing here?"

Her sister grinned. "I heard through the grapevine that it's been a stressful week. We have a lot of milk and cookies left over from the youth group's Christmas party, so I thought I would bring it by."

"An hour away?" Hadassah hugged her around the basket. "Ow. Oops." She looked down. "Forgot about the pins."

"We were visiting some elderly congregation members in town anyway." Yocheved glanced back to Leroy, beaming. "Look what happened. I got to meet the star of the show."

His ears flushed crimson. "Not...not really. Just *one* of the leads." He turned to Zinnia and hooked a thumb over his shoulder. "I helped Miss Yocheved set up a table in the green room for the cookies. Is that okay?"

"That's great. Thank you." Zinnia held out her hand to Yocheved to shake. "I'm Zinnia, the assistant stage manager. I assume you're Hadassah's sister—er, one of them."

"That's me. Thanks for letting me invade your space."

Zinnia quirked a smile. "For cookies? Absolutely. Trust me, during tech week, we're all hopped up on caffeine and craving sugar."

"Sounds like the youth group party last night." Yocheved turned to Leroy. "Want to help me set these out?"

The two of them headed for the green room, chatting like old friends. Hadassah's brow wrinkled. "Wow. Leroy isn't usually much of a talker."

"Guess they hit it off." Zinnia clapped her hands. "Okay, give me that skirt. Griffith will want to start soon."

Hadassah carefully shimmied out of the pinned garment. She felt bare in just her shirt and black leggings, but they couldn't afford to be too modest.

She pulled on her usual denim skirt over the leggings. "I want to apologize to Griffith for what happened with Byron, if I get a chance. To explain things to him." She took a deep breath. "You're right. It doesn't matter what my parents say, or if this seems like the easiest course of action right now. I need to tell Byron I'm not interested, once and for all."

I hope I don't tear our families apart in the process.

"Good." Zinnia's jaw firmed. "Right now, Griffith could use all the allies he can get."

"What do you mean?"

Zinnia hesitated. "Well, you don't like Byron anyway." She glanced at her watch. "We have five minutes. Let me give you the extra push you might need to leave that bad news behind."

And, as Hadassah's horror grew with each sentence, Zinnia spilled the story of Byron's treachery.

Two syllables could cause Griffith's ears to burn with the intensity of a thousand suns.

By-ron.

There the two syllables—well, the person—was. Standing in the auditorium, barking orders to the actors as they completed their warmup for today's dress rehearsal. Thespians roved on and off the stage in costume pieces. One complained of a tear in her skirt.

Griffith exhaled and let the tingling heat subside from his face and neck.

Someone tapped his shoulder. He orbited and couldn't help but crack a grin at his new crew behind him. They promised to march into the auditorium, entourage-style, in case Byron happened to be in here.

"Ah." Griffith put on his best stage voice. "My new volunteers, I am so glad you made it."

Sure enough, when Griffith glanced over his shoulder, he caught Byron blanching.

"Okay." Griffith dug into his jeans pocket and pulled out a folded list from the meeting at She Brews the other day. "Does everyone remember what their new role is?"

Aside from his friends Elijah and Liv, who had a worship practice at Elijah's church, everyone had made it to the theater early. Nods of assent rippled through the group. Just in case—and loud enough for Byron to hear—Griffith read the sheet of paper.

"List for the New Crew Assignments

Andy—Running the second spot. May be the only spot-op if our dramaturg can't figure out his spotlight.

Caroline—Will move sets in between scenes. May also be a runner during dress rehearsals (see Charlize's role below).

Derek—Will also move sets. May also have him pull the curtain.

Charlize, Derek's Girlfriend—A "runner." Will make sure actors have props, get changed into their costumes, and fill any extra need we have backstage. She'll also be helping with hair and makeup.

Ryan—The person who pushes the 'Go' button in the light booth. Zinnia will give him cues.

Elijah—An usher, will be trained on Wednesday night, our final dress rehearsal.

Liv—Also an usher."

"Yes." Charlize, bedecked in winged eyeliner, rolled her eyes. "We got your several texts explaining these roles to us ahead of time, Griffith." She smirked, folding her arms. "We're prepared."

The doors to the back of the auditorium swung open. Lilian marched in with a box in her arms.

"Christmas came early." Her fingers prattled against the package as she set it in one of the seats. "Ready to see your programs?"

Griffith's heart catapulted into his throat.

No matter how many shows he put on, a feeling so otherworldly took over him when he opened a box of programs. When he got to hold one in his hands. He imagined it was like a slice of heaven that greeted him for just that moment.

Lilian pulled out an X-ACTO knife and sliced through the tape. She dug inside, pulled out a playbill, and handed it to Griffith. His fingertips glided up and down the smooth surface. He beamed and flashed the design at Andy.

"You made this, bro."

"Nah." Andy clapped his hand on Griffith's shoulder. "It's your vision. I'm just happy to be a part of it."

Griffith flickered through the pages, eyeing the headshots and bios of each of the cast members. Reality tugged him back when he heard Byron calling his name from the stage.

"Earth to Griffith. We finished the acting exercise. Are we going to get this rehearsal started sometime this week?"

His ears flamed again. Griffith exhaled and counted to five. "Yes. All right, everyone, places. Let's take it from the top."

He hadn't had a chance to slip into his costume yet. Maybe he could run backstage during the "intermission." His entourage had disappeared, meaning they'd gone to their designated areas. Lights faded to black in the auditorium.

Good, that meant Ryan was following Zinnia's cue calls to a T.

Jogging, Griffith headed backstage and halted when he heard Hadassah begin her monologue. Chekhov yipped on stage, but silenced moments later. She must've found his good belly rub spot.

He thanked the Lord that the people in the hair and makeup crew volunteered to take care of his dog backstage while he began preparations for the day. *I can only imagine how much more work having a kid would take.* No wonder many people in the theater were either empty-nesters or waited many years to begin families of their own.

Will this make me a horrible father?

The thought stung his skull.

If he followed a call for theater, would that mean he could endanger any future with a beautiful wife and family? Would any woman even want to marry the likes of him if he spent more hours in the auditorium than at home?

Maybe it was for the best that Hadassah was with someone else...even if that someone else was Byron.

Hadassah's speech halted as the lights went from a bright blue to near-darkness.

Ryan must've hit his cue early. Hadassah continued her monologue. From his spot backstage in the wings, Griffith watched her grip Chekhov's leash tighter. *She must be having a hard time seeing in this lighting.*

"What do you think, buddy?" Hadassah cocked her head at Chekhov. The dog mirrored her. She continued her lines. "Should I direct this play? Or will I be giving up everything I worked so hard for—"

Before she reached the last word, the lights flipped to a wan yellow, a cue that shouldn't be happening until the next scene.

"Ryan, what in the world?"

Griffith hardly finished the question before he spotted a building sliding onto the stage. Derek puffed out heavy breaths as he shoved the set piece forward.

"Come on, Caroline." He paused and wiped his forehead with the back of his hand. "I can't move this thing by myself. It's heavier than it looks."

Caroline, meanwhile, had her hands clasped over her mouth. She dropped her arms.

"Derek," she hissed, still loud enough for Griffith to catch her words across the stage. Perhaps he should suggest she audition for a future show, because she certainly had projection prowess. "We're not supposed to move sets until Byron tells us to."

Griffith had positioned Byron at the other side of the stage, because most of the sets remained there during the show.

Derek shrugged. "Well I can't find Byron anywhere backstage, so I figured I'd squint at the script in the darkness and try my best to figure it out. We are supposed to move this building when the lights go yellow."

A "hold" called from the audience. Griffith recognized Lilian's voice.

Everyone on stage froze.

Great, we're off to a horrible start. So much for showing off his new crew. A few lines in, and they already caused Lilian to pause the show.

Rolling his fists, Griffith marched onto the stage and peered out into the audience. The brightness of the lights caused the rest of the auditorium to be shrouded in shadow.

"Let's take it from the top. Again." Lilian's silhouette said this, and then sighed. "Also, Griffith, can you have one of your crew members get me a cup of coffee? I feel a headache coming on."

He stared offstage at Derek and Caroline. No way he could ask the former to pour her a cup of Joe. Knowing Derek's jump-the-gun nature, who knew what would transpire? Would he throw in six cream packets? Accidentally spill it on her when he rushed down the aisles of the auditorium?

"Caroline, would you mind getting it for her?"

He gave her quick directions to the green room. She nodded and bolted out of sight, strands of frayed hair whizzing past like they were stung by electricity. Goodness, she could move fast.

"Before we start the act again, Lilian"—Griffith motioned at the lighting booth—"mind if I check on something?"

He couldn't tell if Lilian nodded or not, but she didn't say "no." So he dashed off the stage, up the ramp, wound up the stairs, and toward the lighting booth. He caught his breath and forced his voice to stay even when he entered.

"Ryan." *Deep breaths, big guy. Deep breaths.* "What in the world?"

Even in the dark lighting of the booth, he noticed how Zinnia's cheeks had harshened to a puce. She gripped her pen like a dagger, knuckles whitening. So she wanted to murder Ryan too, eh?

"I know I'm supposed to click 'Go' when she says 'Go.'" Ryan shoved his glasses up his nose. "I don't know. I was looking at the master script and was thinking of when changing a light cue might have more *impact*." He flashed jazz hands. "No offense, but some of these cues don't feel pizzazz enough in terms of the timing."

"Okay, Mr. Hollywood." Griffith couldn't tell whether to laugh or cry. Typical Ryan. Trying to think of things from a film perspective. "I'm the director this time, so I'm gonna need you to follow my instructions to a T. Otherwise—"

He grimaced at Zinnia.

"—you remember that horror film we watched a couple months ago, in October?"

Color left Ryan's cheeks. "Yeah?"

"Zinnia will do far, far worse than the villain in that. I guarantee it."

Zinnia's lips twitched. Ryan sat petrified for several moments before nodding profusely.

Griffith saluted Zinnia and bounded down the stairs. Maybe they could get their act together when they started over. He swung open the door that led to the auditorium right as Caroline tripped on something in the aisle. Maybe an actor had let a water bottle roam, or maybe she couldn't handle the six-inch heels of death she'd chosen to wear today.

No matter the case, her coffee cup flung from her hands... toward the box of programs.

The brown liquid appeared to move in slow motion, and then all at once, dousing the contents inside the package. Caroline clapped her hands to her mouth and shook her head. Mist filled her eyes.

"Oh, Griffith. I'm so sorry."

"It's okay, we can print more." Could they? Did they have the budget for that? "Go ahead backstage. We'll fix it. Don't worry."

Caroline trembled on her way back to the stage. He noticed how she kicked her heels off, the likely perpetrators of the crime.

As he found his place in the wings, he caught the glint in Byron's eye across the way. Something about his smirk seemed to read, "Nice crew. If I can't sabotage the show, they certainly will."

Chapter Twenty

Byron sabotaged Griffith.

Hadassah clenched her fist on the desk in the school room just thinking about Byron's behavior. She forced herself to relax her grip. She needed to focus on her brothers.

Though the co-op classes had taken a break for the week of Christmas—a welcome relief for Hadassah, in light of the crazy theater schedule—Mom insisted the kids finish any work they had gotten behind on before doing the same.

Elizabeth, of course, had completed all of her coursework, as had the younger girls. The younger boys didn't have as much classwork to begin with, so they finished up by the end of the day Monday. Matthew and Luke...the older boys had a couple days' worth of work yet. So Hadassah sat with them in the school room, making sure they paid attention.

"Matthew." Hadassah rubbed her temple. "The fidget toy is supposed to help you concentrate. It is *not* meant for flicking at your brother."

"He likes it." The toy spun across the desk, hitting Luke's hand. Luke batted the spinner back with his pencil.

Hadassah plucked the fidget from the table. "Enough. Don't you want to finish before Christmas?" She turned to Luke. "Do you need help with any of those math problems?"

"No." He turned a scowling face to the worksheet.

Trust me, I want to scowl too. "Matthew? How's the essay?"

He heaved a sigh. "Fine. Can I take a walk break?"

"Two minutes."

Matthew got up to take a lap around the house. Hopefully the stroll would give him new energy for his work.

Hadassah pulled her phone out of her pocket and stared at the home screen. Despite the boys' reluctance, she hadn't had this much peace in days. Mom and the rest of her younger siblings had headed out to do some last-minute Christmas shopping. In fact, her life had been so hectic that she hadn't been able to talk to Griffith or Byron about their situation last night at rehearsal.

Zinnia was right—Byron wasn't worth her sanity. Her family would recover. After what Byron had done to Griffith, he'd shown his true colors. He was willing to sabotage the theater they all cared so much about just to get back at Griffith.

Chances were, she wouldn't get a chance to talk to either of them tonight either. Griffith planned to do a full run-through of the play. She needed to confront Byron before then. Maybe if he knew Hadassah had no interest in either of them, he wouldn't consider Griffith a rival.

How could she make time to confront him? She could ask him out to coffee this afternoon to talk.

Her hands trembled at the thought. Could she look him in the eye and reject him? Half the time, she was too afraid to string more than five words together, let alone craft a breakup speech—and make it all the way through without interruptions.

Yocheved had told her once about a guy before Aaron who had tried to convince her they were meant to be together. Yocheved had laughed. "I spent an hour *arguing* with him to convince him that I wasn't interested. He seemed to think maybe I was confused about my own feelings. We weren't even dating."

Hadassah didn't think she could laugh something like that off. Especially since Byron considered their relationship serious, she could only imagine this conversation would be worse.

I guess I'll commit the cardinal sin of dating. Time for a breakup via text.

Hadassah: Hi, Byron. I wanted to talk to you about our relationship.

I first want to apologize for addressing important topics over text. As you probably know, I'm not very good at saying things in person. I get too shy and frazzled. Because of that, and to communicate the things I want to say, I'm writing it out.

I respect you and your experience, and I appreciate your time and attention. I know how important our families are to each other. You and your family are practically family. I hope you will understand when I say that I don't want to be involved romantically.

I don't think we feel the same way about each other. Though I appreciate you as a friend, I don't feel that we're compatible.

I hope we can move forward without any hard feelings. I wish you only the best.

She re-read the text several times. Finally, with a shaking finger, she hit send.

Matthew bounced back into the room, whistling. "I had an idea on my walk." He plopped down at his desk.

Hadassah raised an eyebrow. "That was longer than two minutes."

He shrugged. "When inspiration strikes, sometimes you have to take another lap, and eat a cookie." He wiped his mouth with the back of his hand.

Her laugh came out breathy, anxiety sending her heart and lungs fluttering. "Okay, I'll accept that. Get to work, D-Four."

"Can I take a walk too?" Luke sprawled back in his chair dramatically. "I think my brain is dead."

"Yes. Go a—" Her phone buzzed, vibrating the tabletop. Her heart ricocheted against her ribcage. "Go ahead. I'll follow you. Matthew, stay productive."

She scooped up the phone, wandering out of the school room on wobbly legs. The device continued to buzz, a name blazoned across the screen—Byron.

Her heart pounded. Could she pretend she didn't hear it ring?

She held the device in front of her like a fragile bomb, not daring to move.

Finally, the ringing stopped. A "missed call" notification flashed across the screen.

Seconds later, a text popped up as well. She slid to open.

Byron: Please call me back. Are you okay? What's going on?

No chance on the call back. She didn't know if her voice would even work. She tapped out another message.

Hadassah: I'm perfectly fine. Nothing bad is happening. I just don't feel that we're right for one another.

She headed for the kitchen. She needed a glass of water.
The response came seconds later.

Byron: This seems to be coming out of nowhere. Did you talk to someone? Is this about Griffith?

She stopped halfway to the kitchen, a fist clenched. Byron thought the only reason she could possibly not be interested in him was if another man had stolen her affections?

Hadassah: This isn't about Griffith, or any other guy. I just want to be truthful with you. I don't think this relationship is going to work.

She filled a glass and took three big gulps. The third swallow went down the wrong pipe, and she coughed, thumping a fist into her chest.
Eyes watering from the mishap, she read the next text.

Byron: Call me.

The two words floated in front of her vision. Panic caught in her throat.

Hadassah: Sorry, busy.

Then she turned off her phone and dropped the device in her pocket.

Two hours later, her hands still trembled as she entered the theater. She hadn't worked up the nerve to turn her phone back on.

Zinnia waved her backstage. "You don't know stage makeup, right? We need to get your hair and makeup done. Charlize will help you."

"Oh, okay." She let Zinnia herd her into a director's style chair near a table and mirror, where a woman with a blue streak through her dark pixie cut had laid out an array of brushes and palettes.

The ASM tapped a pen on her clipboard. "Okay, Hadassah to makeup, now to find Griffith..." She strode away.

The makeup artist raised a hand. "Hey. I'm Charlize." She reached into what looked like a tacklebox, pulling out more makeup. She handed Hadassah a cloth headband. "Can you put that on for me? Want to get the baby hairs out of the way."

Hadassah accepted the headband and slipped it on, still recovering from Zinnia's whirlwind. Luckily, she hadn't seen Byron on the way in.

Charlize picked up a makeup sponge. "All right, let's start with foundation. You aren't wearing any makeup already, are you?"

"No. I don't have any." Not that Mom would have stopped her, but she had no one to learn from, considering most women in her home school circuit didn't use cosmetics.

"I apologize in advance, then." Charlize dabbed with the sponge, cold, gloppy cream hitting Hadassah's face. "Stage makeup is nothing like regular makeup. Really thick so the lights don't wash you out, and overdramatic so the audience can see it. It's going to look weird up close, but trust me."

"Okay." She began to relax. Maybe she could get to the run-through without encountering Byron at all. As Charlize worked, Hadassah's heart began to return to a normal rate.

"Hadassah."

Her spine stiffened at the male voice. Her eyes darted to the side, toward the door. Byron's rigid shoulders filled the entrance.

He strode toward her. "We need to talk."

She kept her back straight, fingers trembling. Charlize hadn't bothered to stop applying makeup, probably used to interruptions backstage, so Hadassah didn't move. If she could remain here, with someone else, even someone she hardly knew, it would be better than being alone with Byron. "I don't think right now is the best time."

"I don't want to interrupt anything with the play either, but you haven't been responding to my calls." He stopped five feet away. "This is too important to wait."

Her hands clenched on the armrests of the chair. She bolstered all of her courage. *Remember, he doesn't care about this theater. He sabotaged us all.* "I need to be on stage soon." Charlize turned to gather more supplies, giving Hadassah a chance to speak without worrying about holding still. "If there's something urgent, you can tell me here."

Hadassah closed her eyes while Charlize brushed powder on her eyelids. Maybe not just to avoid powder in her eyes, but also to hide.

"All right." His voice rumbled low. "What's going on? Did someone put you up to this?"

The brush ceased and Hadassah opened her eyes. "No, Byron. I stand by what I said. No one else even knows I sent those messages."

Charlize grabbed eyeliner, grumbling, "This isn't awkward at all."

Byron ignored her, eyes fixed on Hadassah. "Hadassah. Please." His brows furrowed in a semblance of tenderness. "I don't know what's happened, but we can always work through things."

Hadassah focused on moving her lips as little as possible as Charlize applied the eyeliner. "That's just it, Byron. I don't want to work through things. There's nothing to work through. I don't want to be together."

"He can't take a hint, can he?" Charlize muttered, too low for Byron to hear.

"Hadassah." He gave a short laugh. As if she were being foolish, childish. "Is this a fit of nerves? Your father has already given us his blessing. Don't worry, he was delighted."

Her vision tunneled. *Already given his blessing?*

"Just mascara and then you can get out of here." Hadassah couldn't tell if Charlize was talking to herself or to her.

Hadassah held very still, trying to form words while Charlize applied mascara. She didn't want to move and be poked in the eye.

He had talked to her father, and Dad said yes. Realization dawned. That must have been where he and Byron went off to on Sunday. They had made a deal about her, like a prize cow.

Blood roared in her ears. Was this her fate? Passed off from maintaining one home to another, her opinion or desires not taken into account by anyone? Her parents never asked if she wanted to do something else. Byron never asked if she wanted to date. He didn't even ask before kissing her, before he and her father decided her future.

When Charlize capped the mascara, Hadassah stood. "Thank you, Charlize." She turned to Byron, locked gazes with him, and spoke past the tightness in her throat. "How many camels was I worth? Or do we deal in apprenticeships and job offers now, like modern, forward-thinking people?"

His head tilted. "What are you talking about?" He reached forward, as if to take her hand. "I plan to propose after the Christmas season, when it's less hectic. I think you'll find it quite nice."

She snatched her hand out of his reach. "Don't touch me."

"Hadassah..."

"No." She stepped around him, making for the door. Her voice rose. "You aren't listening to me. I'm sorry, but I never wanted to date you. You never asked me. You just assumed."

Two feet from the door, two feet from freedom, he caught her arm. "If you would calm down—"

"Stop." She yanked her arm out of his grasp, glaring up at his condescending expression.

"Whoa, hey." Charlize snapped her makeup tacklebox shut. "Hands off the lady, dude."

Byron flashed a smile at her. "It's okay, we're just talking." Turning back to Hadassah, his countenance morphed from feigned compassion to anger. He spoke through clenched teeth. "Calm down. You're being irrational and making a scene. Everything is already decided."

"You're right, it is." Her volume rose. "Because *I've* decided. How dare you assume what I want? You think you know better than me?" She realized she was shouting, but she couldn't stop. "I will *never* marry you!"

She whirled around and stormed out of the room, almost colliding with a wide-eyed Griffith.

"Pardon me." She ducked her head and scurried around him, toward where she could hear Zinnia's sharp voice issuing orders.

Her heart pounded, but hope floated in her chest.

She'd done it. For the first time in her life, she had stood up for herself. Without the help of Yocheved or anyone else.

Now, she could only hope her family wouldn't disown her.

Miracle of miracles, they were about to finish their first run-through of the play and hadn't run into a single hitch.

Leroy shoved his hands into his pockets and beamed at Griffith and Hadassah. "Wow," he said, in-character. Soft, but with a boldness that Griffith had yearned to witness since the day of auditions. "We pulled off that play, mister and missus. What now?"

Griffith grinned at Hadassah, trying and failing to blink away the memories of the confrontation that happened an hour and a half ago in the hair and makeup room.

Hadassah's voice, from that fight between herself and Byron, echoed in his skull. *"I will never marry you."*

Zinnia had guessed right.

The two of them never courted—or at least, one of the parties didn't agree to be engaged to the other. Byron dismissed the crew only because he felt threatened by Griffith.

Why?

He could only be jealous if there's something to be jealous of.
Was there?

Griffith joggled the thought away and declared his final line. "I think I have a few ideas."

Here, he and Hadassah were supposed to stage kiss. He watched her stride across the stage toward him, then halted. She stared out at the audience. Although Griffith didn't follow her gaze, he could feel the glare from Byron out there.

Usually, during dress rehearsals, Byron, as stage manager, was supposed to be working back stage. Lilian kept having him roam the theater to make sure he could catch every word from the actors from every seat in the auditorium. "We need to make sure everyone who buys a ticket gets their money's worth," Lilian had said. "That includes actually being able to hear the lines."

Hadassah whitened. Her bottom lip trembled. "Sorry," she mouthed. Mist filled her eyes.

Griffith wanted to answer back, "It's okay," but a blackout from the lighting booth obscured Hadassah from being able to read his lips. Before rehearsal, Griffith instructed Zinnia to kill the lights if Hadassah couldn't go through with a kiss.

Moments later, the auditorium filled with wan beams once again.

Griffith planned to work with the cast at the final rehearsal on the curtain call, so seemingly uncertain what to do, the actors milled about the stage.

"Great job, everyone." Griffith planted his hands on his hips, like a man who'd just finished constructing a house and stood back to admire his work. "There are chicken sandwiches out in the lobby. Go ahead and take a half-hour break, and then we'll run through the play one more time."

Aromas of chicken, pickles, and a super-secret recipe sauce from the restaurant "Wingin' It" stirred Griffith's stomach. Did he remember to eat breakfast or lunch today?

Dizziness overtook his brain. Ah, that answered that question.

An auditorium seat squeaked as Lilian lifted herself from it. She raised a hand, as if silencing any speech Griffith had prepared. He didn't even realize his mouth had opened. He clamped his lips shut.

"That ran really well today. Leroy has made amazing progress."

Leroy stood in the back of the crowd clumping up the aisles to get to the auditorium. He whirled around, perhaps hearing his name, and grinned at Griffith. With a running start, he charged back to the stage and shook his head back and forth, pompom on his cap flailing.

"That was awesome today." The pompom bobbled in agreement.

"You got that right, Leroy." Griffith had to focus on anything but Leroy's hat, because the thrashing tassels threatened to spawn a headache in Griffith's skull. "You got every line down today. I can tell you've been working hard at memorizing."

Leroy nodded, his hat slipping down his forehead onto his eyes. He pushed the cap back. "I really think this is gonna be the best play put on by this theater ever." He craned his neck over his shoulder at the withering line of people. "Anyway, gotta get food. Thanks for believing in me, Director Griffith."

Warmth exploded inside of Griffith.

Lilian watched Leroy rejoin the queue, an amused expression

imprinted on her face. Then she turned back to the remaining actors on stage—Griffith and Hadassah.

"It *could* be a very good play, one of the best we've had in a long time, if"—she eyed Hadassah—"we could clean up that ending."

Hadassah stilled, shoulders jutting skyward.

Toward the back of the auditorium, a silhouette halted, mirroring her motions. Byron. Why hadn't he gone with the rest of the cast and crew to get his chicken dinner? Zinnia, up in the lighting booth, flicked on more lights in the auditorium. Byron's face flickered to life. His eyes glinted, fixated on a certain actress on stage.

Ah, that would explain why he hadn't moved.

"I." Hadassah clasped her hands and hunched her neck. "I'm sorry. I just don't feel comfortable with doing a real kiss."

"That's fine. We don't have to do it."

Hope flickered in Hadassah's pupils when she stared at him.

"Unfortunately"—Lilian tapped two nails against her clipboard—"you do. At least, a fake one. The show ends on a flat note without it. Is there any way you can work with her on making it look real, Griffith?"

He swallowed.

His gaze bounced back between Byron, Lilian, and Hadassah.

"Sure, but maybe I can have Zinnia help demonstrate. That way Hadassah can see how it's done, and then try it herself."

Hadassah's neck uncurled. She tugged a strand of hair behind her ear, and a faint grin flickered. "I think that's a great idea. That'll help soothe my nerves. If someone else goes first."

Griffith called Zinnia down from the lighting booth. He noticed a glow behind the glass. Ryan must've brought his laptop to the theater to work on editing photos during breaks.

Zinnia jumped on stage and tapped her lips. "All right, Griffith, I didn't gloss these bad boys for nothing. Give me a kiss I'll never forget."

Hadassah broke out into a laugh, doubled over. Zinnia winked at Griffith and flicked her glance at Hadassah. He nodded, understanding. Zinnia was doing everything she could to melt Hadassah's tension.

"Okay, Hadassah." Griffith motioned for Zinnia to stand counter to him. "There are two types of fake stage kisses. You and I will probably do the first one, since it requires no lips actually touching. We'll demonstrate both. For the first one—"

He placed his hand on the small of Zinnia's back. They both nodded at each other, indicating they were ready to do the motion. He dipped her and leaned over, their lips an inch apart.

"—I dip her. From the audience's perspective we look like we're kissing. See how we're not actually touching?"

Hadassah emerged in his periphery. She nodded.

"Great." He lifted Zinnia. "Now the second one does require physical touch. I'm going to put my thumb on the center of Zinnia's lip."

He did so. Yikes, she hadn't lied about dousing her lips with balm.

"I'm going to press my mouth against the back of my thumb." He demonstrated the motion. Then pulled his finger off of Zinnia's lips. He wiped his finger on his jeans to get off the sticky sensation from the lip gloss.

Zinnia winked at the lighting booth. "Don't worry, Ryan, there's plenty to go around."

Once the laughter died from Griffith and Hadassah's throats, Griffith turned to Hadassah.

"Are you feeling up to practicing the first one?"

Hadassah exhaled. After two seconds, she nodded.

"I'm going to position myself to be with my back to the audience. You stand right in front of me. Yes, like that." Electricity shot through his fingertips when he grazed the small of her back. "I'm going to dip you, but only when you're ready. So nod at me when you are."

Two seconds later, she bobbed her chin. He lowered her and leaned over her face. Wondered if she could feel his breath on her cheek.

"About two seconds later, I'll lift you." He helped her up. "Then Zinnia will hit the blackout in the lighting booth." He clapped his hand on her shoulder. "You did great."

She no longer trembled. "I think...I think I'm ready to practice it again." A flush shot up her neck. "You know, to get used to it."

They ran through the motion five more times. After the fifth, Hadassah laced her fingers together.

"Griffith?"

"Yes?"

"Maybe we could work on the second one? The one with the thumb on the lips?"

Something like the sound of papers slamming erupted from the back of the auditorium. Scarlet filled Byron's face. Whoops. Griffith had forgotten all about him.

"I'm not standing around and watching this." He jabbed a finger at the stage. "Good luck finding yourself a new stage manager. I quit."

He clenched his fists and stormed out of the auditorium.

A mixture of relief and dread swirled in Griffith's gut. The former because, well "ding dong the wicked" Byron had left. Dread because...who would fill in for Byron backstage? *Someone* had to hand actors props, tell the cast members when to enter stage, and call into the headset whenever something went haywire.

Zinnia, who stood off to the side near the curtain during Hadassah's practice kisses, folded her arms, shrugged, and then chewed on a loose hangnail.

"Easy, Griffith. I'll take over for Byron. I was doing more stage managing than he was, anyway."

Griffith's mouth went dry. He motioned at the lighting booth. "What about—"

She held up a hand. Then cupped both of hers to her mouth and directed her handmade megaphone to the booth. "Ryan, do you hear me?"

The door to the booth swung open. Ryan stumbled out, annoyance imprinted on his expression. "Yes."

"If I am not in the booth during the show, do you, Ryan, solemnly swear to click the light cues exactly as they are written in the script?"

"I do?" Ryan cocked his head. "That's a really weird way of phrasing the question. It's almost like wedding vow—"

"Do you, Ryan, solemnly swear to talk into the headset I have up in the booth if anything goes wrong?"

"I do."

"Do you, Ryan, swear to defend the lighting booth with all your heart, until death, or the final performance, do you part?"

"I do, and I'm very scared to find out what happens if I don't."

Zinnia grinned at Griffith. "Well, it's a match. I now pronounce Ryan 'ASM' to the lighting booth."

Chapter Twenty-One

"THIS IS SUCH A MESS." MOM worried a dishrag between her hands.

Hadassah took a deep breath, gripping the edge of the kitchen counter. "It's okay. The truth is out there and everyone can work on moving on. The Wrights and Youngs are such good friends, this shouldn't change anything."

She had fallen into bed late last night post-rehearsal after the rest of the family had already gone to sleep. Which meant it took all of a few hours this morning before everyone knew everything, thanks to Mrs. Young telling Mom exactly what happened—the Byron version, anyway.

Dad scratched his head, sitting at the breakfast table with his coffee. Work had given him half the week off for Christmas. "I thought you liked him. This is a bit of a surprise, Hadassah."

"I know. I'm sorry." Her attention flicked between him and Mom. "Now you know, and it's all fine."

Mom sighed. "From what I hear, Byron isn't fine. Maureen says he's hardly spoken to any of them." She picked up a recipe card to fan her face. "Hadassah, did you really have to tell him he made you feel like a camel?"

"I didn't say that exactly—"

Dad choked on his coffee. He pounded his chest, then cleared his throat and calmed himself under Mom's withering glare. "Sorry." He lifted his mug and muttered to himself, "A camel."

"Maureen is beside herself." The recipe card in Mom's hand fanned faster. "She said Dave is acting angry as well. She called to make sure *we* weren't mad at them. I apologized for your behavior and assured them none of it came from *us*." She gestured between herself and Dad.

Hadassah gripped the counter harder. "Of course. None of this is about you and your friends. This is between me and Byron only."

"Is there another man?" Mom offered what Hadassah thought was meant to be an understanding look.

"No." She took a deep breath, trying to calm the heat in her chest. Some floodgate in her had broken when she rejected Byron, and now the fires of indignation burned within, making it difficult to keep her emotions in check. "I have interests outside of men. I have dreams. Aspirations." *Calm. Speak calmly.* "I was never able to go to college. I don't regret staying here with the family, but I feel like God is calling me to something different. Something more than only marriage and kids."

Mom's hand flew to her chest. "You don't want marriage and kids?"

"I don't think that's what she's saying." Dad slurped his coffee.

Hadassah's eyebrows rose in surprise, and she shot him a grateful look. "Dad's right. I do want those things, someday. But I want other things too."

Mom slumped back against the counter. "Like what? Missions work? Children's ministry?"

"No." Hadassah fidgeted. "Theater."

Dad's brow furrowed. *Slurp.* "Byron wanted you to do theater with him."

"I want to do theater on my own. Without Byron making it happen for me. I feel like God has called me to this."

Another sigh from Mom. "I thought this would be your last show. You're gone so often. Are you sure it isn't a fun hobby for now?"

"Mom..."

"I think you should reconsider things, is all. Don't throw an excellent match away because of a hobby."

Her mouth opened and closed. The two had nothing to do with one another. She clenched her fists. "I don't like Byron and I do like theater. I'm going to go check on the boys." Then she stalked away before she said anything she would regret.

As she drove to rehearsal that evening, she replayed the conversation in her mind, muscles tense. *Will they ever understand?*

Her fingers clenched around the steering wheel. Meanwhile, without Byron there as the stage manager, how would the production go? Zinnia was a more than capable leader, but such a drastic change so late in the process...had Hadassah sabotaged the play as well? Had her rejection of Byron thrown a wrench in the project they had all worked so hard on?

I certainly hope not. If she had ruined her family's friendships *and* the play...

The moment she stepped inside the theater, Leroy ran up to her, red-faced and breathless. "I lost my script. Can I borrow yours? I didn't mean to lose it, I set the book down on the table and—"

"Whoa, whoa." She held up her hands. "It's okay. You have all your lines memorized, right? If you can't find it before today's rehearsal, you can look for it after."

"I don't know if I do. What if I forgot them all?" He rocked on his feet, brow furrowed. "What if I mess up the whole play?"

"Hey, it's okay. First of all." Hadassah reached into her bag and pulled out her copy of the script. "You can use mine for now." Leroy accepted the packet eagerly. "Secondly, you've worked hard. You've done everything you could to make this an excellent performance. Anything after that? It's in God's hands. Even if you did mess up and forget all your lines—which I don't think you will— you did the best you could, and that's what matters. That's what brings glory to God—giving Him your best, whatever that means for you."

He blinked. "Wow. I guess I never thought of it that way."

She paused for a moment as well. She had done the best she could to be faithful in following God's leading—in theater, in being honest with Byron. Was she taking her own advice? Did she really believe that everything was in His hands?

"How are my favorite thespians?"

Hadassah whirled around at the familiar voice. "Yocheved?"

Her sister waved, striding forward to give Leroy a high-five. "There's my favorite actor."

Hadassah raised a teasing eyebrow. "Excuse me."

"My favorite act*ress*." Yocheved gave her a hug.

She hugged her sister back. "What are you doing here?"

"Eh, I kinda got roped into the brigade on Monday. Couldn't make it yesterday, but figured I'd come today. I'm here helping out with the theater kids and lending a hand to the theater moms and their attempts to get all of you to actually eat meals."

Hadassah put a hand on her hip. "That's a long drive for you."

"I'm very invested in watching the progression of a burgeoning career." She gave a stage wink to Leroy.

He reddened and laughed.

"And." Her expression sobered as she put a hand on Hadassah's shoulder. "I wanted to check up on my sister. I got a very frazzled call from Mom."

Hadassah groaned. "Of course."

"I'm proud of you." Yocheved squeezed her shoulder. "I told Mom the same thing."

Her heart warmed. "Thank you. I—"

"We're running behind, people." Zinnia's voice cut through the conversation as she shouted across the theater at the milling cast and crew. "Let's go. If you aren't getting in costume, you need to be."

"Gotta go." Hadassah hugged her sister again. "Thank you."

We can do this. We'll make this rehearsal the best yet.

It was not the best yet.

The rehearsal started fifteen minutes late, then was delayed another several minutes when one of the children somehow managed to fall off the stage in one of the opening scenes. The boy remained unscathed other than a few bruises, but Griffith had to remind the actors to be aware of their surroundings, and *not* push their friends, even in character.

Leroy recalled all of his lines, but stepped on Hadassah's still-slightly-too-long skirt and tripped them both, tearing the fabric. Hadassah ran offstage between her scenes to grab a different outfit while the original was rapidly mended.

The light crew shone a spotlight at the front row instead of the stage, one of the large candy cane props broke in half, three kids forgot to leave the stage after their scene ended and instead stood watching the play awkwardly from behind, and the deck crew moved the wrong set piece on stage at least twice. Griffith missed his cue to enter the stage for one of the scenes because several actors flagged him with concerns before Zinnia could shoo them off and address the issues herself.

At least the stage kiss went smoothly. Griffith dipped her, a thumb to her lips, and her heart sent up a fluttery beat, starkly aware of his hand on the small of her back, holding her like she weighed nothing, his face so close to hers. A flutter so very different from the alarm bells that rang when Byron kissed her.

As the lights dimmed, closing their very last run-through of the play before the performance, the buoyancy in her chest morphed to an anxious thud.

Next time they took the stage, it would be in front of an audience.

As Griffith corralled the cast into lines to practice the curtain call for the final dress rehearsal, one thought boomeranged. Over and over again—

Why did our last rehearsal have to be a disaster?

Coming on the heels of yesterday's practice, Griffith's hope had ballooned in his chest. Finally, everything appeared to work in order. Derek had moved the sets during the right time. Ryan clicked the lighting cues at the appropriate moments. Lilian barged in, halfway through rehearsal, with another armful of programs.

Caroline made sure to have Andy go on any coffee runs during breaks instead of her. After all, they used the spotlight only a few times in the show.

Today...

Griffith sighed and motioned for some of the ensemble to step upstage.

"Okay, as I mentioned before in prior rehearsals, we are going to practice the curtain call. I've arranged you in rows." He gestured at the lines of actors. "Based on how many lines you have. Our ensemble goes first. Then the line behind them. Then our supporting roles. And then Hadassah, Leroy, and I will step forward. We'll each take individual bows. Any questions?"

A hand shot up in the back. Its owner, Leroy, shrunk into his turtleneck costume for the last act.

"Yes, Leroy?"

"I haven't done much theater. Is there a reason why there's a curtain call? Don't our friends tell us after the show that we did a good job in the lobby?"

Oh goodness, he could talk for hours about the importance of any element in the theater.

Griffith glanced over his shoulder at the clock in the auditorium. They'd already gone fifteen minutes over. Thankfully, Griffith's parents swung by twenty minutes prior to take care of Chekhov until Griffith returned to his apartment.

Although they'd said very little in their exchanges with him, sadness pierced his mother's eyes. She looked like she wanted to say something but shut her mouth and led the dog to her car.

Best keep the explanation short and sweet. Then maybe I can have a chance to connect with my parents tonight before tomorrow's performance.

"Sure, Leroy. Even though we will have a meet and greet out

there"—he motioned to the doors at the back of the theater—"traditionally, actors don't often get to hear the response of the audience. It can be hard putting in all those hours of work without having a clue if the people who watched the performance enjoyed it. That can be really hard for an artist if they don't know if people liked their work or not."

He signaled the curtains.

"A curtain call is a moment for the audience to share their appreciation and for the actors to feel that their hard work paid off."

Griffith noticed a figure leaning against the side of the stage. Caroline. Dark circles ran under her eyes. She'd been a trooper tonight with all the mishaps and such. All of the stage crew had.

"Caroline."

She jolted when he called her name.

"I know you don't do acting, but you are in an artistic field. Is there a curtain call of sorts in the book world?"

"Oh." She fiddled with a dangly earring in her lobe. "Hmm. I suppose book reviews are like that. Andy and I had no idea how the public would react to the picture book we collaborated on. Some of the words people wrote about it." She clasped both hands to her chest. "It made all the hours absolutely worth it."

"Exactly. Thank you, Caroline. For us, it's a little like a book review, but for the theater. Let's practice our bows. Starting with the first row."

They ran through the curtain call a handful of times. Although it didn't take too much direction from Griffith to get it right, he had to correct minor errors.

"Kathy, make sure to keep your head down when you bow. The audience will get weirded out if you look at them the whole time."

"Ty, make sure to bow with everyone at the same time."

When they finished the final run-through, a buzz filled Griffith's veins. They'd arrived. All the last pieces had been put together.

Now...tomorrow determined their future.

Had they sold enough tickets to justify Griffith earning a full-time position at the theater? Would there even be enough of an audience to clap the actors on their way out? What if they had a repeat of tonight?

Griffith glanced skyward and threw up a quick prayer. *I thought this was what I was supposed to do.*

His nails dug into his palms. He forced a grin at the actors.

"Great work, everyone. Get a good night's rest, and I can't wait to see you for tomorrow's performance. Zinnia will email you your hair and makeup times."

Zinnia, perched in a chair in the audience, flashed a thumbs up. "Already done."

Warmth flowed through him. Even if tomorrow went up in flames, at least he had wonderful friends who went down with him, working as hard as they could to pull off this show.

Once the cast cleared out, Griffith and Hadassah hung back to put the props in their proper places. When Griffith ambled onto the stage to snag a large candy cane one of the actors had left behind, light pierced the back of the auditorium.

Two figures shuffled in, still shivering. Flurries of snow swirled off their coats onto the carpet.

"Griffith." Elijah's strong voice seemed to echo even more in the darkness. Moments later, Ryan, up in the booth, flooded the theater with light beams. "Sorry Liv and I are late." He motioned to the tall girl beside him. "Practice for the Christmas Eve service at church went long. Anyway." He bit into his gloves to pull them off his fingertips. "Can you walk us through how to be ushers tomorrow?"

Oh man, Griffith had forgotten about ushers with all the disasters that struck the stage today.

"Sure." He noticed Hadassah in his periphery and passed the candy cane to her like a baton. "You mind putting this away for me? Thanks, Hadassah, for staying back."

After she uttered a "no problem" and ambled away, Griffith met the two ushers at the base of the stage.

"If you two will follow me, I'll show you where you'll be handing out programs before the show."

He led them back up the center aisle and into the lobby.

"These are the only doors that will lead into the auditorium, so we'll have you both positioned here. There's no uniform, but just dress nice. Like what you two are wearing today."

Liv had bedecked herself in a sweater dress and leggings, and Elijah, his typical dark skinny jeans and button-up shirt.

"Also, I may have you both stick around for intermission. Our house manager runs concessions and may need an extra hand back there. Get here about an hour before the show, in case we have some audience members arrive early. Any questions?"

Elijah held up two fingers.

"Two questions, why are you talking a million miles an hour, and why do you look like you haven't slept in a week?"

Classic worship leader, always able to diagnose when someone felt off, spiritually and mentally. Griffith wiped a palm down his face, as though attempting to wipe away his exhaustion.

"I—we had a rough rehearsal."

How much time passed? Griffith couldn't say. Several moments later, he found himself, and the two others, on the lobby couches, recounting everything from his parents' disapproval of his calling to how tonight's rehearsal fell apart. Hadassah must have joined them at one point, because he noticed her sitting beside him, a cushion's length apart.

Heat prickled his face.

This was embarrassing. Him spilling his guts to her, to Liv and Elijah—the latter two who had started a budding indie music career for themselves. In fact, this past summer they won a music competition together, which included a twenty-grand prize and a record deal.

He expected pity to mar their faces. Instead, the two of them nodded, seemingly with understanding.

When Griffith finished, his throat felt parched. He reached for his water bottle and sucked in a gulp. Once again, Elijah tossed up two fingers.

"One—Griffith, when you're doing the Lord's work, this is to be expected. The enemy wants to suck dry any hope you have, so you don't perform your best tomorrow. Last rehearsals always end in disaster. Trust me." He winked at Liv. "We should know. I don't even think she was able to be at our last one, and we didn't know if we'd have the whole band for the performance."

Griffith almost choked on the liquid. He swallowed.

Wait, the Lord's work?

"But—but my play doesn't have a distinctive Christian message. It's nowhere close to the missions work my parents do."

"Griffith." Elijah practically chuckled on the word. "The theater is your mission field, and although you may not have a nativity scene up there, Andy has told me plenty about the play for me to know that you are still glorifying God with it."

He ticked off several examples.

Griffith had thanked the Lord in his bio that appeared in the programs.

One of the characters in the play was a Christian and consulted the Lord for help often.

The play promoted good values such as patience, love, forgiveness, and sacrifice.

"Two"—Elijah flashed his fingers again—"when you act, you feel God's pleasure. You don't need the approval of the audience or your parents to tell you where your calling lies. Just continue to follow that call, and God will continue to open the right doors."

Griffith's chest swelled.

Maybe they both needed to hear this right here, right now.

"Thanks, Lij."

"Don't thank me." Elijah glanced upward. "Now, let's give them a show they'll never forget tomorrow."

Chapter Twenty-Two

"Come on, Chekhov." Hadassah shivered as a bitter winter wind blew into her face. "It's time to go potty."

The little dog circled the patch of slush, sniffing. Hadassah suspected she might be standing in the frigid air for a while. Something she hadn't considered when she offered to take Chekhov for a pre-show walk.

Her fingers trembled, not only from the cold. Soon, they would take the stage in front of a crowd. Would they mess up? Would it be enough for Griffith to get the job?

Lord, I trust you. Please be with us all.

Her pocket buzzed. She pulled out her phone and saw a text from Mom.

Mom: Break a leg. (I read that's what you're supposed to say in theater instead of good luck.)

Hadassah chuckled to herself.

Hadassah: Thanks, Mom! Nice theater lingo :)

Just yesterday, she wouldn't have expected the show of support. After this morning...

Hadassah had been cleaning up the breakfast mess with Elizabeth when Mom said, "Liz, why don't you go check on the girls? Hadassah and I can take care of this."

"Sure." Liz shot Hadassah a sympathetic look. Usually, Mom sending siblings out of the room meant the remaining child was about to get a talking to.

Mom stacked the last breakfast dish in the sink and sighed. "I talked with Yocheved, and I realized I might have been a little...harsh about Byron."

Hadassah's eyebrows rose. This wasn't the direction she'd been expecting the conversation to take.

Mom grabbed a sponge. "I knew your dad was the one. Yocheved knew it was Aaron. Maureen knew it was Dave. If you don't know in your heart that Byron is the one, then you shouldn't be pressured to pursue the relationship." She bit her lip. "Maureen and I talked too. About that same thing. We agreed we would never want to push our kids into an unhappy relationship. Just because we're friends, that doesn't mean our kids are compatible—or even need to be friends with each other."

What? Mom and Mrs. Young both had no hard feelings toward her? Both agreed with Hadassah's decision?

Were pigs flying too?

"I'm sorry, Hadassah." Mom turned to face her. "I'm going to try to be more supportive of you finding the man *you* want to marry."

Hadassah broke out of her stunned stupor and wrapped her arms around her mother. "Thanks, Mom. It means a lot."

Maybe it was related to his mother's chat with Mom, or maybe it wasn't, but a couple of hours later, Hadassah received a text from Byron.

Byron: I think you're making a mistake. But I'm also not going to waste my time on someone who isn't interested in a serious relationship.

She had rolled her eyes.

Hadassah: That sounds wise. I wish you the best.

Chekhov broke her out of her reverie with several quick yaps.

He ran to the end of his leash, bouncing in excitement.

"Quiet, boy. That's impolite." She turned to see what had gotten him all riled up.

Griffith strode toward them. He offered a wide smile at Chekhov and crouched down. "Hey, buddy. Are you being good for Hadassah?"

The dog bounded into his arms, licking his face and wriggling for pets. Griffith scratched Chekhov's ears. "Hey, now, don't mess up the nice job Ryan did brushing your coat."

Hadassah laughed. "Even Chekhov has gotten his hair done for the show."

"Ryan insisted, and it was a good idea." Griffith stood. "Thanks for taking him out. I thought I'd check in, since the two of you had been a while."

"Our furry friend has yet to do his business." Hadassah raised an eyebrow as the white furball sniffed a tree trunk.

"The little turkey." Griffith laughed. "Good thing we're here so early. I think most of the cast hasn't arrived yet. Zinnia has everything moving like clockwork."

"Praise the Lord for Zinnia." Hadassah hesitated, then wrinkled her nose. "She does a much better job than Byron anyhow. I heard about what he did. I'm sorry about that, and I think I'm partially to blame."

Griffith sighed and tugged on his scarf. "Don't blame yourself at all. Byron was already...unpleasant to work with, long before the three of us were all involved in this play." He shrugged. "I think he's insecure, feels like he has something to prove. I hope someday he finds that security—not in accomplishments, but in his relationship with Christ."

"Wow." Hadassah's head tilted. "That's a mature way to think about it. To be honest, I..." Her gaze fell to the ground, and she hugged her arms across her chest. "I didn't really consider what he's going through. I was too busy thinking about how I felt."

"Don't feel bad."

She glanced up to see him with a serious expression.

His mouth set in a grim line. "No matter what someone is going through, it doesn't give them the right to hurt other people. It doesn't mean you should allow yourself to be hurt."

Her eyes widened. She had never told Griffith what happened between her and Byron. One moment she and Griffith had been spending time together, enjoying one another's company, and the next they slipped into strained territory, separated by Byron's jealousy. What made him think Byron had done anything to hurt her?

Griffith shifted, rubbed the back of his neck. "Er, not meaning to make any assumptions. Just, you know, in case you needed to hear that from someone. Not saying...I mean..." He trailed off with a sheepish grin as she hid a giggle behind her hand at his stumbling. "You know what I mean."

"I know." She bit her lip. "And...you're right. It hasn't only affected me. It's affected you and this play too. Even in something as simple as me being nervous about a stage kiss." Her eyes widened, and she felt her cheeks burn bright red. She hadn't meant to say anything about that.

His jaw tightened, but she could tell by the faraway look in his eyes that his anger wasn't directed at her. "You're way more important than the play, Hadassah. Whatever you're comfortable with, from a full kiss to no kiss at all, I'm willing. I'll deal with Lilian if she gets upset."

Chekhov tugged toward a car passing by, but Hadassah held tight to his leash and blinked back moisture in her eyes. "I appreciate you, Griffith." Impulsively, she wrapped her arms around him in a hug.

Gently, almost hesitantly, he hugged her back. Then, as if he'd waited to make sure that was okay, he gave her another squeeze. "I appreciate you too, and all of your encouragement throughout this process."

She felt a tug on the leash and stepped away. "Oh look, he's finally doing his business." She smiled at Griffith. "You ready to go put on a show and knock some socks off?"

He grinned. "Let's do this."

Shockingly, miraculously, the show started without a hitch. Chekhov obeyed commands. No one forgot their lines. No children fell off the stage or broke props. The lights hit their cues, and Derek pushed the right set pieces on stage.

The audience laughed, clapped, even gave collective "aww"s. Hadassah couldn't make out the crowd beyond the stage lights, but from the sound, the theater seemed packed.

Best of all, Leroy shone. His performance captivated the audience, eliciting the most audible reactions. At times, Hadassah almost forgot they were delivering a script. She really *was* Emily, trying to help the troubled boy, and he was Oliver, the foster child she finally managed to break through to with the magic of theater.

After both an eternity and only a second, she found herself facing Griffith, the final line of the play leaving her mouth. As she met his smiling gaze, she could tell the sparkle of joy in his eyes was more than just an act.

They'd done it. No matter what came next, after all of the late nights, the stress, the long hours, they had pulled off a production to be proud of.

His eyes seemed to say, *I couldn't have done it without you.*

She hoped hers replied, *I'd do it all again in a heartbeat.*

A lightbulb seemed to pop to life in her mind with realization. Her heart flapped like a spastic chicken. She would. She would be happy to do just about anything with Griffith. Wandering downtown, painting sets, climbing through dusty prop attics, facing each other on stage like this...as long as they could do it together.

Finally, she understood what Mom, what Mrs. Young, what Yocheved had talked about. The things she had never felt for Byron, no matter how hard she tried.

Griffith Williams, I think you're my person.

When they leaned in for the kiss, she placed her lips on his. She felt him start in surprise, then melt, returning the kiss. Holding her closer.

The applause of the audience soared with her heart.

The time for the Curtain Call arrived.

In the wings, Griffith watched as rows of the cast entered the stage and took their final bow.

Leroy, Griffith, and Hadassah waited their turn.

Beaming smiles from the cast members set Griffith's heart aflutter. All this hard work was worth it.

His calling was worth it.

Griffith gripped Hadassah's and Leroy's hands.

"Show time." He should've whispered this instead of speaking it as loudly as he did. But it didn't matter. The audience's thunderous applause drowned out most sounds.

He tugged them toward the stage, and each took their individual bows. After Griffith did his, he made sure to watch Hadassah and Leroy's faces.

When Leroy bowed, well, Griffith had never seen anyone's face light up like a firework...until now. Tears sparkled in Hadassah's eyes as the audience whistled. She gripped her skirt, curtseyed, and dipped her head in a bow.

The audience leapt to their feet. Griffith had no idea how long the clapping lasted...but it didn't die down for several moments.

Griffith's knees wobbled as the curtain drew to a close.

Hadassah had stage kissed him. *Actually* stage kissed him.

Before he could regain his sense of balance, he watched the cast fade to a blur as they jogged backstage and toward the lobby. Hadassah had disappeared amongst them.

Sneaky, sneaky...getting away before he could ask questions.

He shook his arms until feeling returned to them. Chekhov, attached to a leash, glanced up at Griffith as if to ask, "Yo, why are you jostling my harness so much? Calm down, dude."

Easy there, big guy. It's a stage kiss. It probably didn't mean anything.

Then again, why wouldn't his heart stop beating as if a hummingbird had been stuck inside it?

The curtains pulled open again moments later, and most of the auditorium had cleared out. Chekhov's tail wagged as three figures approached the stage—Griffith's family.

His mother carried a bone in her hands, wrapped in a red ribbon. She kneeled to give it to the dog. Chekhov bounded forward and attacked her cheek with kisses. She patted his backside and placed the bone on the stage.

"Who's a good boy? Who stole the show tonight? That's right, you did!"

Had the audience really leapt to their feet when Chekhov took his "bow"? Which consisted of Griffith presenting him with a flourish, and Chekhov taking more interest in Hadassah's shoes as she curtseyed for the patrons.

No, they'd given the standing-O to Hadassah.

In truth, *she* had stolen the show. When she planted that kiss on his lips...the audience whistled and cheered. At moments in the show, even through the darkness, Griffith noticed many in the front row had leaned in any time Hadassah or Leroy gave a monologue, clinging to every word.

They'd pulled it off. Actually pulled it off.

He threw up a quick prayer of thanks.

Griffith's mother cleared her throat as Chekhov started gnawing on his new treat.

She nudged Griffith's dad, who bestowed a potted poinsettia to Griffith.

"You." His mother swallowed. "You looked right at home up

here, sweetheart." She fiddled with a stringed bracelet on her arm. Maybe she'd woven that with the kids in the village on a crafting day. "I don't know if you got my note last night. Left it on the fridge."

Blurs of memories washed over him.

Sure enough, an image of a Post-it with the message danced across his vision.

Hi, Griffith,

We weren't sure how long you'd be gone, so we took Chekhov on a walk and are heading home now. We also went to Ryan's apartment to take care of his animals, since we figured he may be at dress rehearsal late too. He always leaves a key underneath his mat.

Anyway, there's been something on my mind. I wanted to tell you at rehearsal tonight, but figured you were stressed enough as it is.

Can't wait to see your performance tomorrow.

Love,
Mom

Much as he hoped to give the note further musing, sleep overtook him on his bed minutes after.

"Oh." He set the plant beside him on the stage. "Yes, I remember the note."

The last word hung in the air, like a question.

His mother sighed and squeezed Hudson's shoulders.

"There was something I left out of the story about Hudson completing his construction project in the villages—and missing out on his birthday celebration."

Hudson grimaced, as though he'd popped some of the sour candies they sold at the concessions stand during intermission.

"He'd gotten an earful that night. About how we'd spent so

much time planning to celebrate him, and how he dedicated so many hours to the project that he'd begun to neglect family and his friends at the compound."

Mist filled her eyes. She laughed and sniffed, lifting a finger to her waterline to wipe away any moisture.

"He was doing the Lord's work, but he'd gotten so wrapped up in it that...well, it hurt my feelings. I felt so guilty for berating him...and when I confronted you the other day about missing out on family Christmas traditions—"

"About that." Griffith palmed his neck. "Mom, Dad, Hudson, I'm so sorry. I feel awful. You only come to the States so often, and I took so much time to—"

His mother held up a hand.

Griffith stopped.

She took several moments to speak. "I think we were both in the wrong, for different reasons. That wasn't my point." Her eyes glistened. "I wanted to tell you yesterday that I believe you're doing the Lord's work too. We caught glimpses of the rehearsal, and we saw the play during the performance, and I can see His glory shining through your script."

She laced her fingers. He noticed some chipped polish. His mother did have a habit of biting her nails when she got nervous.

"We want to support your mission field here. Your calling. Because the Lord has given you a gift, and heaven help me, I better not get in the way of Him using it." She motioned at the stage, and a watery laugh overtook her throat. "Goodness, you made us cry so much during the show. Even your father."

After recounting some of their favorite moments in the show, the family finalized Christmas plans. Griffith said he'd meet them at home after the cast tore down the set in something known as "strike" and they grabbed a cake to eat during the cast party held in the lobby later that night.

A tap on his shoulder caused him to jolt.

Lilian already carried an armful of props, commencing strike early as the cast spoke to their families in the lobby. "Well done, tonight."

Although her face read stony—since Lilian was never one to hint much at emotions or expressions—the slightest of smiles played on her lips. From what Griffith could tell in the shroud of darkness during the show, most of the seats had filled up. Perhaps the numerous family members of the large cast who showed up in support accounted for the ticket sales. Maybe the audience turnout and their reception of the show guaranteed him a spot in the theater on their full-time staff.

Then again, after all the obstacles Lilian threw at him, maybe he'd read into the night all wrong. Perhaps the performance hadn't gone as well as he felt.

Lilian vanished backstage, replaced by Hadassah moments later. She grappled two electric drills. "I've been put on drilling duty for strike." She clicked the trigger, and the drill bit whirled. "Care to join me?"

Griffith grinned and took the extra tool she'd brought for him.

Now, the cast and crew filed into the auditorium as Zinnia doled out strike assignments for them. Griffith knelt beside Hadassah near one of the wood boards for a set piece and unwound a screw from its place.

"Hadassah." He cleared his throat as her machinery cut off. "Why did you go for an actual stage kiss tonight?" Crimson bled on her face, and he quickly added, "I mean, obviously a stage kiss doesn't count as the real thing, and it's whatever..." *Play it off as cool, man. She probably didn't mean anything by doing the real thing.*

Amusement played on her face, twitching her lips.

She untwisted a screw from its place and dropped it into a bucket between herself and Griffith.

"I know we hadn't done the real one in rehearsals, but as you've mentioned in practice, any movement on stage is all about trust. I think I finally trusted you enough to know you'd handle it well."

Hadassah wedged her drill bit into another screw. She pulled the trigger, but the shrieking noise died down a second later.

"Thank you, Griffith, for being patient with me. I can only imagine your frustration when I had a hard time adjusting to Lilian's changes." She blinked several times, a haze disappearing from her eyes.

"Hey." Griffith set his drill down and fought the temptation to rest his hand on her shoulder. "You take whatever time you need. I'm not going anywhere."

At first, he'd meant the sentiment about the theater.

As the words echoed in his skull...he realized they could've taken on a different meaning.

Was that what I meant? That I'd be as patient as possible until she felt comfortable being something more than friends?

Fires stoked in his stomach. Sure enough, a resolve filled his bones. He would pursue this girl—if she was even open to the thought of the two of them together. Like a stage direction, only when Hadassah felt ready to dive in.

Hadassah brightened. "I have a feeling, Griffith, that you won't have to wait long."

Butterflies stoked in his chest for the remainder of their drill time. Once they disassembled the boards, they returned the plywood to the wood shop and helped Zinnia tag and organize the remaining costumes.

Because of the ample size of the cast, strike finished within an hour—an unprecedented personal best for the theater.

The cast and crew met in the lobby, and Zinnia handed Griffith a large butcher's knife. He praised the Lord that he didn't see Ryan at the other end of the blade.

Heaven knows what would happen if those two worked on another project together.

Bloodshed would ensue, to be sure.

"You do the honors, sir." Zinnia saluted him and flourished an arm to present a cake. Whoever baked the treat had piped the words "Follow Your Call" in blue, cursive icing.

He wedged the blade into the corner of the cake. The room erupted into cheers.

Chapter Twenty-Three

STRAINS OF "WHITE CHRISTMAS" DRIFTED OVER the sounds of laughter and chatter. Mom said something, and Yocheved burst into guffaws. Meanwhile, Isaiah, Enoch, and Obadiah poked around the presents under the tree, whispering and giggling to each other.

Hadassah sat near the radio, munching on a Christmas cookie dusted in powdered sugar, warmth filling her chest. Dad and Aaron bonded over football with animated arm gestures, the girls sang along to Christmas songs near the fireplace... And Matthew and Luke joined the younger boys poking around the tree, mischievous smiles alight on all of their faces, not realizing Mom knew exactly what they were doing. Christmas reminded her how much she loved her crazy, giant family, flaws and all.

"You did an awesome job with these cookies, Liz." Hadassah raised her half-eaten treat to her sister.

Elizabeth grabbed a peanut butter cookie and plopped down on the couch next to Hadassah, taking a big bite. "You did a great job with these." Her eyes sparkled. "I'm excited for you to open your present."

"I thought Mom drew my name this year. Why do you know what it is?" Hadassah gave her a teasing look. "Were you snooping around?"

"I didn't have to. Mom told me." She bobbed her head toward the kitchen. "And Yocheved."

"Wow. Rude. I don't know anyone's gifts." Hadassah chuckled. "Well. Except for Obie's. And Priscilla's. And Luke's. And...well, I helped D-Six through Ten decide on presents."

They both laughed.

"The younger droids haven't installed secret-keeping protocol yet." Elizabeth giggled. "Obie told me what mine is."

Hadassah slapped a palm to her forehead. "Snitch." The grin didn't leave her face.

A buzz rumbled in her pocket. Curious, she pulled out her phone.

Griffith: Merry Christmas!

The message was accompanied by an animated Christmas tree doing a dance. Hadassah snorted.

Hadassah: Merry Christmas to you too!

She sent an animated reindeer doing the disco.

"Is that Griffith?" Elizabeth popped the last bite of cookie into her mouth.

Hadassah's cheeks warmed. "How did you know?"

"Oh you know, the cheesy grin and lovestruck gaze."

Hadassah bopped Elizabeth with a throw pillow while her sister cackled.

"Are you guys, you know, a thing?" Elizabeth waggled her shoulders.

Her cheeks flamed. "Well. Not...officially. I think?"

She and Griffith had talked during the cast party, after all. And agreed they wanted to see each other outside of theater functions. While Griffith awkwardly stuttered about how they didn't have to be dates if she didn't want them to be, but they also could be, but they didn't have to be.

"I just..." he'd said, shifting on his feet, "I enjoy spending time with you. However that may be."

Controlling her humor at his adorable bumbling, she nodded, clasping her hands behind her back. "I feel the same way." A slight smile broke through. "And I think I'm happy to call them dates."

His ears had reddened, a goofy grin blossoming.

Before he could say anything else, Ryan raised a cup filled with sparkling grape juice and called out, "To our fearless leads! Griffith, Hadassah, and Leroy!"

The cast cheered.

"That's adorable." Elizabeth broke Hadassah out of her reverie. "And so much better than Byron."

Hadassah laughed. "You got that right."

Twenty minutes later, the family had gathered in a large circle in the family room, perching on chairs, couches, the coffee table, with a few sitting on the floor. The kids passed around the Bible, each reading a verse of the Christmas story at a time.

Yocheved recited the final verse, then set the Bible on an end table. "Aaron and I have some news."

Hadassah raised an eyebrow and leaned forward.

Yocheved glanced at her husband with a smile. "Do you all remember the boy in Hadassah's play, Leroy? The one who is in a group home?" Her smile broke into a grin. "Aaron and I are in the process of becoming his foster parents. It's going to be a long journey, but we hope we'll eventually be able to adopt him."

Hadassah exclaimed and clapped her hands. Mom, Dad, and Elizabeth all burst into excited chatter.

Mom wiped a tear from her eye. "Now that's a Christmas present for all three of you—and us too. I can't wait to welcome Leroy to the family."

As soon as Mom gave the go-ahead, the kids dashed for the tree, rustling branches to find the Christmas pickle. Enoch found the ornament first, starting off the gift-opening. After him, they began opening presents from youngest to oldest. Tabitha shrieked in delight over the doll Hadassah had gotten her, which came with multiple outfits. Priscilla was almost as excited as Tabitha.

When it came to Hadassah's turn, Elizabeth placed a wrapped box the size of a toaster in her hands. "Merry Christmas."

The package felt light, almost...empty?

Hadassah tore away the wrapping paper and opened the cardboard box to reveal a single slip of paper.

She picked it up and unfolded the sheet to read the contents.

You deserve to follow your dreams too. Love, Mom

Beneath the message was a picture of an advertisement for a tutoring service.

Hadassah looked up at Mom in confusion. "I don't understand."

"You've done so much for all of us." Mom reached for Dad's hand and clasped it. "Your father and I agreed, and Yocheved and Elizabeth helped us figure out the details. You should have enough time to pursue your dreams and interests. We're hiring a tutor to help with home schooling, so I can depend less on you and Elizabeth." She dabbed at her eyes. "You both deserve to spread your wings and fly anywhere you want—college, theater, marriage, even to the ends of the earth, though we'd certainly miss you. I want you to be able to be honest with us about what you want to do, so we can support you as much as we can."

"We learned some things from the Byron incident," Dad added. He glanced at Yocheved. "And your sister helped us realize we hadn't really been listening to you."

Moisture filled Hadassah's eyes. She didn't know what to say, so instead she jumped up and wrapped her arms around her mother, then Dad, then Yocheved. She spoke past a lump in her throat. "Thank you."

"When we saw you on stage, we all knew." Yocheved grinned. "You come to life in the theater. In a way none of us have ever seen."

"You're *really* good," Elizabeth added.

Hadassah laughed through her tears. "I hope you'll get to see me in plenty more plays. Thanks to all of your support."

"Enough mushiness." Yocheved lifted a present to her ear and shook it. "Let's open these gifts."

To the sounds of music, rustling paper, and exclamations of delight, Hadassah's heart danced all the way through opening gifts to piling into the van, heading for the Roseville Christmas Carols event, her favorite tradition of their town.

Thank you, Lord. For everything.

She was ready to sing her heart out.

"Cinnamon roll-flavored popcorn? Why, Mom, I would have never guessed."

Everyone in Ryan's apartment dissolved into a fit of giggles. Griffith had suggested his family hold Christmas there since Ryan didn't have relatives with him for the day. This involved Griffith and his family finding any items they could on Christmas Eve to gift-wrap for Ryan, so he wouldn't feel left out as others tore into presents.

Griffith's mother shrugged and balled up the striped wrapping paper Griffith had removed from his newest present. "They let me try a sample of that in the popcorn shop. I must say, the flavor is growing on me."

Griffith opened the plastic seal that held in the cinnamon-sugar goodness. White vanilla frosting drizzled the popcorn. He passed the bag around the circle for others to try as Ryan reached for another gift under the tree.

Lights danced on the brim of the branches. Sparse bird ornaments and red balls hung from the plastic bristles.

Ryan had expressed allergies to real Christmas trees once in a conversation with Griffith.

Speaking of Ryan, he frowned at the label attached to the gift. "Another one for me? When did you all have time to do this?" He squinted at Griffith, adjusting his turtleneck on his reindeer sweater. "I haven't seen you leave the theater once."

Griffith shrugged. "Christmas miracles happen. Now open it. It's from me."

A crock pot full of hot chocolate—a recipe Ryan's mom sent to him the night before—steamed on the kitchen counter. Next to the fridge, Ryan's cat, Buttercup, batted at a catnip mouse Griffith's mom located in a pet store yesterday.

And Ryan's husky, Balto, gnawed on a rawhide. Griffith imagined in his apartment that Chekhov had nestled up to his bone his parents gifted him that morning.

Carefully, Ryan unfolded the corners of the wrapping paper. Back in college, he spent a semester in Japan. According to him, the slower you unwrapped a gift there, the more you held the gifter in high regard.

Minutes passed, and finally, he unsheathed a vintage camera. Little did he know Griffith found it in a thrift store.

"I actually bought this in October. I tend to do all my shopping then, since the winter play takes up so much time."

Ryan's fingers grazed the shutter-speed dial on top of the camera. He grinned and nodded at his bookshelf, which housed several others from other eras. "Can't wait to add it to the collection. Thanks, Griffith."

"Of course. Trash, please." Griffith grinned and held up a garbage bag. Ryan balled up the wrapping paper and swished the makeshift "ball" into the "hoop."

"Speaking of the play." Ryan glued his gaze to the camera, tinkering with every other knob. "I can't believe it's over. It feels sad, you know? After all, it seems like you'd gotten started on auditions just yesterday. And I was simply working at the tech booth, and I got attached. I can only imagine how the ending of your show has affected you."

Certainly, a cloud of nostalgia had already accumulated in Griffith's chest. He felt the swell of a sadness during the cast party. Everyone did.

His college director often labeled this the "post-show blues."

What had that man said during one of their last classes together? "After you've put so much work into something—you've poured your heart, your tears, your time, your everything into it—it's natural to feel sorrowful once the show has ended."

"I won't argue with you, Ryan." Griffith fingered the spine of a collection of plays his parents had gotten him for Christmas. "When a story ends, you can't help but feel a sense of longing for it to go on forever."

Images of Hadassah winked in his mind. His lips twitched.

"That's the beauty of stories. When one ends, another one always begins." He met Ryan's eyes. "And since you've been a big part of mine, I can't wait to play a role in yours."

Once they finished uncovering the presents, Griffith's father read from a passage in Luke 2. He made Griffith and Ryan act out the parts of the shepherds and Joseph. Ryan couldn't break a monotone for all of his lines.

"Acting isn't my forte." Ryan shrugged. "I'm meant to be behind the camera, not in front of it."

"Well, I do know a certain stage manager who has been trying to break into film. Should I send her to the next audition you hold for an indie movie?"

Griffith grinned as Ryan shrunk into his turtleneck.

After the reading of the passage, Griffith twined a scarf around his neck and said he'd meet his family in the parking lot—for the famous Roseville Christmas tree lighting— after taking Chekhov for a quick jaunt outside. He armed himself in his coat and swung his keyring around his finger.

When he reached his apartment, Chekhov greeted him at the door, all cozy in his doggie Christmas sweater. Snowflakes patterned the fabric.

"Who is the most dapper of boys? You are! Now where did I put your harness?"

By his laptop, nestled on his bed.

He rushed over to his comforter and a strange feeling niggled his stomach. Everything poking his insides said, "Open your computer."

He did and prayed that no more work emails had polluted his inbox during the holiday. To his surprise, one from Lilian blinked on the screen. But the subject line caused his stomach to drop.

"A Christmas Gift from Me to You"

He tapped on the email and read.

Griffith,

You'd said something over a week ago that refuses to give up permanent residency in my mind. "I've done everything you asked...I can only do so much with what I've been given."

To be frank with you, when you said this, my blood boiled. My first thought was, "Typical younger generation. Wanting to take the lazy way out and make excuses for why they can't finish the job."

But then it struck me. I had doled out quite the task. The disastrous showing of Willy Wonka Jr. several years back proved to me that asking for someone to have a large cast of kids can already derail a show.

Let alone me requesting dogs, last-minute kisses, very little rehearsal time, etc. Honestly, I think the only trick-shot I didn't pull on you was making you add musical numbers. Trust me, I fought the temptation.

And yet, you persevered. More than I can say for Byron who left at the last-minute. Remind me never to let him help with another show again.

You sold a healthy amount of tickets, and I had so many people tell me after the show about how they laughed, they cried, they didn't want it to end.

Griffith, you have proven yourself more than capable of executing a play under the direst of circumstances. I can think of no greater successor for my role at the theater.

I plan to send more details and paperwork once we emerge from the holiday season.

Consider this a well-earned Christmas gift. You have exceeded all expectations and have a bright future in the theater.

Lilian

Snowflakes outside muffled all sound except for the quick tempo of Griffith's heart. He collapsed on his bed and allowed joy to burst within him. He felt like a marathoner who completed a race in record time.

Griffith pumped a fist in the air. Christmas miracle, indeed.

His knees and hands wobbled as he took Chekhov for a walk, overflowing with so much happiness that it might have exploded like confetti from him. But he managed to get his dog back inside and shared the news with his parents in the parking lot. They engulfed him in a tight group hug.

On his way to driving to downtown for the annual Roseville Christmas Carols event, his breath fogged up his windows. Goodness, the excitement pounded in his fingertips.

A director. *An actual theater* director. *A theater* director *with a full-time salary.*

He wedged his car into a spot in a parking deck, and his family strolled to the downtown square where a woman at a table handed out music folders. His family clustered, with the crowd, around the largest tree the town had to offer. Multi-colored lights wove around the huge branches.

Close to the tree, a woman huddled in a large family. He recognized that long hair and the swish of those skirts. Hadassah.

His heart ricocheted.

Next to him, his mother caught his eye and then stared in Hadassah's direction.

"Who knows?" His mother smirked at him. "Maybe there will be more than one Christmas miracle today." She nudged his shoulder in Hadassah's direction.

He inhaled and marched toward her. Hadassah must've heard the crunch of his boots against the snow, because she whirled around, and a misty breath trailed from her lips. She glanced over her shoulder at—Griffith assumed—her mother. The woman gave a slight nod.

Good enough for Hadassah, it seemed, because she jogged over to Griffith.

"Merry Christmas, Griffith."

"Merry Christmas." His throat went dry. Oh boy, this girl knew how to make him tongue-tied. "Uh, nice tree, eh?"

She snickered and sidled next to him. They stood in the quiet for several moments. Soon the music would begin, and they'd get lost in the notes.

"So, Griffith." Hadassah clasped her gloved hands. "You said a stage kiss doesn't count, right? As the real thing?"

His heartbeat jolted. Where was she going with this?

"Uh, yeah. It doesn't really count."

"A shame. Don't you think?"

Despite the wind, heat flared through his face and neck. Was she—? Did she want to—?

"Griffith."

He glanced at her. Without a moment's hesitation, she slid her arms around his neck, balanced herself on her toes, and planted a kiss on his lips. He hoped to stay suspended like that forever.

They pulled apart. Her eyes sparkled.

"Does that one count?"

He grinned. "That one deserved a standing ovation."

AUTHOR'S NOTE

Right before we wrote this book, we wanted to quit. Quit publishing. Quit writing. Quit everything. Alyssa and I (Hope) would take turns alternating phone calls where we had to assure the other person that they could not, in fact, throw in the towel and that we wouldn't let them.

We may sound like wimps, but we do want to explain something that may encourage or discourage writers and creatives—depending on how you spin it.

We have more than twenty books collectively under contract or published. We've worked as agents, publishers, editors, and just about every other role in the industry. We've helped over one hundred authors find homes for their books, edited hundreds more to help them hone their writing, and have taught hundreds of classes at this point to help creatives get set in the right direction.

And often, we still want to quit.

Because God called us to something very hard. We had no idea how difficult publishing was until we entered it. At times, when we get a new contract, we peel yet another layer of "hard" we didn't know existed before.

Alyssa had thought she was supposed to be a doctor, and me, a teacher. Turned out Alyssa hated math, and I couldn't, well, teach.

God made our calling very clear to us, and He opened the right doors at the right times. We could tell you countless stories of us wanting to quit right before a contract slid into our inbox, or us having to turn down a deal, only for another publisher to swoop in minutes later.

He really has come through, but that doesn't make this any easier.

When I (Hope) received my first royalty check, I cried. And not because I made impressive sales. I'd done all the right things in marketing, had countless people telling me they couldn't wait to get a copy, etc. And then the royalty statement proved they had either forgotten or would, as so many told me, "Wait until it's free."

And even then, they didn't get a copy.

We really wrestled with the idea of calling. Because yes, we write because we experience joy when we do so. And yes, we write to glorify God and to do so with our utmost ability and strength that we can muster.

But it also is really hard to do a calling when the audience doesn't show up. Or when the crowd didn't give feedback after the "show." Or when even friends and family wouldn't come to the performance.

This book not only encourages everyone to follow the calling that God has placed on their hearts—but also serves as a reminder to myself and my co-author why we got into publishing in the first place.

Because we've seen so many writer friends, burnt out by horrible critique groups or rejections, quit.

And we can't allow that to keep happening.

Your calling is far too important to forsake.